A Psychic Surveys Supernatural Thriller

Jed

ALSO BY SHANI STRUTHERS

A Psychic Surveys Supernatural Thriller

Jed

SHANI STRUTHERS

ISBN: 978-1-7392469-1-4

www.shanistruthers.com

Authors Reach
www.authorsreach.co.uk

To Florence – a pure bundle of love, the very embodiment of Jed.

Foreword

Animals are, I think, the best of us. Certainly, with dogs, their love, loyalty and optimism seem to know no bounds. How they greet strangers with such enthusiasm; can't wait for another day to get started, and their complete lack of judgement is just so inspiring. I grew up with dogs, but am now the tired lackey of five cats! One day, though, when life is quieter, it's dogs I shall return to. Jed is one of the most loved characters from the Psychic Surveys universe. A spirit dog, that attaches itself to young psychic, Ruby Davis, I didn't intend for him to be such a big character in the books. He was only ever meant to appear for one case in the first few pages of the series' first book: **The Haunting of Highdown Hall**, when Ruby and a member of her team are called to a house in Heathfield that's being 'haunted' by the spirit of a dog. But lo and behold! A few pages later and he appears again in the book, much to Ruby's surprise and…ahem…mine. And from thereon in, through nine books so far, Jed remains very much the star of the show! Florence (a Retriever), to whom the book is dedicated, was most definitely an influence behind his character, along with other dogs I have loved and known, including Smokey (mixed breed), Wolfgang (dachshund), and Herbie (dachshund). Lately, there's Murphy – a black Lab who lives across the road from me and who also appears in this book. There is a scene in Jed where Murphy acts out of character BUT rest assured, the real Murphy is a complete sweetheart, who'd love you to death, given the opportunity (and he's very good in coffee shops!)

Acknowledgements

No doubt about it, Jed is a character that captures the imagination! A real live dog in this story, whereas in the Psychic Surveys series, he has passed into spirit, and is something of a guide instead, Ruby's knight in fur rather than shining armour (although he can shine when he wants to!) Ruby always suspects, though, that when he's not by her side, he's off saving others. A lot of readers have wondered about this too, and written in to ask me if I'd consider writing a standalone about Jed, revealing more of his history. Well...here it is, but with such a *huge* character, it can only ever be an insight into what and who he is. So thank you to my readers for the idea! Also, a huge thanks to Rob Struthers, Kate Jane Jones, Lesley Hughes, and Sarah Savery (who owns the real Murphy of the story and is also a complete sweetheart!) Your feedback is always invaluable, helping to craft the story. Thank you also to Rumer Haven for another fantastic edit, I'm so grateful for all you do. I'm also very grateful to Gina Dickerson of RoseWolf Design, who brought Jed to life on the cover.

Chapter One

"God! He's adorable, isn't he? I mean, look at those eyes. How they shine."

"He's not a puppy, though. That's what we wanted, remember? What we discussed. A family dog to grow up beside little Jamie. A faithful friend. A guardian."

Ava raised an eyebrow. "Oh, so we're calling the baby Jamie now, are we?"

Her husband, Paul, chanced a smile. "Well…I've been thinking. Damien has…connotations, you know? And not the best kind. If he lives up to his name, we're in trouble! Seriously, Jamie's cool as well. I think it'll suit him better."

With Ava six months pregnant, she and Paul had waded through just about every baby-name book in existence, growing more and more confused. At least the twenty-week scan, which had confirmed a boy, had cut the load in half, but she liked Damien. There was something…*regal* about it, and to hell with *The Omen.*

Before she could argue her case, the dog that had had her in his sights ever since she'd walked into their local rescue centre, barking and barking to get her attention, only stopping when she looked his way, started up again. Now at his pen, and no matter how awkward and uncomfortable it was, she knelt before him, sliding her hand through the bars so she could touch his shiny, wet nose.

"Ava," Paul hissed. "Be careful!"

"Don't worry. I will be."

A Labrador. Black. Male. A stray, according to the rescue centre, picked up on the streets of Eastbourne and no one coming forward to claim him. A dog you'd need to be careful of if you didn't know his history. That was Paul's concern: they'd need to exercise extreme caution if rescuing a dog *and* having a baby. There'd been some terrible things reported in the news lately about how vicious dogs could be. *Mistreated* dogs, she'd reminded Paul, adding that if you hit something enough, could you blame them if they eventually hit back? Despite this, she agreed with him. She'd never put a child of theirs in jeopardy, but the eyes of this dog, brown like her own and such a deep shade, were something else. She could spend all day staring into them and never tire. Trust. It was there immediately. This dog did *not* have it in him to savage anything or anyone. What he was, was love. A big furry bundle of it. How was it possible, she wondered, to fall in love like this, in a flash? It had never happened before, not even with Paul. Only with this creature, who was wagging his tail furiously from side to side, his gaze, like hers, adoring.

"Paul—"

Even though she hadn't asked him, he hooked his hands under her arms to help her stand. "Ava, we can't. It's a stray, an unknown."

"It's a *he*," Ava returned, "and he's perfect for our family. I know it. I *feel* it."

A woman approached them. "Hey there! I see you're looking at one of our newest residents. A beauty, isn't he?

Not sure if you know anything about him, but—"

Again, Paul saw fit to interrupt. "The other assistant, I think her name's Josie – she mentioned something about him. Said he was a stray from Eastbourne."

"Well, he was found wandering," the woman replied, a name tag identifying her as Iris, "about six weeks ago now. We've tried everything to unite him with his owner, but, so far, no luck. You know," she continued, Ava noticing how her eyes lit up whenever she glanced at the dog, "it was funny, really, because it was me who found him. He like...came out of nowhere and just...*welded* himself to me. I'm not joking when I say that. He followed me all the way home, then refused to budge from my doorstep, barked until I took him in. I offered him some food, and he was so hungry, he demolished it! The next day, he accompanied me quite happily into work. We've had him checked, of course, scanned for a chip – he doesn't have one. We've put posters up everywhere, notified all the vets, the pet shops, he's got front page on our website, and he's regularly splashed all over social media. Nothing but tumbleweed. A good job it *was* me he attached himself to, someone who could help him. He lucked out on that part, almost"—a smile enlivened worn but kind features—"as if he knew. Oh! You're going to have a baby."

Ava touched her stomach. "A boy. He's due end of December."

"Wonderful! And, phew, glad I got it right!" A burst of laughter escaped her. "I've a tendency to speak before I think sometimes. Really, though, that's a neat bump you've got there. I've two sons myself, teenagers now." Iris grimaced. "Make the most of them whilst they're little, that's all I can say. It's such a precious time."

3

"So…teenagers aren't as precious?" Paul said, playing along.

"It's *all* precious," Iris amended. "It's just some stages can be a little more…challenging, shall we say? And teenage boys eat you out of house and home! Be prepared for that." She laughed again, a throaty chuckle. "Ah, you'll find out for yourselves in the fullness of time. So, it's Jed you're interested in, is it?"

"Jed?" Ava questioned, turning to him again. "That's his name?"

"It's the first name I thought of when I found him, or he found me or whatever. Somehow he just…looks like a Jed, don't you think? Like I say, he's been here about six weeks, and during that time he's become a firm favourite with the other dogs. We walk them together, you see, those that can tolerate it, and he's the leader of the pack, a real character that keeps the more wayward ones in line, herding them. I swear he thinks he's a sheepdog, not a Lab. Like I said, no one's claimed him, and no one's shown that much interest in him either. As an older dog – we think he's around five or six – he tends to get overlooked. We may be a rescue centre, but people still want the younger animals. Less costly at the vets, you know? S'okay, we don't hold it against them. These are hard times, the cost of everything soaring."

"I'm afraid that's what we're after too," Paul told her, "a puppy."

"Well, we do get them from time to time, sure, but we've none at the moment. I can add your names to our waiting list, though."

"Yes, please, if you don't mind…"

"It's him we're interested in. Jed."

"Oh," Iris said, looking from one to the other, clearly unsure who to respond to.

Paul took the reins. "We just think it's safer rescuing a puppy, that's all. You know what you're letting yourself in for, then. No nasty surprises."

"Paul—" Ava began, but this time Iris interrupted.

Moving towards Jed's pen, she retrieved some keys from her pocket. "I know what you mean," she said, "and I agree with you, I do. We have to be careful too when homing dogs with families with children. But as there's still a few months before the baby arrives, that'll give him time enough to settle, for you to get the measure of him. I really don't think you'll get any nasty surprises with Jed. If I didn't have a couple of dogs of my own at home, and a cat, all of them as demanding as my boys, I'd have kept him myself, let me tell you. This one is…special. Really is. Would you like to come inside with me and say hello properly?"

"No."

"Yes."

Again, Ava and Paul spoke simultaneously, Paul subsequently sighing as Ava waited expectantly by Iris's side.

"Be careful, Ava," he repeated, but she was no longer listening.

As soon as the pen door was opened, she made a beeline for the dog, the dog meeting her halfway, jumping up but gently, as if he knew she carried precious cargo, not trying to lick her face, just staring into her eyes, the bond between them strengthening. Deep in her heart, joy sparked like she'd never known it. Not only that, the baby was kicking too, *excitedly*, when all day he'd been quiet.

With a big grin on her face, she turned her head to where Paul was standing outside the pen. Or where he *had* been standing a few seconds before.

"Where's he gone?" she asked, addressing empty space instead.

"He…um…he's just left," Iris replied, equally baffled.

Ava returned Jed to four legs and scanned the premises.

There were a few other people at the rescue centre, couples mostly, young and old. A child of one of the couples, about seven or eight years old, was running and up down the corridor that divided the pens. Of Paul, though, there was no sign.

Anxiety replaced joy. "I'm so sorry. I suppose I'd better go and find him."

"Of course. Of course," Iris replied, guiding Ava out of the pen.

Bereft. That's how Ava felt at leaving Jed. The howl that escaped him as the cage was put back into place indicated he felt the same.

As they stood in the corridor, the child in the room began whooping as he ran and banged at his legs, more feral than anything else there. The other assistant, Josie, came forward to tactfully restrain him whilst his oblivious parents cooed over a far smaller, some might say cuter, canine than Jed, covered in fluffy white fur.

Before Ava could rush off, Iris laid a consoling hand on her arm. "I'm sorry too about, well, you know. So, I won't be putting your name down for Jed?"

A split second was all it took for Ava to decide.

Her head whipped back round to Iris, a gesture so abrupt that the woman stepped back. "Oh yes, put our names down," she said, and in the pen Jed barked again as if spurring her on. "It's Paul and Ava Kent." Her hands gravitating to her stomach, she added, "And you can put his name down too, Jamie Kent." If she had her way in this, adopting Jed, then Paul could have his way regarding the baby's name. Marriage, after all, was about compromise.

Iris had not only stepped back, she was frowning. "But your husband…"

Although she didn't complete the sentence, her voice drifting off, Ava could sense the woman's misgivings well enough, and all of them justified. If Paul continued to object outright to Jed, then this was a highway to nowhere. Alternatively, if he conceded but the two didn't get along, or rather Paul *refused* to get along with Jed, then Jed would be back at the rescue centre pronto. Iris had found this dog and had also bonded with him. If she could, she'd adopt him herself, she'd already said, but inside Ava grew something else besides the baby – desire, as well as an increasing certainty. Jed belonged to *her* family, come what may.

She had to convince Paul, but first she had to convince Iris. As the woman had reached out to touch her arm earlier, now Ava did the same, gently squeezing.

"You won't be making a mistake if you give him to us, I promise. My husband *will* come to love him. It's just…a dog like Jed is not what he'd imagined, and so of course it'll take some thinking about. All I need is time. As it's Friday, can you give me the weekend to make him see what a good idea this is?"

"Yeah…sure. I can do that," Iris replied, although she was still clearly uncertain.

"Great," Ava said, certain for both of them. All three,

actually, for Jed too – four if you counted the still-kicking Jamie. She looked again at Jed behind bars, who was no longer howling or barking but sitting obediently, the hope in his eyes something raw. "We'll speak Monday," Ava continued. "The day I'll be taking him home."

Chapter Two

A new house, a new dog, and a new baby. Each following on the heels of the last.

Jamie was born earlier than expected, not in December but November. Ava had been alone in the house they'd moved into that summer – a mid-terraced family house in Heathfield, boasting three decent-sized bedrooms – when labour pains started. As a business analyst, Paul worked in London, leaving home early, usually, before 7:00 a.m. and coming home about twelve hours later. On that particular day, the twenty-fifth of November, exactly a month before Christmas, she'd been pottering around at home, not doing anything too arduous, cleaning, tidying, and admiring the newly decorated nursery which had been painted in such bright colours. Nesting was the term for it. She'd even had a nap. Gone into hers and Paul's bedroom, which had also been revamped with plain white walls, white curtains, and white painted floorboards too. She loved it, how serene it was, almost sacred.

"Sacred?" Paul had said when she'd first described the look she'd wanted. "You think it's going to stay sacred with a new baby in the house?"

"Of course," she'd replied. "Like the dog, he'll have impeccable manners."

"Really? You promise?"

"I promise," she'd said, kissing the tip of his nose.

"We'll see," he'd murmured but smiling nonetheless.

She'd known she could do it, persuade him about Jed, insisting over and over what a gentle soul he was, that he'd be an asset to their family. "Gentle but also protective," she'd insisted, "looking after me and Jamie when you're not there."

He'd agreed to a trial, on the proviso that if the dog was still with them when Jamie arrived and showed even a hint of jealousy towards him, he'd be back in his pen at the rescue centre faster than his four feet could scamper.

She'd agreed. She had to. Quietly confident any kinks could be ironed out should they occur, which they wouldn't.

How quickly Jed had settled in! And, for a supposed stray, he did indeed have impeccable manners, leaving Ava slightly worried. What if his previous owner simply hadn't noticed all the effort the rescue centre had gone to and were still out there, pining for him? Nothing she could do about it, though, except pray they *wouldn't* surface, because no way she could bear to lose him now.

Even when Ava saw her mother, Carol, and friends during the final weeks of her pregnancy, Jed accompanied her. They spent every waking minute together, constant companions. She taught him tricks, admiring how he took a treat so gently from her fingers afterwards. They'd walk...well, he'd walk, and she'd waddle. Her favourite times, though, were when they lay slumped together on the sofa in front of the TV, she, Jed, and Jamie-to-be, the wood burner fully ablaze. Jed would rest his head on her stomach, his tail wagging whenever the baby kicked, as though the two of them were engaged in the sweetest of games.

Idyllic. The life she'd hoped for, that she'd dreamed of ever since she could remember, filled with love and happiness. Blessed was how she'd describe herself. She'd met Paul and, after a whirlwind romance – they'd only known each other a year – married him, becoming pregnant exactly when they'd planned, the house they'd coveted falling into their laps without a hitch, and now Jed to complete the picture.

Sometimes, as they lay on the sofa waiting for Paul to return from work, she'd wonder: What if it all went wrong? If something bad happened? Life had its ebbs and flows. Everyone knew that. One day you had everything, the next...

The possibility could draw tears. With one hand on Jed, the other on her stomach, she'd feel so bleak suddenly. *Terrified.* Having never been tested – she'd had a great childhood too, with doting parents – what if the one thing she wasn't was strong? If something marred her perfect world, would she simply crumble?

Dear Jed. During those pendulum moments when she swung from one emotion to another, he seemed to sense it. He'd lift his head and nudge her gently but persistently, as if saying, *It'll be all right. Believe me. Everything will turn out fine.*

Wishful thinking? Perhaps. But he always brought her back from that strange place she kept disappearing to. The moods, of course, were all down to hormones wreaking havoc. No need to bother Paul about it. It was a passing phase. Once the baby arrived, she'd settle, go back to normal. God, she couldn't wait for Jamie! She'd be such a show-off when he arrived, cherishing every indulgent smile rained on him.

What she didn't expect, though, was that Jamie couldn't wait to be born either.

After pottering that morning and twenty minutes' shut-eye, she decided on one last chore before assuming position with Jed on the sofa: heaving a sackful of rubbish from the kitchen to the bin outside the front door. No doubt about it, she was exhausted again afterwards, even after such brief exertion, thankful that on days such as these – grey-skied and drizzly – Jed didn't seem to mind if a long walk wasn't on the cards, not if he could frolic in the garden.

She was half in this world and half out of it, pleasantly drifting, when the pains kicked in, bringing her rudely back to full consciousness. The next thing she knew, water gushed from between her legs. Water streaked with blood.

"Shit!" she said, trying to sit upright but for a flash of searing pain which rendered even that simple movement impossible.

Poor Jed! He'd been trying to nudge her awake for a while, she realised, but she'd been fending him off. Now he was as beside himself as she was, barking and running around in circles, the pair of them completely at a loss what to do next.

Paul. She had to phone him. It was an ambulance she needed but him she wanted – to have him tell her what was happening was completely normal, even though every fibre in her body screamed it wasn't. She was confused, bewildered, and terrified, this time for justifiable rather than fanciful reasons.

Regardless of who she called first, she needed her phone, which both hands searched for. Where was it? Where the hell had she put it?

The phone wasn't beside her on the sofa, although she was sure she'd slung it there earlier. Had it slipped down the back? If so, not for the first time. Trouble was, she couldn't turn to check, could still hardly move. It was as though her body were caught in some kind of giant invisible clamp, the baby, who'd also been slumbering earlier, every bit as distressed as she was and kicking, *violently*, prompting an overwhelming urge to push, which she fought against. This wasn't supposed to happen for another three weeks or so, and then in a controlled manner, an epidural on hand or gas and air, at least.

"Aargh!"

Her scream tore at the atmosphere.

Wherever her phone was – if not on the sofa, then in the kitchen, maybe – it didn't matter, because if she couldn't move, she couldn't reach it. Even if it were in front of her on the coffee table, she doubted she'd be able to grab it.

This was labour, *full-blown* labour.

She could try screaming louder still, yelling for help, but she knew that her neighbours either side worked, unless by a miracle they were off sick or something.

Another urge to push, this one undeniable.

"No, no, Jamie, don't. It's not your time yet." *Don't ruin this!*

She was further bewildered. How could she think such a thing? This wasn't the baby's fault! It wasn't hers either. It was nature. *Merciless* nature.

Tears filled her eyes, which she angrily blinked back. Crying would get her nowhere. Nor would screaming, but she didn't stop that either.

She couldn't do this. Not alone. *Both* their lives were in peril, hers and Jamie's. They could die here in the living room of this house that she and Paul had coveted, and the first he'd know about it was when he eventually returned home, walking through the door to find…what? Blood splattered over everything.

Tears and screams were as unstoppable as the baby, panic clouding her mind, making it impossible to think, only to react, the body all-powerful.

Perhaps this *was* her fault after all. She'd done this, brought it about with all her morbid thoughts lately, somehow heaped catastrophe upon them.

"Help! Help! Help! Jed, help."

All doors and windows were closed. It was November; of *course* they were closed. And even if they weren't, what could a dog do? If he ran up and down the street barking, people would get angry with him, think he was a stray again, vicious, and either keep their distance or call the police or the rescue centre. If only they'd do the latter! Iris knew Ava was pregnant. She knew too that Jed was a good boy, that he wouldn't act like that without reason. She might investigate, get Ava the help she needed. But even if she did, the whole thing could take hours – and Ava didn't have that. No point in crying, and no point in clutching at straws either.

She slid onto the floor, her back against the sofa, and had another urge to push. "Jed, help. Help. Please."

The dog, who'd been howling and howling, ran out of the room and left her.

"Oh, Jed," she whispered, trying not to blame him for taking fright and abandoning them both, probably seeking refuge in the hallway or a bedroom.

If only she'd kept her phone closer, especially at this stage of the pregnancy, but there'd simply been no hint anything like this was going to happen earlier.

Should she push or not? What was safest? She had no idea. Shit, it had all been going so well! A blessed life, charmed. Sheltered. That too. She couldn't deal with an emergency like this, was absolutely not strong enough. *Think, Ava! Think! Women have given birth since the dawn of time, and many, many of them have done it alone; some even choose to. Calm down and listen to what your body is telling you.*

She was trying so fucking hard to calm down, but a counter voice was screaming all things opposite: *You can't do this alone! You'll die. The baby will. Jamie...*

The blood! The sofa and carpet were indeed saturated in it, a mix of darker and much brighter blood. Should there be this amount of it? She hadn't wanted to know too much about the birth beforehand, had actively ignored it, deciding to deal with it at the time, or rather let hospital professionals deal with it, as though they were gods, putting herself entirely in their capable, experienced hands.

How could anyone endure this pain? Go on to have more children? If she lived through this, if *they* did, there'd never be another.

Ava screamed, screamed for Jed too, she was sure of it, but she was also becoming strangely distant from all that was happening – those screams sounding as if she were at one end of a tunnel and they were reaching her from the other side, no longer shrill but muted. Everything, the stench of blood and fluids, was fading. She was pushing, she was struggling, but, like earlier, she was also drifting, unable to keep herself tethered. Just too afraid to face the consequences.

What was she drifting towards, though? Why was

everything so dark? If she was dying, wasn't it normally a light that people saw at the end of the tunnel, something tantalising that encouraged them onwards?

Nothing was tantalising about where she was. It was a hopeless place. Cold and unforgiving. No baby with her. Not anymore. No shred of comfort.

Hell. Perhaps that's what this place was. But why? She didn't deserve hell! She'd always tried to do right by those she knew and loved, never knowingly caused harm. How was it she even knew about places like this? Could conjure them so readily?

"Jamie?" Her voice was, like her, distinctly weaker. "Paul? Someone. Anyone. What's happening? Is the baby okay? Is he?"

In this other place, a *shadow* place, she could move more freely, and so she hunkered down, her arms wrapped around herself, trying to force comfort. Her life was ordinary, that was all. No crime in that, surely? She'd met Paul and started a family. Did everything a person was supposed to, what society encouraged you to do. She'd even insisted on rescuing a dog rather than buying one from a breeder; *that's* how good she was. And look where it had led her…to this. Somewhere cursed.

Her head fell back against the sofa, sweat pouring from her forehead. She'd given in, pushed and pushed, so why was there no baby yet? That first cry bellowing.

Everything slipped further as the darkness increased. Such a greedy thing; she could sense its hunger, how it wanted to feast on her when she finally succumbed.

Oh, to die like this…both of them.

Jed? Jed, where are you? Don't leave me. Leave us. You're supposed to protect us. Please, Jed. You're all we've got.

Drifting…deeper and deeper. Into the abyss. Such pain. Such…torture. Arms at the bottom of it, a multitude, all eager to welcome her as one of their own.

No screaming, not anymore. A few whimpers was all she could manage. Although there *was* sound. Jed had started up again from wherever his refuge was. Was *maniacally* barking. It was still a muted sound, though. As was another that joined it.

"Hello? Hello? Is there someone there? Oh my God! Oh, look at you! Don't worry. Oh shit, please, please don't worry. I'm here. You're not alone, not anymore. That's it. There you go. Let me see what's happening. Oh yes, yes. The baby's coming. The baby's…stuck. Okay, okay. I know what to do. I…um…don't keep pushing. Try not to. Not yet. Listen to me, hear my voice. Whatever you do, *do not push*."

Ava had had her eyes closed, feeling some comfort after all in that dark place she'd entered, a sense of belonging, of sweet defeat. For what was the use of fighting? She would indeed succumb. It was just easier.

"I don't know your name, but whoever you are, listen to me. Relax your legs further, but don't push. I need to unhook the cord; it's wrapped around the baby's neck. I'm a midwife. Well…a trainee midwife. But I know what I'm doing…kind of. Relax your legs and don't push. Not until I tell you to. Then, when I say, give one big almighty push. The *last* push, okay?"

Such an urge to push, though, now more than ever. Another voice too, beside that of the stranger, one that hissed in her ear: *Do it. Push! Right now. Push! Push! Push!*

Irresistible, and Ava responded, *You're right. I have to push.*

A feeling of wetness, other than that between her legs, snapped her fully back to the moment, to the living room, the weak light of day, and the intense agony. A tongue licking at her face and a nose pushing against her cheek.

It was Jed. There was also a woman right in front of her. She was the one who'd been speaking. And she was young, *impossibly* young, about twenty.

Ava's voice returned too. "What's happening? I can't…I have to push. Now."

"NO!" the girl roared. "Not until I've removed the cord from around the baby's neck. Please, Miss—"

"Ava. It's Ava."

"Please, Ava, you must listen!"

There were tears in the stranger's eyes, as if she was just as terrified as Ava, her gaze entirely focused as her hands worked furiously.

"Oh God," Ava said again. A midwife, is that what she'd said she was? A *trainee*. How had she got into the house?

Ava clung to Jed, gleaning from him the strength she needed to follow the girl's instructions and not the hissing voice.

"Almost there, almost there," the girl muttered. "Wait. Just wait. Both of you."

A trembling voice, and Ava's body shuddered too, resisting what was so powerful.

Not just clinging to Jed, she'd sunk her nails into him, just as you would a birth partner, digging so hard and the dog withstanding it, holding strong.

"Did you do this, Jed?" she whispered. "Bring her here?"

"PUSH!" the girl yelled. "PUSH NOW!"

Closing her eyes and screwing up her face, Ava did it, felt a terrible burning sensation, was again sure she couldn't survive the pain of it, just felt so weak, so depleted, and then...relief. Incredible relief! The pain was gone, as if someone had left a tap running, then quickly turned it off. A cry. The one she'd yearned for. The midwife cried out too, as did Ava, with Jed barking and chasing his tail.

"A boy," the midwife said. "It's a baby boy. A...*big* baby boy."

"Jamie," Ava whispered.

"Jamie?" the girl, the angel said. "Oh wow!"

"You like it?" Ava managed, knowing she'd hold her baby in good time but right now simply enjoying the relief.

The girl laughed. "Yeah, yeah. Love it. It happens to be my name too."

Chapter Three

Paul was mortified he hadn't been with Ava and Jamie at the birth. He hadn't known anything about it until three hours *after* the baby was born, because that's how long it had taken him to return the midwife's calls – an unknown number – due to a meeting he was in.

Even so, they were trying to leave it all behind them, not the wonder of it, though, the rescue that had come out of nowhere. Even in the fog that Ava's brain was still engulfed in after Jamie's arrival– a fractious baby, he wasn't overly keen on sleep – how events had played out amazed her and Paul alike.

Basically, Jed had saved Ava and Jamie, because without him Jamie would have died and she'd likely have bled out. The cord had been wrapped tightly around his neck, and the midwife – not her first delivery but certainly her first *difficult* delivery – had desperately tried to unhook it but later confessed she hadn't been sure if such a thing was possible, not without the necessary medical equipment to hand. She'd been scared. As scared as Ava. If she'd failed…if *they* had… So much had been at stake.

She'd done it, though, succeeded, delivered him safely, swaddling the baby and Ava in clean towels and blankets, keeping them as warm and as comfortable as possible until an ambulance arrived.

Jamie had tried to explain why she was on the scene. "I was on my way to the Eastbourne Midwifery Unit to do a shift there. I was heading to the bus stop and saw your door was open, and I just…I couldn't make myself walk past it."

"You heard Jed barking too?"

Jamie nodded.

"And the door was wide open?"

"Uh-huh."

"But I'd shut it," Ava said. "I'd taken the rubbish out earlier, I remember that much, and then I closed the door behind me."

Jamie just shrugged. "All I know is it was open." She'd then leant her head to the side slightly. "Want to know something even weirder?"

"Weirder?" repeated Ava, holding Jamie in her arms at last, stunned by the beauty of him. "What could possibly be weirder? You two even share the same name!"

"I know, but, okay, here goes. Normally I get a lift to the hospital with a friend who works there," Jamie continued, "but I missed it this morning because I was stuck in the bathroom! No, seriously. The lock had jammed, and it's never done that before. Never! I couldn't even ring for help, 'cause my phone was in the bedroom, in my bag. So I missed my lift – no way Lana could wait for me or she'd be late. She just presumed I wasn't coming, was ill or something and had slept in. And so, when the lock finally gave way and it just released – honestly, like it had never been stuck in the first place – I went straight to the bus stop instead. It's a quiet street you live on, isn't it? I was literally the only one around." She adjusted her gaze to the newborn baby. "It's a miracle how it all happened.

21

Nothing less."

"Thank you," Ava had whispered back. "Thank you so much."

A miracle, absolutely, but one not entirely without explanation, Paul had insisted.

"When you took the rubbish out, you didn't close the door properly. And a gust of wind blew it open."

"If I'd left the door open, I'd have felt a breeze earlier in the living room."

"You had the fire going, so perhaps not."

"I closed the front door, Paul! I know I did. But, yeah, it flew open, and the one in Jamie's bathroom somehow jammed itself shut when it never had before. And then there was Jed. He'd slunk off, gone quiet, but suddenly, at the same time Jamie's walking past, there he is, barking for all he's worth, getting her attention, the way he did with me and Iris too. The *right* person's attention. A midwife, for God's sake, trainee or not!"

Paul had shrugged, making her feel like she was talking to herself. All he wanted to do was focus on the fact Jamie had been delivered safely, not the finer details. Fine, fair enough. She supposed that's what she should focus on too, certainly not the trauma, that feeling she'd been drifting, the place she'd been heading to. So scary!

Following Jamie's birth, Paul took two weeks' paternity leave, an industry standard, Ava supposed, but it wasn't enough. The days flew by. Soon it was just the three of them again: Ava, Jamie, and Jed, Paul doing his utmost not to work long hours initially but also insisting he had very little choice, not if he wanted to progress through the ranks and provide well enough for them.

Ava used to manage a local coffee shop. Being a barista

was her passion, but in the last stages of pregnancy, she'd given up, she and Paul agreeing that they wanted to bring up their child themselves, not hire a nanny or put him into day care. Ava *did* have plans for her career in the future. She wanted to own a coffee shop eventually, in a more vibrant location, and market her own small-batch coffee, but for now, life was all about family, the family she'd dreamed of. When Paul returned to work that first morning, however, when the door shut behind him, Ava standing there with Jamie in her arms, a *squirming* Jamie, and Jed by her side, she once again felt scared, cold and bleak – those same feelings she'd experienced just before and at the time of birth refusing to wholly let go even though she willed them to.

When another couple of weeks passed, she talked to her mother about it.

"It'll pass," Carol assured her, round at her house and holding Jamie, the baby more content in his grandmother's arms than Ava's, not squirming at all. "Your hormones will settle in time. The birth was difficult, plus you're not getting as much sleep as you'd like either. Then again, what new mother does?"

The birth was difficult? That was an understatement, but Ava let it go.

Carol reached across. "You wanted this, remember? Your own family? And look at him, he's such a handsome fella."

"I know, Mum. I know."

"And you are…loving it, aren't you? You love little Jamie?"

"Of course I do! What a daft question."

On the living room sofa – a brand-new sofa and brand-new carpeting too – Carol leant back, satisfied. "Good. Good. If you carry on feeling a bit out of sorts, just let your health visitor know. They'll be able to sort something out. But honestly, love, I know what it's like; every new mother does. It can be overwhelming. The more time that passes, the more you get used to it. It becomes normal. The *new* normal."

"Yeah, yeah, sure," Ava replied, her mother handing Jamie back to her, declaring she had to go but assuring Ava she'd pop in again at the weekend, with Ava's dad in tow – the doting grandparents.

At nearly twenty-nine, Ava was the first in her circle of friends to have a child, friends who could meet her, who wanted to, but only once the working day was done. Trouble was, the evenings were Jamie's worst time, when he was at his most irritable, Ava pacing the floor with him, wearing a hole right through the new carpet if she wasn't careful. She could hand the baby over to Paul, she supposed, then head out, but he was often exhausted after a long day working and commuting. Besides, right now she could barely think straight, let alone hold a coherent conversation. If fortune was favouring her and Jamie *did* settle, then all she wanted was to collapse on the sofa in front of the wood burner, cuddling Jed, or head to bed herself and grab what sleep she could, realising what a precious commodity it was.

A new normal, but also a transient phase. Jamie would grow, start playschool several mornings a week and eventually school full-time. Then she'd regain her freedom. It wasn't lost forever. For now, though, it was all about trying to get through the day, Ava sometimes taking them all on several short walks in the park, kicking through leaves, Jed chasing them, Jamie sometimes screaming, sometimes sleeping, then screaming when he got home instead.

If the baby was growing more averse to sleep as the days and weeks went by, so was Ava. It was proving too fitful to be refreshing. If anything, she'd wake feeling worse than ever. Plus, the darkness that sleep brought with it had subtly changed, not offering the promise of respite, but instead reminding her more and more of what it had been like when she'd been drifting when giving birth. Not the gates of heaven waiting for her, but the spikes of hell, the demons it contained counting her amongst their own. Dramatic thoughts. *Stupid* thoughts. Especially in the cold light of day. At night, though, they were thoughts that persisted.

Paul was right. Painting the bedroom white – a sacred space – was a mistake. Obviously, Jamie slept in there for now, in a cot beside their bed, but Jed was not allowed in the bedroom. If Paul would only relent, it might make all the difference. With one hand nestled through the bars of the cot, resting on Jamie's stomach, and the other on the dog, soaking up his warmth, she might feel warm inside too.

Evenings came around so quickly in winter. And in the day there was very little blue sky to speak of, the sun weak and watery, if it bothered to show at all.

That evening, Paul had made an effort and came home early. Funny how Jed always knew when he was on his way. He'd mosey on over to the front door, sit and stare at it, and every so often wag his tail. Five minutes later and in would walk Paul, Jed pleased to see him, Paul, in return, offering a cursory head rub.

It was Jamie Paul was excited to see, naturally. He rushed down the hallway and into the living room, where Jamie was lying on a playmat whilst Ava tidied.

Hoisting him up, he covered his face in kisses. Only then, a few moments later, did he acknowledge Ava, who stood there watching. *Briefly* acknowledged her.

She didn't mind he did that, not at first, but lately it began to grate. Paul came in with the darkness, and with his presence, the darkness intensified. *Everything* he did was annoying her, especially that voice he used, reserved solely for Jamie, such a...*stupid* voice, high-pitched, squeaky, every nerve ending she had firing in response. He'd use it relentlessly, again glancing at Ava now and then, seeking a smile from her, some form of approval. If he *really* looked at her, the way he used to, drinking in every inch, he'd notice the smile never quite reached her eyes.

She left them to it, headed to the kitchen, and got on with preparing dinner. Jed sidled up to her, gave her a nudge, and settled close by. Now *there* was a creature that noticed her, that...monitored her, she sometimes thought. She supposed she could force the issue of him sleeping in their bedroom, but Paul...if he gave in at all, wouldn't do so gracefully. She'd need a certain amount of energy to argue the case, energy that right now she simply didn't have.

Still with Jamie in his arms, Paul followed her into the kitchen.

"What's for dinner?" He'd said it without even looking at her, his eyes all for Jamie.

She clutched tighter a wooden spoon she was stirring some sauce with. Could it be...was it possible she was *jealous* of Paul and Jamie's relationship? Just as Jamie was more settled in Carol's arms, so it was with Paul. And yet whenever she held the baby, he struggled, his face growing puce with anger.

It was unforgiveable to be jealous. Just mad. Completely.

"Ava?" Paul prompted.

"Curry. I'm making a curry," she announced.

"Fantastic. Chicken?"

"Um...tofu. I thought we'd have a break from meat for a few days."

His reply wasn't so enthusiastic this time. "Oh. Okay. Right."

"Hope so," she said, although she had to admit, the bean curd wasn't as firm as she thought it would be; if anything, it was disintegrating in the mixture before her. "If you bathe Jamie and give him a feed, I'll get it ready for around eight."

"Bath time? You hear that, Jamie? Splashy fun! Me and you are going to mess about in the water. Bubbly wubbly water. Lots and lots of lovely bubby wubblies."

Ava's nostrils flared as she continued stirring, her breath also a little heavy. Jed got to his feet too, reacting to Paul's high spirits, wondering if he could follow.

"Stay," Ava told him, knowing Paul would only tolerate him so far.

Giving up on the sauce – it was a disaster; she'd shove something in the oven instead – she turned to watch her husband and son leave the room. Paul had made an aeroplane of Jamie, zooming him gently through the air, Jamie slightly alarmed, but he'd grow to love it. Soon enough he'd squeal with laughter at his father's antics, the pair of them partners in crime. Would she feel a part of that team? Included?

She could still hear Paul talking in that ridiculous high-pitched tone as they climbed the stairs, a model father who would try to be there for Jamie as much as he could. And every moment filled with enthusiasm.

Where was her enthusiasm? Why had it deserted her so spectacularly? She had everything to be grateful for. *Everything.* No way she could continue like this. She had to dig deep and find the person she used to be.

Jed had done as she'd commanded and settled down.

Dropping to her knees, she flung her arms around his neck and just breathed him in, his fur slightly damp from a walk in the rain earlier. The weather really was atrocious lately, but they'd still go out in it, the three of them, trudging along the streets and byways, the new house not so much a sanctuary anymore, more like a prison.

She hugged Jed, and there it was, a glimmer of much-needed comfort. The night was coming, though, and sleep. She the one who mustn't fight it.

Chapter Four

Extra splashy fun at bath time meant Jamie went off to sleep with barely any fuss. Now they must sleep too, Paul declaring what a day it had been, quickly giving Ava a peck on the cheek and then turning over and switching the light off.

The bedroom was plunged into darkness, so much of it. It seemed to cling to her nowadays, Ava fearing that perhaps she was clinging to it too, just as hard. Lying there in the stillness of the night, she turned from Paul to face the cot beside her. She could hear Jamie, the snuffles he made, such a reassuring sound. She loved him, completely; that was without question. But *dealing* with him, day in, day out, all day, that's what she found tough. His arrival had wrought so many changes that, strangely, she'd never anticipated all the while she was pregnant. She'd just never seen that far ahead. A protection mechanism, maybe, or plain idiocy.

Because Jamie had gone straight to sleep after his bath and feed, she and Paul had enjoyed a quiet, uninterrupted dinner together – sausage and oven chips rather than her attempt at tofu curry, but at least they were veggie sausages. It had been the perfect opportunity to talk to Paul, and so she'd told him that although she was physically taking more walks in the park than she'd ever done before, she wasn't, metaphorically, finding her situation a walk in the park. It was harder than she'd imagined, or rather hadn't.

In between shovelling ketchup-drenched food into his mouth, Paul had frowned. "But surely you must have realised life would change drastically. I mean, even when Jamie's grown up, he's still going to need us. That's parenthood. It's a forever thing." Before she'd even had a chance to formulate an answer, perhaps defend herself because there'd been something accusatory in his tone, he'd added, "I know you think my life hasn't changed much because of work, but it has. No way I can go for after-work drinks as much, network, because you want me here at home."

"*I* want you home?"

"Yeah, of course, to help with Jamie because you're tired. And I don't mind, honestly. I love coming home to this, our family. All I'm trying to say is, life is different for us both, but we'll get used to it, grow into it. Ava, come on, I can see you're getting riled, but just remember, it's amazing what we've done. We ought to embrace it, not…I don't know, focus on changes all the time. There's no need to be miserable. Tell you what, I think I can come home early tomorrow too. That big project I told you about, remember? It's been put off till next week now."

And that had been it, the extent of their heart-to-heart. Effectively, he'd shut her down. *Blamed* her. Just as she was getting used to Jamie, she also had to get used to this new version of Paul, someone who expected her to toe the party line.

Still on her side, still staring at the outline of her baby in the darkness, she sighed.

Paul was right, though. She was playing this all wrong, should absolutely lighten up, not be so serious about everything or scared. Just accept she was on a learning curve, a *steep* learning curve, but one that was glorious too. Cut herself some slack. Turned out, it wasn't just babies that suffered from teething problems.

Suffer?

She rolled her eyes.

Go to sleep, Ava. You just need some decent sleep, that's all.

If she could get three or four hours straight, she might feel differently to how she did right now, more able to cope. Jed wasn't with her, but he was nearby, keeping guard. She knew he did that, patrolled the place at night, and there it was again, momentary comfort in that knowledge. More than momentary, actually; she was finally relaxing, drifting, encouraging that sense of ease to linger as her eyes closed.

More darkness. Plain, ordinary darkness.

Every limb felt heavy, as though cast from lead. It was like she was sinking into the bed now rather than drifting. Sinking into the depths. A proper level of rest, hopefully, akin to a whiteout. Exhaustion was of course the reason she was so highly strung lately. No one could function properly without quality sleep, and there it was – an explanation for everything. Nothing was ever that much of a mystery.

Her mind would still soon, as well as her body. Also, maybe with a bit of luck, Jamie wouldn't wake till dawn, until the first rays of light entered the room, heralding a new day she'd embrace rather than shrink from.

She loved her baby. Her husband too. Her dog.

One of the lucky ones. You know you are.

Extraordinarily lucky. Some people just are.

Apart from the birth, it's all been effortless. So far…

Silence. Utter silence.

Her mind still at last. A suspension of sorts. Death in miniature.

Death?

Instead of sinking, she was now climbing. Or at least trying to, clawing her way back to the surface. Wherever she was, this place of descent, that's what it promised: death. She *had* to wake. Couldn't stay there. It was as much a prison as this house was.

Up and up she pushed through thick, muddy layers. Something was wrong. *Very* wrong. Although she had no idea what. Too much silence, perhaps?

The silence of the grave.

No longer silence, there was commotion.

A dog barking. What dog?

It rose and dipped, then rose, was off the scale.

"Huh? What is it? What's going on?"

Forcing her eyes to open, Ava tried to work out where she was and what was happening. She was at home, in her bedroom, and a dog was barking…*her* dog…Jed. Usually he was so quiet, a good boy, the best. Never made a sound unless… Was someone trying to break in? Had they done so already and were heading upstairs, a dark figure, malevolent, intent on destruction?

"Paul. Paul." Her voice was so weak! She had to work harder to inject it with more strength. "Paul! Wake up. Something's wrong. Jed, can you hear him?"

Paul stirred, but only lightly. Amazing what the man could sleep through. All the nighttime feeds she'd done, all the pacing, the baby agitated, screaming and screaming.

And Paul just slept through it.

Her head whipped to the side as, finally, she realised.

Jamie wasn't making his usual snuffling sounds.

"PAUL!"

Nothing weak about her voice this time – she demanded he sit up and take notice, Jed still barking frantically below. An intruder was *not* the reason, though. If that were the case, they'd have silenced the dog by now. A quick hammer blow to the head would do it. The reason was Jamie. Something was wrong with him.

With the aptitude of an athlete, she leapt from the bed, landed on her feet, and bent over the cot, grabbing him. No longer a fighter, he was floppy in her arms.

"Jamie! Jamie!" she screamed this time, over and over, shaking him as fear, such an ice-cold thing, rendered it almost impossible to breathe. She begged him to breathe, though, as tears of desperation rolled down her face.

Someone was by her side: Paul, although she barely registered him, his hands reaching out too, trying to wrestle the baby from her.

Her grip was like iron. No way he'd succeed.

"Jamie, you have to breathe! Oh, please breathe, please."

Seconds. And in each an eternity.

"Jamie, come on!" Paul's voice joined hers. "Shit, this can't be happening. It can't!"

A cry at last. A scream. And not from either of them. A scream that was…indignant as Jamie, animate again, kicked his legs and waved his arms. Ava's own breath was heaving. Just when she'd thought life was lost, it returned, Jamie crying now rather than screaming, the three of them equally shocked.

A baby's cry… She'd read somewhere it was pitched at

exactly the right level so that a mother couldn't ignore it; instead, they'd do anything to quieten them down. A survival technique that nature had created. The sound did indeed pierce her, and she always tried to bring it to a halt, never leaving him to cry. Now, though…now the sound was like a *melody*.

"What happened?" Paul kept saying. "What just happened?"

"I don't know. I was in a deep sleep. It was the barking that woke me. Jed was barking so loud."

"Did Jamie just stop…breathing? Why?"

"I don't know. I just…I don't know." There it was, hot on the heels of elation, that same sense of bleakness, the *hopelessness* of before. "Oh shit, I've no idea!"

Although Jamie went back to sleep that night, Ava and Paul didn't, this despite Jed being allowed into their room, Paul still a little reluctant but Ava giving him a look that told him if they didn't, just for that one night, there'd be all kinds of trouble. Going downstairs to fetch Jed, she'd thrown her arms around his neck and thanked him for saving Jamie a second time and, by proxy, her and Paul. She'd then brought the somewhat bemused dog upstairs, where he settled immediately on the floor beside Jamie's cot, his ears pricked all the while.

Would Jamie really have died if Jed hadn't alerted them? She shuddered to think it.

A trip to the doctor was scheduled the very next morning, Ava insisting Paul skip work and accompany them.

"An anomaly," the doctor concluded. "We don't know why this happens, and certainly we'll run more tests. But there's no reason to think it'll happen again."

"It might!" Ava insisted. "We need urgent tests. A monitor of some sort."

"Sounds like you already have a pretty good monitor," the doctor replied. "From what you've told me about Jed, he's a bit of a hero."

Still Ava pleaded. "He is, but please. We want every test you can throw at him."

The doctor continued to reassure her. "He's a fine boy and a healthy weight, but of course we'll carry out further checks. Meanwhile, it's a baby breathing monitor you want, there are plenty to choose from on the market. I agree, that'll certainly help to give you peace of mind. It's been a shock, Mr and Mrs Kent, I completely understand that, but if you stress about it, you're going to make yourself ill. Mrs Kent, can I ask, do you still see your health visitor?"

"Yes. Yes, I do. Not weekly, of course, not anymore, but I do still see her."

"Good. If you do need more regular appointments, that can also be arranged."

"I'm fine," she said, embarrassed suddenly, afraid. Did he think she couldn't cope? And if so, what would he do? Force an intervention? She kept her smile in place. "We'll get a breathing monitor straightaway, after we've left here, this morning. Thanks for letting us know about them."

"Good," he said again. "That all sounds very good."

After they left the surgery, Paul, who'd been so pale last night after what had happened, as fretful as her, was back to his normal self, totally reassured.

"Best get back to work," he said. "Too much to do to take the rest of the day off. You sure you'll be okay? You'll manage?"

Riled by what the doctor had said, and now Paul, she couldn't help but snap back. "Of course I can bloody manage! Looking after Jamie is what I do; it's my job. But...do you really have to go back? We need to research those monitors."

"Just look online, then buy the one with the best reviews. Easy."

Easy? From being so worried, he was now so dismissive?

Jamie, in his pram, was fussing, wanting their attention. Ava bent down to release the harness, picking him up and jiggling him, which only made him scream louder. She had to raise her voice as she begged Paul further. "I'd really like us both to choose a monitor, and it has to be done today. Plus, I thought we could fetch Jed and go for a walk in the park. I really don't want to be without you. We've had such a shock, and, well...we need to make the most of what we've got." *Still* got, she wanted to say but couldn't bring herself to.

Paul's shoulders slumped as he shook his head. "It's manic at work. I have to go in. It'll be frowned on if I don't. I'm sorry. I really am. Tell you what, I'll research a monitor on the train and pick one up before I come home. You just focus on having a lovely day, making the most of the fact it's not raining for once." He smiled as he looked at Jamie, who was still crying, his back arched and fists flailing. "Nothing wrong with him at all. A fine, healthy boy. That's what the doctor said. Believe it, okay? Who knows, we may even have overreacted."

Overreacted? As *incensed* as that comment made her, she knew better than to continue pleading with him; it would fall on deaf ears if she did. All she could do was agree, Paul taking Jamie in his arms now, the baby calming, and the three of them enjoying a walk home together, at least. Then she waved Paul off from the doorstep once he was suited and booted, staring long after he'd disappeared.

Happy. She should be. *Especially* happy. Another crisis averted, and a cure-all breathing monitor would be put in place before Jamie's bedtime.

She also had Jed, loyal and constant, who'd earnt his keep a hundred times over.

As the three of them returned inside, she sighed.

Why was happiness something she could no longer remember?

Chapter Five

"He's lovely! How old?"

If she were honest, Ava's smile felt more like a rictus grin. "Coming up for three months. And thank you, I think he's lovely too. How old is your little one?"

"Same! Nearly twelve weeks. Sorry, I hope you don't mind me stopping you for a chat. It's just I've seen you in the park several times with the buggy, just like me, and I thought… Anyway, I'm Sarah Savery, this is Leo, and the dog's Murphy."

"Oh, right? Gosh! Murphy looks just like my dog, doesn't he? His name's Jed."

Both women smiled as Jed and Murphy, although on leads, gravitated towards each other, Jed really tugging, wriggling his backside and emitting an almost seallike sound from his mouth – a cry of excitement, she assured Sarah. On reaching Murphy, his excitement only became greater, Murphy a little unsure of such boundless enthusiasm, but gradually relaxing into the meet and greet.

"You don't fancy a coffee, do you?" Sarah asked. "There's a café just across the road, the Brew Box. Do you know it? It doesn't mind dogs." As Leo opened his mouth to emit a wail, Sarah shrugged wryly. "Or screaming children, for that matter."

"Sure," Ava replied, the pair of them turning in the

direction of the café. "I'm...um...Ava Kent, by the way, and this is Jamie."

"Well, hello, Ava and Jamie. It's very nice to meet you. Always reassuring to know others in the same boat, don't you think?"

As they walked the short distance to the café, Sarah chatted easily, and Ava was thankful for it – feeling rusty, if she were honest, about the mechanics of friendship, having mainly only texted friends recently. Shortly after Jamie was born, there'd been a flurry of visits, everyone eager to see the new arrival, but then visits had died down, work commitments keeping everyone busy. She couldn't blame them. She remembered well enough those days when she'd worked in the coffee shop, the hours that flew by so fast, always on your feet, always knackered come the evening. They were good times, though, full of hustle and bustle, with an ever-changing sea of faces. And now it was replaced by this, being grateful for the talk of strangers in the park. Different times. Not lonely, she couldn't say that, she *mustn't*, but Sarah was right – it was nice to meet someone in the same position, who perhaps understood what it was like, some of the grey areas.

On reaching the Brew Box, they ordered their coffees at the counter, then picked a table by the window to sit at. Quickly it became clear that, for Sarah, there were no grey areas. She was a woman *born* to motherhood, just so competent.

Expertly, she juggled feeding Leo with drinking her coffee, one hand also reaching down regularly to pat Murphy, who was under the table with Jed, Jed nuzzling him and still emitting that seallike sound, both of the women laughing to hear it, even Jamie, she was certain. It was typical Jed. When he wasn't busy saving them, he was always trying to coax a smile. No mean feat sometimes.

Sarah continued to chat, telling Ava she was on extended maternity leave from her chef job and that she'd been married for seven years. She was thirty-two, and her husband was an electrician, working across Sussex. Ava listened intently despite being aware that Jamie's good mood was on the decline. He was growing increasingly fractious in his pram, and then when she held him instead, he squirmed in her arms too.

Her own coffee went cold as she continued to look for any chinks in Sarah's armour, an admission that, actually, life with a new baby was a tough gig, the way it left you feeling tired and grumpy, hormones *really* taking their time to settle. Ava had also been unable to shift the baby weight. No surprise, really. She snacked on chocolate digestives like they were going out of fashion, trying to seek energy from them rather than sleep, which had become even more scarce since the incident with Jamie, despite the installation of the breathing monitor.

In contrast to herself, with her lank brown hair and sallow complexion, Sarah looked fresh. *Glowing*, in fact. Her peaches-and-cream skin was complimented by multitoned blond hair, which fell into a natural curl at her shoulders, and sparkling blue eyes. She was smart too, wearing a far clingier jumper than Ava would chance such a short time after the birth, and a short woollen skirt over tights. A pair of boots finished the look, extending to just below the knee, *shiny* boots, whereas Ava wore scruffy trainers.

Compare, despair. Ava knew that phrase. Never had it seemed so poignant.

"So, yeah," Sarah continued brightly, "we've just finished decorating our third bedroom, getting it ready, you know."

Ava frowned. "For another? So soon?"

"Absolutely," Sarah replied, nodding. "We just think, Dave and me, that if we're going to have two, then have them close together, get it over and done with. Here's the thing, though," she added, leaning forward, "Dave wants to stop at two, but me, I'd like three, maybe even four. What about you? When are you having another?"

Ava was stunned. Here she was, talking with another mother she'd only just met, both of them having just had babies, and now they were on the subject of producing yet more.

In her arms, Jamie screeched, a sound that sliced its way through the air, no doubt drawing the attention of other customers, although she didn't dare look.

"Sorry," Ava said, hanging her head, jiggling him in her arms even harder but only adding to his distress. "It must be colic, something like that. There, there. Come on, Jamie, calm down, eh? There's a good boy. Just…calm down."

She was saying the words so sweetly – trying to appear just like Sarah: adept. Deep inside, though, there was another voice, one growing louder, also turning into a scream: *For God's sake, stop it, will you! Just bloody calm down!*

Jed stopped frolicking beneath the table and sat up to stare at her. Sarah – perfect Sarah, with her perfect cooing child and well-mannered dog, able to contain his excitement far better than Jed – reached across.

"Here," she said, having placed Leo back in his pram

and sporting a smile that Ava couldn't help but think bore traces of pity, "let me try."

Before Ava could object, assure her she was fine – just as she'd assured the doctor, Paul, and her own mother – Sarah's hands were around Jamie's body and gently tugging. She had no option but to release him, let Sarah take over, Ava's shoulders slumping as she was relieved of her charge. *You really are so useless*, that inner voice said now. She'd done her best to appear unruffled, but it was all too clear that beneath her forced grin and sickly voice was one hot mess, who couldn't get to grips with motherhood no matter how hard she tried.

Dear Jed. He'd come forward, laid his head on her lap, and was now busy staring up at her, no pity in his eyes, just devotion. She'd heard that, with rescues, their loyalty to those who'd liberated them from the kennels could prove undying. *His* loyalty was evident in those chocolatey eyes and his love, *such* love – for her, Ava, when she felt she didn't deserve it, couldn't even love herself, not anymore. He was a miracle; Jamie was too, and yet tears squeezed from her eyes even when she shut them tight, trying to prevent herself from having a meltdown in a busy café with a stranger, who was looking at her as perhaps everyone was – pity not so disguised this time.

"Sorry," Ava said, knowing she couldn't just sit there, mute. "I'm just…gosh, I must be tired! You know how it is. Or perhaps you don't. Perhaps…you actually don't." *Perhaps Leo, the perfect baby, sleeps perfectly bloody well too.*

Thankfully, she stopped herself from voicing those last words, quickly wiping at her eyes, noticing not just pity in Sarah's expression but also a hint of embarrassment and confusion. Ava swallowed, knew with absolute certainty that despair – *unwarranted* despair, *selfish* despair – was definitely a mystery to this woman. She had to stop herself from melting entirely and focus on Jed, only Jed, on what he was trying to tell her: *You're lovable, despite everything. Motherhood can be hard, but you're doing fine. You'll be okay. You will. In time.* She'd so hoped Sarah would say those things to her, the pair of them huddled together in an almost conspiratorial manner, applauding motherhood but also being honest about it. Sarah, though, had now averted her gaze, her attention solely on Jamie as Leo – the perfect sleeper indeed – began to doze despite the perceived turmoil.

"That's it. See? It's not so bad, is it? It's not so hard."

Ava stiffened. What Sarah was saying to Jamie, who was – incredibly – *beaming* back at her, was it really aimed at him? Or her? *It's not so hard.* Well, it was! It was fucking impossible sometimes! People were encouraged to start a family. It was the thing you did. The procreation of the race. What you *existed* for. But what if you were crap at it? If you weren't a natural? If you felt so damned bleak all the time, the darkness that had entered your soul even before the birth only ever increasing.

"Ava?" Sarah's voice pulled her back to such a blisteringly cringeworthy moment. "Are you okay?"

"Yes!" Damn her voice for sounding squeaky! "It's like I said, I'm tired, a bit emotional. It gets like that with babies, doesn't it? Difficult at times."

An opening for Sarah, another chance, and Ava silently pleaded with her.

Sarah handed Jamie back. "Well…the thing is, Leo's so easy. Has been from day one. I have to wake him for his feed sometimes. Imagine that?"

Ava held on tightly to Jamie, perhaps a bit *too* tightly. *Imagine that*, Sarah had said. Well, no, she couldn't. And Sarah knew it. Smug Sarah, who now reached towards Leo, her slumbering child, to give his cheek a pat, Ava's mouth tightening.

This woman, this stranger that had accosted her, was no friend, no confidante. She was someone who would only make Ava feel worse than she already did.

Waves of hot and cold washed over her. More tears threatened, which she continued to blink furiously away as she turned from Sarah to strap Jamie back in his pram. So content when he'd been handed over, he was back to struggling, making it so damned difficult to fasten the straps. Abruptly, she stood up, trying to get a better grip, and as she did, she nudged the table, hard. Coffee spilt over the edges of both cups, the cups themselves rattling against the saucers, a sound that grated every bit as much as Jamie's cries, which echoed throughout the café, a din. With the child finally secured, she bent down to grab Jed's lead and tugged at it. To her horror, Jed tugged back, clearly reluctant for the meet to be over. Tough. She and Sarah were *not* friends. No point in pursuing the matter.

Sarah during this time had also risen, not just confusion but concern on her face. Murphy likewise got to his feet and started to bark at Ava when he'd been friendly enough before. Not just barking, he growled, his teeth bared.

Again, customers stared, not just at Ava this time, at them all.

What was wrong with Murphy? Like Jed, he'd seemed so gentle. Why was he now acting this way? *Re*acting.

It's the darkness in you.

The thought arrived unprompted and wouldn't fade.

He sees it plain as day.

His eyes…they were as brown as Jed's, as deep, could see as far.

"Jed, come on." Ava didn't just tug at the dog's lead, she yanked it. "Come on," she repeated, her voice loud enough to combat the commotion.

If any solace was to be had in this entire sorry debacle, it was that Sarah was clearly as baffled by how events were unfolding as Ava was. Her cool demeanour dissolving at last, she was every bit as flustered, her pale cheeks red.

"What's going on?" she muttered, a frown creasing her forehead. Leo was awake again and matching Jamie in the squirming stakes.

Ava's eyes still on Murphy, she didn't answer but began to backtrack. The minute she did, the dog reared up. To do what? she wondered. Lunge, then sink his teeth into her? Right there, in a coffee shop in Heathfield? An ordinary place, an ordinary situation becoming *extra*ordinary and in the worst way.

Shocked by this latest development, Ava froze. Sarah did too, her mouth forming a perfect oval. Murphy *was* going to attack her, jump up and tear at her throat. A vision erupted in her mind of the savaging that would take place, and she'd be powerless to stop it, maybe even…*deserving* of it.

Still, she was motionless as Murphy was about to spring. *Come on, I'm waiting*, she challenged, albeit silently, surprised to find a feeling of relief on the rise. Maybe the spiked gates of hell wouldn't be waiting this time, the only thing pearly about them beads of blood. There might be nothing afterwards, sweet nothing.

Galvanised, she let go of Jed's lead, pushed Jamie's pram

away, and braced herself for the inevitable. As soon as Jed felt his lead go slack, however, he was the one that lunged. Aiming to do what? Protect her? Or would he be savaged too?

She closed her eyes, balled her hands into fists, and took a deep breath.

"Oh, look at that, look at that. Good boy, Murphy, good boy! Something spooked you good and proper, didn't it? But that's okay, not to worry. Whatever it is, it's over."

Ava's eyes flew open. What was Sarah talking about?

Jed hadn't lunged at Murphy. He'd bounded towards him not to attack but to frolic further, his look-alike companion not growling or preparing to pounce either but frolicking right back, the pair of them emitting playful yelps and licking each other, knocking the table and spilling more coffee, making puddles on the Formica top.

"Jesus!" Ava breathed. "What was all that about? Your dog…"

"Oh, like I said," Sarah replied breezily enough, "something must have spooked him. He's never acted that way before. It's a one-off, I'm sure of it. He's such a good boy, normally. The best."

"The best?"

Ava looked at the playful dogs, questioned everything that had just taken place – if it was even *her* who'd spooked Murphy or someone else, someone just behind her, getting up to leave, whom Jed appeared to have noticed too, inclining his head slightly. Seconds, that's all it had been, and yet for her those seconds continued, her heart racing, her chest heaving.

She grabbed on to Jamie's pram. "Your dog is nuts," she said at last. "And don't try to deny it. Despite how you're trying to brush it off, your voice is shaking every bit as much as mine. Jed. Jed! Come on, it's time to go." As Jed complied, she bent down to grab his lead. "The best, you called him?" she continued. "I don't think so. If it wasn't for Jed—"

"Excuse me," Sarah said, clearly indignant, "but I think you're blowing this up out of all proportion. It was just a couple of crazy seconds, nothing more—"

Ava wouldn't let her speak or continue to lie. "Keep away from me, okay? You and your dog. I'll find another park to walk in from now on."

"Ava, please! This is ridiculous, don't go. Let's grab another coffee, discuss it."

Ava, though, was in no mood to prolong the agony. She hauled all three of them out of there, Jed obedient this time and Jamie quiet for once, although behind her, Leo – the perfect baby from day one – showed he could kick up a storm when he wanted to.

Jed trotted meekly by her side as she continued down the street towards home, now and then glancing up at her, emitting a whine.

"Stop it, Jed," she said, her voice harsh, which she immediately felt bad about.

Jed was the best dog. The one who, yet again, had saved her. Diffused a potentially dangerous situation not via a counterattack but with love and kindness. A lesson in there if she was in the headspace to receive it.

Tears filled her eyes as she walked faster and faster. For whatever reason, Murphy had been spooked by her, had got ready to attack.

Hadn't he?

Finally reaching her own street, she couldn't help but

glance behind her.

It was a gloomy day, rainy, early afternoon, but already the light was fading.

Darkness.

It was in her and…behind her?

Looking back several more times, she squinted. Was someone following her? Twice now, she'd caught sight of a figure, one that darted just out of sight whenever she looked, behind a tree or a car. Nothing distinguishable about them. From the distance the figure maintained, she couldn't tell if it was a man or a woman, just someone dressed in black from head to toe.

Jed pulled on his lead and barked loudly, desperate for her attention.

She focused on him, shivering, and not entirely because of the cold. If someone was stalking her, what did they want? Was it simply another imagining, or was there truly someone intent on livening up this gloomy day with the most macabre of games? If so, if *truly* so, was she its focus or, worse still, Jamie? The menace she felt coming towards her in waves, was that also to be trusted?

Jed continued to pull on his lead towards home.

He was right; they needed to get there, forget this morning had ever happened.

She picked up speed, the knuckles of her hand white as she clutched at the pram.

Having reached her front door, she struggled to release the key from her coat pocket and then fought to insert it into the lock, cursing such clumsiness under her breath.

When the door finally yielded, she got them all inside, slammed it shut, and then fell against it, a sob escaping her, quickly followed by more. Jamie wasn't passive any longer either but crying too. As for Jed, his entire body trembled.

Chapter Six

Crazy. Absolutely crazy to think someone had been following them. Not someone but *something*. What, exactly? An entity of some sort? A demon?

The evening had passed with Ava feeling so cold inside, so scared. Paul had come home an hour or so later than usual, his train having been held up due to signal failure. He was tired and grouchy, doing that thing he did lately, which also set her teeth on edge: letting her know *exactly* how tired he was by heaving a deep sigh as soon as he stepped inside the house. What did he hope to achieve from it? she wondered. Did he want her to rush to him, say something like 'Oh, darling, you poor, poor thing. Come on in, sit down, that's it, nice and warm by the fire, and let me do everything for you. Absolutely bloody everything. Take your coat. Remove your shoes. Fetch you a drink. Can't have the breadwinner lifting a finger now, can we?' As tempted as she was to say that, she wouldn't, of course. She simply stayed where she was in the living room, with Jamie asleep beside her on a nest of cushions. Jed stayed too, which was odd; he hadn't bothered going to the door this evening to greet Paul, as was the norm. She was grateful, though. She *needed* him by her side, her anchor.

He hadn't actually left her side since they'd got home. All afternoon, she'd been swinging between thinking she was crazy and then being certain, absolutely certain, that what she'd seen was all too real. Murphy with his teeth bared, intent on attacking her, then someone following them home with that same intent. Jed sticking to her like glue seemed to prove the point, indicating he was worried and upset too.

The *three* of them had stuck together – her, Jed, and Jamie – which was why the baby was beside her sleeping and not in his cot yet. Ava had closed all blinds and curtains, terrified that if someone had stalked her, they could find their way round to the back of her property, jump the wall – it was low enough – and try to get in the house the back way. Nothing of the sort happened, of course. There'd been no rattling of the door handle, no knock at the window. It had been a quiet afternoon. Silent.

When Paul finally entered the living room, she was surprised to find she *wanted* to run to him, felt a desperate need to have his arms around her, some human comfort. It was…lovely to see him. A normal, down-to-earth, straightforward guy – a pain at times, admitted, but who didn't have their flaws?

Whilst he held her, she could tell him what had happened with Sarah and the stalker, listen as he dismissed Sarah as readily as Jed. 'Someone who just loves to interfere,' he'd say, 'to show off. Just ignore her.' As for the stalker, he'd assure her no one would harm her; he'd make certain of it.

Or…there was the other scenario. The more *likely* one. He'd say those things about Sarah, but about the stalker, something else entirely. 'Don't be silly, of course no one's following you. You're just tired, that's all. Creating nonsense.'

She wouldn't run to him and confide. She didn't.

She must be normal too.

Imagination was the culprit indeed, potent when combined with so much tiredness. No one stalked anyone in a place like Heathfield.

The evening passed, Ava insisting the baby remain beside them whilst they ate dinner on their laps and watched TV. He was sleeping so soundly, the last thing she wanted was to risk waking him and have more screaming.

A great evening, in fact, on the outside. Inside Ava, though, so many emotions stirred, just wouldn't settle, no matter the normality of her current situation. All she could remember was what was *ab*normal, how she'd met someone today, another mother, a potential friend, who'd reached out. And it had all gone so horribly wrong.

Finally, all three went to bed, not late, around ten, Ava saying goodnight to Jed, watching as he settled by the patio doors close to them – *very* close, in fact. How forlorn he looked as she left him. How she wished Paul would relax house rules and allow him to accompany them. To hell with the white bedroom; she could always paint it another colour, throw a few rugs down, cover those stupid floorboards. She was beginning to hate the white anyway, blaming it as much as Paul for Jed's ban – sacred space indeed. She'd definitely change it up as soon as she could, then argue the case for Jed further. Why should Paul have the last say? Had he forgotten so quickly what Jed had done for Jamie? *Nothing* was better than having him in the room with them, keeping them safe.

Having reached the bedroom, Jamie was stirring in her arms, and she stiffened, wondering if he'd kick off, already anticipating hours of screaming. Paul, though, quickly took him from her, rocked him gently from side to side, and then, just as gently, lowered him into the cot, Jamie settling, his eyes closed and head turned to the side.

They hadn't switched on the light when entering the room for fear of disturbing him further, and so it was under cover of the darkness that they got into bed, slowly, quietly, Ava holding her breath, even, until she was beneath the duvet.

All quiet. All good. Paul lying on his back in his space, Ava lying on her back in her space. No touching whatsoever.

She was just about to whisper 'goodnight' when she heard it from downstairs: a growl. Remembered too how Jed had settled himself so close to the patio doors, as if…he knew something. Something they didn't.

"'Night," Paul said, turning over. Evidently, he hadn't heard Jed growl, but Ava remained silent, listening out for more.

Within seconds, Paul was asleep. How he did that, drifted off so fast, she'd never know. Only she was awake, in between husband and son. Jed awake too…

Another growl. She was sure of it. Low. Guttural. Paul snoring now, Ava having to strain to hear, fury building, wishing he'd shut up, fear on the rise too.

A bark. Something *was* wrong downstairs. Terribly, terribly wrong.

Ava shot into a seated position. Her hand came out and thumped Paul hard in the side. "Wake up! Wake up!" she said.

Paul might've struggled to regain consciousness, but Jamie didn't. Pulled so rudely out of sleep, he started screaming.

"What the hell?" said Paul eventually.

Ava jumped out of bed and grabbed Jamie, the baby only screaming louder. "Someone's outside," she said. "Go over to the window and check."

"Outside?"

"Jed's growling. Go on, Paul! Quickly! Check."

"Fuck's sake," he muttered, although he did as commanded. At the window, after craning his neck from side to side, he finally turned back to face her. "No one there."

"Go downstairs! Double check!" she said.

"Okay. All right. Look, try to calm Jamie, okay?" As he left the bedroom, he muttered, "And yourself. Just...fucking calm down."

She *did* try, but not for his sake, for Jamie's. "There, there," she said. "It's okay. Really. We're safe. Me, Daddy, and Jed will keep you safe."

Paul returned almost immediately.

"No one's trying to break in. Everything's fine." With one of his dramatic sighs, he held out his hands. "Give Jamie to me."

"Is Jed okay too?"

"Everything's fine," he insisted. "Look, can we just get Jamie settled and go back to bed? I've a busy day tomorrow."

He wrenched Jamie from her rather than Ava handing him over, the baby's screams by this time at fever pitch. Even so, it was now or never, the reason she was so terrified, on high alert every bit as much as Jed.

"Something happened today, Paul. Something really scary. I'd met someone, and we'd gone for a coffee. Afterwards, I was on my way home, and it felt like, it really, really felt like I was being followed. All the way home."

Paul was bouncing Jamie up and down, wincing at the noise he was making, enough to lift the rafters. "You what? You met someone? Who? Then someone followed you home? The same person you met or what? Bloody hell, Ava, why are you telling me this now? It's hardly the time. Why not earlier?"

"I just...I wasn't going to tell you anything, actually. Because...because I wasn't sure about being followed. But, given the way Jed's behaving downstairs, the growling, it's best you know why I'm on edge. It isn't as if it's for no reason. He knows something's wrong as well as I do. *Badly* wrong."

"Fucking hell," Paul swore, briefly screwing his eyes shut, the assault on his senses from all angles clearly proving too much. "I can't hear myself think!"

"Give me back Jamie."

"NO!" he said, hanging on to the screaming child tighter. "It's fine. He's settling. Who was this person you met?"

"A woman. Sarah. She's got a baby too."

"And who do you think followed you home? Her?"

"No. Someone else. A lone person. Like...darting behind trees and stuff."

"Darting behind trees and stuff?"

"Yes!" Ava insisted. "Look, can we have the dog up—"

"What the bloody hell—"

"Don't swear in front of the baby, Paul!"

He rolled his eyes at the admonishment. "It's not as if he understands, Ava!"

"Not yet, but... You don't believe me, do you? About

being followed home."

"I just want to get some sleep, okay? Whatever happened, no one's trying to break in. We're safe. Quite safe. And look, Jamie's quieting at last. Let's take advantage of it, discuss all this in the morning. For now, everything's under control."

It isn't, Ava wanted to scream. Everything was careering *out* of control, even more so than before. But for her, *only* for her. Quite clearly.

Paul was right about one thing, though: Jamie was quieter, grizzling still, but such a tired grizzle, every bit as exhausted as they were. Of all of them, he had to sleep. And so Paul was right, no more discussing anything, no more paranoia.

Downstairs, Jed was quiet too. Perhaps...he'd sensed a fox or a squirrel, a bold one, coming right up to the door, and tapping on the glass. And that's what had set him off.

No need to discuss anything further. Not even in the morning. With Paul getting up early and rushing off to work, there'd be no chance to anyway.

With Jamie back in his cot, Paul returned to his side of the bed. Again, at no point had they turned the light on; it was all done in darkness.

"'Night," he said again, turning over, away from her. No reassuring hug, nothing.

"'Night," she replied, soon listening to him snoring and Jamie snuffling.

Downstairs, Jed was quiet.

She should just close her eyes, force sleep to come. Could you do that? she wondered. Just like...*insist* on it?

How she wished Paul had held her before drifting off, even briefly.

She turned on her side, back to Jamie, studied the outline of him in the darkness.

If Paul *had* hugged her, it wouldn't have been brief. She'd have hugged him right back, clung to him.

Held on for dear life.

Chapter Seven

Huddled beneath the duvet, 13.5 tog, she'd been plenty warm. So how come Ava wasn't anymore? She was cold. The room like an icebox.

What if Jamie was cold too? *Deathly* cold. She should rise, see to him, make sure that wasn't the case, but somehow…she couldn't. She was frozen in place.

A dream. That's what this was. She'd fallen asleep despite her fear and worry, forced it after all. No way the room was cold – they also kept the heating on low all night. You had to in winter with a baby in the house; his wellbeing depended on it.

In the dream, she was murmuring Paul's name and reaching out, expecting to feel his skin against her palm, the soft smoothness of his back, more warmth. She breathed deeply too to inhale the scent of him.

His smell was one of the things that had attracted her in the first place. They'd met in a pub; he was there with his friends, and she was with a bunch of hers. They'd got chatting at the bar, both of them ordering a round. It'd been such a noisy pub, and so she'd had to lean in close to hear what he was saying. That's when she'd noticed it, a clean smell with a hint of musk, natural, not synthetic.

When they'd first got chatting, she'd thought him good-looking but at the time wasn't searching for a boyfriend, just enjoying some time out, everything just being…hassle free. She'd had a few duff relationships and no desire to keep repeating the process. So, when Paul had started talking to her, she'd been polite but distantly polite. He might've been good-looking, but so what? Plenty of men were. It didn't mean you had to fancy each and every one. But that smell…it did something to her, *captured* her. She'd reared back and looked at him properly this time, noted the sweet curve of his mouth as he smiled, hazel eyes with brown flecks, and the endearing floppiness of his fair hair. And there was no doubt about it, she'd wanted him. Could see that something in him had clicked too, that he didn't just fancy her, the brunette at the bar; it was deeper than that. Their friends had to wait so long for their drinks that, in the end, they'd collected them themselves.

She'd been with Paul for six years. *Glorious* years. Now more than ever, surely? After all, look what they'd produced! And, like Sarah, they could have another baby, and another. A football team! She'd grow into her role as a mother, was bound to become an expert at it. Years down the line there'd be cards on Mother's Day with *Best Mum in the World* emblazoned across them in swirly gold letters. That her children would think that would of course prompt tears of joy. She'd done all right after all. Had had nothing to be afraid of.

Some people were just…born lucky. So why feel guilty suddenly? *Persecute* herself because of it. It was just the way the dice rolled and the cookie crumbled.

"Paul," she said again, able to move a little now, reaching out both hands to find him. The gulf between them, however, was wider than she'd thought. Maybe he'd rolled right to the edge of the bed, and so she inched that way too, hands still grasping at nothing and growing colder. The duvet must have slipped, so she kicked her legs. *Bare* legs.

There was no Paul. No duvet. No bed at all, it seemed.

"Jamie?"

Her eyes flew open as she whipped her head to the side where the cot should be. There was only darkness, as if her eyes were shut still.

She blinked, not once but several times. Harder and harder. Faster and faster.

Darkness was everywhere. She was suspended in it.

Panic set in. Was she awake or still dreaming? It was hard to tell anymore. She felt like she was awake, but then dreams could confuse you, make you think that way, fool you.

"Jed?" she called out instead. "Jed!" He was the one she needed, above Paul and Jamie. The one that kept saving her. "Jed, are you there?"

No response, just frosty silence.

You're asleep. This is a dream.

If that was the case, she needed to wake as soon as possible, *truly* wake. This was not a place she wanted to be. On high alert. Waiting. For what, exactly?

No point in forcing her eyelids to open. In the dream they already were, and she was staring blindly. Maybe she could pinch the skin on the back of her hand. That might catapult her from this, bring it to an end.

The pain registered as she did it, caused her to yelp, even, but nothing changed; her surroundings and situation remained the same. Or was it…could it be…that the darkness had become more intense? Something that bore down upon you, could crush you. She'd taken a breath earlier, and now she exhaled, then tried to inhale again. All she was capable of was shallow breaths, unable to fill her lungs to capacity.

Ava had had dreams before. And nightmares. Nothing like this, though...as extreme. As vivid. How could darkness be vivid? And emptiness so heavy?

If only she could breathe, if she could see, sleep without such torment.

"Jed," she repeated. "What's happening?"

A noise, echoing in the silence. Not that she could place where it was coming from, not at first, or what the sound was, even.

A door handle? Rattling?

Did that mean she was in the bedroom still?

She was freezing, and yet she was burning too, not suspended but on a pyre, a woman accused of something she was innocent of but punished even so.

Wake up! Wake up! Wake up! The command in her head became more urgent. *Wake up before...*

Before what?

Before the door opened. Whatever sought entry into her own personal darkness, she mustn't gaze upon. There were many mysteries in the world, she knew that, acknowledged it, although in a remote sense. So much to discover on life's journey, to marvel at and unravel. But this – whatever *this* was – needed to stay behind the door in the darkest part of the shadows, the umbra, never to emerge, for there was no place for it elsewhere. It simply didn't belong. Despite this, it would want her to gaze on it. She could feel how much it wanted that, its longing so profound she found herself almost...*empathising*. That need for connection.

If their eyes locked, it would never let go. There'd be darkness forever, then, and a madness as sticky as molasses. *Not so lucky, then, eh?* She'd lose everything.

Including Jamie.

Wake up! Wake up!

Desperation had as strong a hold on her as the darkness, and still the door rattled, creaked too, as if opening at last.

Helpless, but she couldn't afford to be.

She moved her body further, thrashed her limbs, calling out – where was Jed? – although her voice was as weak and as pitiful a thing as she was. She *thought* she was thrashing her arms and legs but feared she was lying limp instead. In this nether-world she'd woken into, nothing was as it seemed.

The door was indeed opening, and with it came a sliver of light. Nothing comforting about it, though; it was crude, yellowish, sickly. Enough light to see by and therefore cruel. What sought entry was *not* a thing to empathise with. How could she even begin to think that? *There's no connection between us.* She was ordinary, a wife and a new mother. Jamie needed her, perhaps even Paul. *Jed, where are you? Will you save me a third time?*

She tried to turn her head and close her eyes but couldn't, immobile again, held rigid like she'd been that day in labour. The thing that would soon appear – taking its time, *arrogant*, enjoying the fear it provoked – was it from another realm or dimension? Or…something worse still: her shadow self. Now separate.

I have to wake up! Someone help me!

If only she could turn from it, not be in its thrall.

She couldn't see it, not yet, but she could hear it well enough.

"Too late. All too late."

It isn't! It can't be.

Whoever it was begged to differ, delivering words she now expected:

"You're already mine."

Chapter Eight

March was but a day away, and although Christmas and New Year's had passed in a haze, Jamie so tiny then and Ava still recovering from the birth, it was *still* a new year. One she must face with more confidence. She'd been fragile after the birth, and so had Jamie, but with every passing day they were becoming stronger. He was changing, as babies tend to do, becoming more robust, no more holding-his-breath episodes and scaring the life out of them. And she would change too.

After the nightmare she'd had, if she didn't swim, she'd sink, and so she made a pact with herself: *I won't give in to this, whatever 'this' is, let the darkness overwhelm me.*

Jed had wandered up to her whilst she was deciding this, her jaw set firm, her hands clenched tight, and he jumped up on the sofa beside her, leaning in. Immediately, she unfurled her hands and held him close. They sat there, the pair of them, for an age, not moving. And then she kissed the top of his head.

"Thanks, Jed," she said, "for always being there. For understanding."

Jed whined briefly before settling down in the same spot. This was unusual for him; he tended to go towards the patio doors and settle there, facing the garden. Today, though, he was happy where he was, and so she let him be, thankful Paul wasn't there, as he hated Jed climbing onto furniture, had rules about that too.

A new year and a fresh start. Time to get ready and face the day. They had found other places to walk to avoid Sarah and Murphy, heading to the shops sometimes when the weather was bad, at other times just ambling aimlessly along the streets, the dog by her side and the pram in front of her. No one following them, of course, and eventually she stopped checking.

Today was a *big* day. Firstly, Jamie was moving into the nursery this evening, still monitored to the hilt, and secondly, she'd had a leaflet through the door earlier in the week, advertising a music class for new parents in a church hall nearby – being held this morning, Thursday. A chance to introduce some structure to days which otherwise blurred into one another and, of course, make new friends. If, like Sarah, they embraced motherhood, if it was all hearts and flowers for them too, she wouldn't hold it against them, not anymore. Wanted it to be that way for herself too. Jed couldn't come, which she felt guilty about. They'd been inseparable since she'd got him; he'd wonder where she was. But she'd hurry back afterwards, make it up to him with a good long walk and some of those treats he loved for being such a good dog, cheese-and-beef nibbles. He'd be okay – she'd only be gone for a couple of hours. Rushing about getting ready, she felt almost giddy with excitement, proud of herself for summoning up the courage to do this.

In the hallway, Ava slipped on her coat, Jamie already in his pram, fastened in. Jed trotted up to them, wagging his tail, full of excitement too whilst eyeing his lead. She bent to pat his head. "Sorry, boy, you can't come this time.

We've a music class to attend, and, sadly, they don't allow dogs. I know, right? Crazy! But I'll make it up to you, I promise."

She hoped he'd be fine about it, but he started barking, whining too, endlessly nudging at her coat with his nose. He'd only just been to the toilet, so she knew it wasn't that, more like separation anxiety kicking in. As she watched his performance, guilt threatened to change her mind. Perhaps she should stay. Jamie was too young for a music class, for God's sake, would likely scream his way through it, disrupt proceedings spectacularly. But then, she reminded herself, it *was* for babies, and so they might all scream at some point. If she went, what was the worst that could happen? She'd come away with a headache? She *would* go, and Jed...well, Jed would have to learn about staying home alone.

Before she could talk herself out of it further, she opened the door and quickly hauled Jamie outside, Jed continuing to protest as she shut the door.

A swift half-hour walk along streets slick from a downpour earlier and she arrived on church grounds, a path in front of her dividing into two, one leading to the church itself with its tall spire, the other to a much smaller, squat building: the church hall. It was there she hurried to, to a set of doors with peeling and flaking white paint.

As she opened them, a blast of much-needed warmth engulfed her. Entering the building, she stepped into a foyer, a fusty smell in the air, she noticed, and another set of doors directly in front of her, these ones wide open. Although there was another ten minutes before the class was due to start, she could see people milling about in there already. People who...knew each other, it seemed, all women, all holding babies, and all chatting amiably. On a table to the side of them were facilities for making tea and coffee, and a plate of biscuits.

She shouldn't linger but get in there, introduce herself, grab a coffee, and begin chatting too. She *willed* herself to do that, but her feet refused to obey. She continued to stand there, paralysed. No way she could just saunter in. She didn't belong amongst such cheery people, *genuinely* cheery, not just faking it to make it. *Is that what you're doing, Ava?* she asked herself. *Faking it?* She was determined to be happier than before, sodding Mother Earth if needs be, and yet how quickly such resolve could fall apart. Since the nightmare, she'd taught herself to feel her smiles, to laugh from the belly, to think only of nice things, not take any notice of the news or any events that could bring her down, TV shows too – everything had to be lighthearted. And it had worked. She was certain of it. Was excited about coming here earlier. So standing like she was in the foyer, something caught in the headlights again, fucking Bambi come to life, peering in, frightened, an outcast, *untethered*, should not be happening. Of course she belonged; she was a bona fide mother. The people inside weren't strangers, just friends she hadn't met yet.

Stranger... The word kept repeating. *They won't want you here. They have enough friends. You'll remain the stranger. Strange. Strange. Strange.*

Tears filled her eyes as Jamie began agitating in his pram, fighting against the restraints. In another two or three months, he'd be crawling, able to get away from her, unstoppable, sensing too how strange his mother was.

No way she could go any further, continue this charade; she had to get them both out of there. *Sorry, Jamie. I'm so, so sorry. I'm a terrible mother. I know it.*

She shuffled backwards. All she wanted was to be home, where she could shut the world out again, bury her face in Jed's fur, her screams muffled against his skin, the dog allowing her to just…vent, let all the fake stuff out, the real stuff too. An animal never judged. *Jed* didn't. *Leave before you make a fool of yourself!*

She'd almost fully turned when she heard a voice behind her, a voice that, strangely, made her spine tingle.

"Hey, there! You okay? Not going already, are you? We haven't started yet."

As much as she wanted to, she couldn't just ignore whoever was speaking to her. No choice but to swing back round to find a man who was just a little taller than her, well-built with broad shoulders. He had dark hair and a closely trimmed beard, was around her age, either late twenties or early thirties, and casually dressed in jeans and a navy jumper over a blue-collared shirt. An ordinary man but for his eyes; so brown they were practically black.

"I…um…I was just…" She wished she could stop spluttering! *Take a deep breath, Ava, relax!* "I had a leaflet put through my door about the music class," she said, pleased – and surprised – when her voice did indeed hold steady, "and I thought I'd come along. I'm not sure, though…can you just turn up?"

"Yes, yes, absolutely! I think it actually says so on the leaflet, doesn't it? If not, my apologies. It's a drop-in class, all very casual, not something you have to commit to week after week. Donations only, all of which go to the church, of course. Look, as I say, we're about to start, so come on in. You'll enjoy it." His grin, with something of a boyish quality about it and therefore endearing, grew wider.

"Well, he will, your little man. The name's Ben, by the way."

He held out his hand, Ava forcing herself to take it, registering the firmness of his grip as she introduced herself.

"I'm Ava, and this is Jamie."

"How old?"

"How old? Um…oh, you mean him, not me."

Ben stood there, still with her hand in his, caught between frowning and laughing.

"He's…just over three months old, actually. And there I am, thinking you meant me when you asked about age. I guess…I guess I need another few months to adjust to being a mother. Some people do, though, don't they? Not just being a mother but a father too. *Everyone* needs time to adjust to new circumstances."

Ava forced her hand from his and briefly closed her eyes, felt even more embarrassed for babbling now instead of spluttering. This man – Ben – with his dark, piercing eyes, must think he was dealing with a fool and no doubt silently wish she would leave.

When she opened her eyes, however, Ben was standing closer than before.

"Don't go," he said. "Come on in. We don't bite. Really, we don't. Well…*they* don't."

Despite herself, she laughed. He did too. He was being so friendly! The joke he'd just made was an ordinary one, the kind anyone might make, that she might've too in the days when she used to joke. So why was her spine still tingling?

Ava, stop this! Act normal!

Or what? She'd end up in a facility somewhere? Locked

69

in a room and the key thrown away? It was just a music class she and Jamie were attending. And Ben was just a man. All very ordinary, nothing terrifying about it. *Smile, Ava, as widely as Ben.*

She allowed herself to be led from the foyer into the hall, a somewhat gaping space, Ben having taken her arm and gently steering her. Everyone turned as he did. The music teacher, he had to be, holding court.

"Shall we begin?" he said, finally releasing her and clapping his hands instead. "Grab a cushion and an instrument, form a circle, and, Ava and Jamie, why don't you sit by me?" His attention back on his adoring crowd – clearly, he *was* the teacher, a church volunteer or something – he added, "Thanks for coming today, everybody. It really is lovely to see you. I can tell already this is going to be the *friendliest* group."

* * *

Ben Miller was not a church volunteer but the vicar himself, Ava found out after class, presiding over the church that the hall was attached to. Just like people might after a mass, so the group of mothers gathered again to chat following thirty minutes of lusty singing. And she was right, a few of them did indeed know each other already, the easiness between them something forged over time. Even so, they introduced themselves to Ava, complimented Jamie, and showed off their own babies. She was met with a flurry of names, trying to catalogue each one but losing the battle. *His* name, Ben's, was easy to remember. Not just the only man of the group, he was also the friendliest, the warmest. *Charismatic.*

She was grateful to him for easing her into this first session.

"You will come again, won't you?" The eagerness she saw in his eyes touched her. "We aim to meet every Thursday. God willing."

What could she say but yes, she'd love to, mentioning also how much Jamie had enjoyed it, his eyes wide throughout and not one hissy fit, only a series of smiles. He needed this kind of interaction, and so did she. Paul would be so pleased when she told him later what she'd done and how well it had gone. In fact, she *couldn't wait* to tell him, resolving to dig her mobile out of her pocket as soon as she left the hall.

At last, people drifted off, waving or shouting their goodbyes, issuing promises they'd be there next week too. Some left in pairs, going to grab lunch somewhere, maybe, at that café she'd gone to with Sarah, the Brew Box. God, she hoped no one who'd been in there during that time was here. If so, she could imagine the conversation now taking place: 'It is her, isn't it? The one that caused all the commotion. I wasn't sure at first, but the more I looked, the more I realised I'm right.'

This paranoia! It would eat her alive if she let it.

Everyone was leaving, but she wasn't, not yet, as Ben was still standing with her, talking to her, and even though Jamie was getting fidgety again, clearly exhausted from all the activity but fighting it, the vicar continued chatting, even directing her to where there were some chairs stacked up against a wall. It wasn't long until – with the exception of Jamie, whom sleep was finally managing to overpower – they were on their own entirely.

Once seated, his gaze lingered on hers, his

eyes...searching?

Feeling examined under a microscope, she searched for something to say. "How come music classes? You're a musician as well as a vicar?"

His cheeks crinkled when he laughed. "No. Can't you tell? I'm not a musician, although I can play a few chords on the guitar. Sadly, though, I've a voice like a foghorn, and so I let the parents and children do all the work regarding that. This class was the brainchild of the previous vicar, Moira Lintern. She ran it originally. Moira was a very hands-on vicar, as I aspire to be. She ran a number of community projects, some successful, some not so much. This one proved very popular, and so when I took over recently, I thought I'd continue it. Took on board what she told me, that for some new parents the class is a lifeline."

"A lifeline?" Ava mused. "I see."

Ben sat back in his chair, crossed his legs and shrugged. "I take her point. Parenthood can be a lonely place. Although you've added to your family, indeed, to the world in general, some can feel...isolated because of it. If someone is the first in their circle of friends to have a baby, they can feel out on a limb, an outcast."

"An outcast?" Ava's voice reduced to a whisper as she once again echoed him.

Ben nodded, gestured around him. "And so this is a safe space for them to come, babies *and* parents to have some fun and just relax. Again, like Moira, I feel it's important to make sure everyone feels included. Ava..." he continued, hesitating now, she could tell, causing her to stiffen, to feel another surge of panic. This hall seemed even bigger with just the two of them in it, the air

72

weighing heavily when before, during the class, it had been filled with lightness, the lightness of energy, she supposed, something now depleted. It was also, despite electric lighting overhead, gloomier, the sun not streaming in as much, clouds outside no doubt gathering, trying to hide it. He said her name again, perhaps noting she'd drifted. "How are you since having Jamie? He's a lovely lad, very bonny. Are you…okay?"

"Okay? Yes. Yes," she replied, a wave of heat engulfing her. "Of course! Why?"

As soon as she'd added 'why', she regretted it. She didn't want to know why he'd asked and was sure he'd heard it as plainly as she had, that crack in her voice when she'd said it.

She'd found his eyes piercing before, as if trying to see beyond mere skin and bone to what lay beneath. She'd found it uncomfortable, troubling even, a *violation*, but how could she have thought that? There was such concern on his face. As a vicar, it was his job to care for others, to interact. To help where he could.

"I…I…" With no distraction of any kind, Jamie sleeping, not grizzling, and Jed at home, not tugging on his lead, she had no option but to continue. "I'm fine," she reiterated, but her eyes betrayed her, she knew they did, her whole demeanour. "Sorry. I'm just…tired. You know how it is." She almost laughed at this; he was a vicar, a man. Could vicars marry? Have wives and children? She didn't know. Glancing at his hand, she noticed no ring on his finger. "Jamie's sleeping now, but he doesn't always. In my house, sleep's become a rare thing. And there it is, the reason I'm *not* always fine. Because I'm tired. Just really, really tired."

Ben placed one hand over the top of hers and gently squeezed.

She'd lowered her head whilst speaking but now raised it, saw something in his eyes which at first startled her. There was pain, a pain she recognised, that which stemmed from loneliness and conflict, reflected right back at her.

Despite having a husband and both sets of parents visiting often, no one could see what she was going through, let alone understand it.

But this man did. The vicar. Ben.

Not just touching her hand, he reached for her, there in the silence of that vast hall, and drew her into the circle of his arms.

The tears came then, no way to stop them, the floodgates opening. So much pain in them, so much guilt, shame, and bewilderment, and all such heavy crosses to bear. She was ungrateful, undeserving, and so bloody frightened.

This close, the smell of him was like the hall, a bit fusty, and at first she stiffened because of it. She grew used to it, though, in his arms, until it was no longer noticeable. If only Paul would hold her like this, if only he understood. But she knew what Paul was like; he'd judge her, be...*appalled* by her. He loved being a parent, and she did too, she was certain of it, deep down, but all these other feelings were masking the joy. Would Ben be able to help her find her way back to her old self? Was such a thing even possible?

"That's it," Ben murmured, "let it out. Let it all out. Remember what I told you, this is a safe space you're in now. The space to do exactly what you're doing. I'm here to help, and I will, Ava. Now that we've found each other,

I'll help all I can."

She was crying, she was nodding, rearing back to wipe at her nose, the storm within gradually easing, a measure of calm returning.

When she finally left Ben, after promising she'd show up the following week, Jamie was stirring and it was raining, the pavements wet again.

She didn't mind one bit.

She not so much walked but *floated* home, something in her that had been absent for months – not just relief, more than that. Happiness? *Euphoria*, even? It was as though…a healing had taken place inside the church hall, a miracle. For that's what Ben Miller was by his very profession, a modern-day miracle worker.

From this moment onwards, everything would fall into place.

Why then, when she opened the door to her house, as she called out for Jed, expecting him to come bounding towards her, was she met with stony silence?

"Jed?" she said again, shutting the door behind her. "Where are you?"

Parking the pram at the foot of the stairs, Jamie awake but babbling to himself, holding his hands up and staring at them in such sweet wonder, as if recalling a memory of her clapping them at class, she left him and hurried into the living room.

Jed was there, but he wasn't the first thing she saw. The first thing was blood. So much blood. Everywhere. The room was drenched in it. A mix of bright red and dark blood, some of it in pools as smooth as silk, whereas elsewhere it was congealing.

The shock of it almost stilled her heart. Disbelieving,

she screwed her eyes shut. How could anyone survive such haemorrhaging?

She could. She *had*.

It wasn't real, what she was seeing, just a memory – of herself, on that floor, bleeding and screaming, an *enhanced* memory, more vivid than ever.

Why? When she was happy, when she felt more like her old self?

There was that smell again, that fusty smell there'd been on the vicar, now on her clothes and getting worse. Why was she also remembering that?

"Jed?" she cried, every bit as pitiful as she'd been in the foyer of the church hall.

As weak.

When her vision cleared, he was there in front of her. But his tail was static when usually it wagged at the slightest provocation. On seeing her, even after a bathroom break in the garden, he'd go into raptures, chasing his tail around and around. A daft dog, *her* dog, eternally grateful, it seemed, that she'd taken a chance on him, that he'd been rescued. Who'd make her smile, give her comfort. *True* comfort. Who asked for nothing in return but some food to eat and a warm bed to sleep on.

Stock-still. No wagging tail.

But growling.

Chapter Nine

Ava and Jamie returned to music class the next week, as promised. And there was Ben, talking to a trio of mothers, all of them laughing at whatever he was saying in what Ava considered to be an affected manner. *Trying to curry favour,* was the reason that formed in her head. *Because in this room, he's not God's representative, he's God.*

His head came up, and his eyes met hers.

As they did, a smile crept across his face – one of relief? More thoughts crowded her mind before she could stop them. Was he bored with the other mothers' conversation? Waiting for Ava to appear? Stupid to think so! Arrogant. Even so, he quickly made his excuses, extricated himself from the trio and came over.

"I'm so glad you're here, Ava! You cut it fine, though. I was worried."

Worried? Really? She wasn't just one of many, an attendee, but more significant than that? He was right, though, she *had* deliberated about coming, so nervous about it. But she was glad she had. Not only would he have been disappointed in her, she'd have been disappointed in herself. There was another reason that had almost swayed her: Jed had been upset again when she was leaving him.

What had happened with Jed when she'd returned from class the previous week had played on her mind. He'd growled at her, when he'd never growled before. Tentatively, she'd approached him, kept calling out his name but softly that time, trying to soothe him, fighting off dismay and doubt. Had Paul been right all along with his concerns? They knew nothing of Jed's history. He'd just been…found and never claimed. Why? Had he turned on his previous family, as he was now turning on her, and subsequently been turfed out? Could it be he wasn't a kind and gentle dog at all, that he'd fooled them?

Unkind thoughts, the very worst, such betrayal in them. Jed was as precious to her as her own child. And yet was he also something to fear?

"Jed, come on," she'd coaxed, holding her hand out, surprised further when he replaced growling with a whine, when he *cowered*. What was wrong with him? Her gaze briefly left him to look outside the patio doors. Had something happened in her absence? He'd been spooked somehow? "It's okay," she continued, bending so that their eyes were level. Another vision entered her head: he'd lunge at her as Murphy had wanted to do, be the one to rip her throat out. All that blood she'd seen, it had nothing to do with what had happened prior in this room, was instead a vision of the future, a premonition.

Despite this, she reached out and made contact, felt the familiar softness of his fur, how smooth it was, wanted more than ever to bury herself in it, to just hold him, cling as though she were drowning and he the only thing keeping her afloat.

"Don't you ever change, Jed. please. You're my one constant. My rock."

He leapt, but straight into her arms, nuzzling her, not tearing her apart, whining still, licking her, *avidly* licking, as if trying to wash her clean.

No longer worried, she was laughing, trying to hold him at arm's length.

"I missed you too," she spluttered when she could.

The moment was broken by Jamie issuing a scream from the hallway, no longer content with his own company. It had been a strange happening, a strange day, some of it disturbing, definitely, but she worked hard to maintain the euphoria of earlier. That night, she cooked. A good meal, successful, a beef stroganoff, which was one of Paul's favourites.

They put Jamie to bed and opened a bottle of red with dinner, sat down to eat and chat like any other normal couple, the subjects touched on ordinary, but nothing wrong in that. Paul told her about his day, the workload that just kept increasing, and she told him more about the music class, which he was indeed pleased about, although the conversation did swing quickly back round to his work again. Ava didn't mind. Best just to go with the flow.

As for Jed that evening, he took up his usual position by the patio doors, his eyes perennially trained on the outside, giving a quiet bark now and then if a squirrel should happen by, or a fox. They got a lot of foxes in the neighbourhood, so that could well be what agitated him, so she closed the curtains, giving him some respite. Might close them too when she left for music class.

In the ensuing days, the dog had stuck close to her.

Days that she'd counted down.

And now, with Ben standing before her, as close as ever, she had to do it before class started: apologise. "Ben, I just want to say, well…first, thank you so much, you know, for listening to me last week. I really appreciated your concern." *Your insight. This connection we have.* "I also want to say I'm sorry. I feel embarrassed, actually, as I really am fine. This week's been great. Fantastic, in fact. It's likely just a touch of the baby blues as well as tiredness, but it seems to be easing. I know what the previous vicar meant about this class being a lifeline, though. I've been looking forward to it all week."

Ben was nodding. The same age as her, or thereabouts, but he seemed so much more mature, worldly wise. She a mere child in comparison.

"Good, good," he replied. "Really glad to hear it. Now, come on, let's get this show on the road. I hope Jamie's in fine form today as well, singing his heart out."

"Singing?" Ava queried, a grin on her face, maybe even a *stupid* grin. "Not sure you can call it that."

"You, then," he said. "You sing to your heart's content." Patting at his chest, he added, "Nothing lifts the soul like a bit of singing."

They laughed again as he accompanied her and Jamie to the crowd, who seemed to have mutated into a single entity rather than several separate people, all of them with their eyes on Ben and Ava as they approached. Just imagination, but Ava was sure she detected one or two of them frowning as they jiggled babies on their hips, a scowl, even, from a dark-haired woman – Heidi. Paranoia. Intent on sabotaging everything. No way she'd entertain it.

Although she'd been introduced to the women the previous week, Ben did the honours again, gesturing for them to come closer to Ava and Jamie, *insisting* on it. If he was God and they were his flock, there was no real option but to obey. Jenna. Leanne. Polly. Lou. Christina. Heidi. Anna. Jo. She must try to remember their names this time, make a concerted effort. Especially as Ben had left her, wandered off, and was now scattering cushions in a circle and placing some instruments within it: maracas, tambourines, and some rather bashed-up rain sticks.

As they'd done before, the women cooed over Jamie, trotting out the same kind of sentiments they had last time, that he was cute, destined to be a heartbreaker, the set routine. Ava tried to match each compliment with one of her own in an attempt at conformity. Of all the women, Lou looked like she might actually be her type, less yummy-mummy, a little more down-to-earth, dressed much the same as she was in jeans, boots, and a jumper.

"Are you a full-time mum?" Ava asked her as others began to drift towards the circle.

Lou frowned initially at her question, then pulled a bit of a face. "Well, anyone who has children is a full-time mum, don't you think?"

"Oh," Ava said, feeling the heat rise in her cheeks. "What I meant was—"

Lou interrupted her. "I know what you meant. don't worry. I'm teasing. I work part-time for a local insurance firm. Holbrooke's. They have offices in Heathfield. Have you heard of them?" Before Ava had a chance to answer, Lou continued. "They're a nice little family firm, a cushy number, if I'm honest, so I didn't want to give it up when I had Lola, couldn't really afford to either, not with the cost of living the way it's going at the moment. So, no, I'm not full-time, per se." With Lola sleeping in a pram beside her, Lou had raised her hands at the 'full-time' bit and wriggled her fingers. "I'm glad, though. I think it's important to have a balance. Work gives you an identity other than just being a mother. Do you work too?"

Ava shook her head. "I did, but no, not right now. I managed a coffee shop, and it's something I'd like to do again – would love to, in fact. When Jamie's older, when I can juggle it all, the various demands. I want to *own* a coffee shop with a small batch roast business; that's the dream. Difficult, though, isn't it? To juggle, I mean? Babies take up so much of your time. There's never a minute to yourself, is there?"

She was babbling, prone to it. But even so, was there any need for Lou to be quite so rude? Her eyes had glazed over after only the first couple of sentences Ava'd uttered; she was also looking around at the other women, finally catching someone's eye and smiling at them.

"Sorry," she said, not bothering to glance Ava's way again, "I think Jenna wants a word. Better see what it is before the caterwauling starts."

Ava tried to breathe evenly as she watched Lou go, tried also to quash the despair she felt, which hadn't miraculously vanished as she'd hoped. Before having Jamie, she'd been popular enough, had an array of friends. People had gravitated towards her, so why now was the opposite true? What was it about her that...*repelled* people? Was it because they could see below the surface, detecting a conflict of emotions? The negativity? *Are you a full-time mum?* What a stupid thing to ask, and Lou not hesitating, not for one minute, to make sure she knew it was. She should never have come here. To hell with it. She was already turning, clutching Jamie to her, heading for his pram, when she caught sight of him, Ben, alternating his gaze between her and Lou, who was now laughing with Jenna. She could hear them – *raucously* laughing. At her? The woman who asked stupid questions?

There was a frown on his face, which was deepening, and something in Ava recoiled to see it. She felt a need, an urge, to go to him and say something like *It's okay about what happened. It was my fault, really. Honestly, it's not a problem.* Before she could, though, and perhaps thankfully so, he brought his hands together in a clap, the resultant boom thunderous. If she had gone to him, said something like that, she'd have made things so much worse! Plus, maybe Jenna *did* have something important to impart to Lou, and it wasn't just a ruse. The pair of them were shoulder to shoulder now, sitting there in the circle, reminding Ava of those women in history textbooks that would huddle at an execution, knitting, cackling, and gossiping, waiting for the guillotine to drop. Women who weren't her type at all. And nor was she theirs.

Ben secured her attention once more.

"Let class begin," he said, definite steel in his voice.

* * *

Despite what had happened at the music class, or what she'd *perceived* to have happened, Ava and Jamie attended for a third week running. Straightaway she noticed something: Lou was absent, and Jenna. The other women were also a little more subdued, the atmosphere not as jolly but somewhat stilted. Ben was his usual gregarious self, however, not even mentioning the absentees. This was a drop-in class, after all, made clear on the leaflets and by Ben himself when he'd first spoken to her: *Come if you like, if you're free.* It was a donation per class; five pounds seemed to be the going rate, dropped onto a plate on the table by the biscuits, tea, and coffee, a bit of profit in it for the church, hopefully. No commitment, though, as Ben had stressed, so no need to comment on the no-shows.

She was late again that morning, turning up just a few minutes before the session began, hoping Ben wouldn't delay the class as he'd done the previous week, giving everyone, *her* particularly, more chance of a chitchat, or rather a chance *not* to be included in it. *Spurned.* Despite trying at times during the previous week to convince herself that hadn't happened, she remained convinced by it. Lou was bored by her, even though she barely knew her, which hurt, deeply. And yet here Ava was, at the class, in spite of them and because of him: Ben.

He beamed when she walked in, and beckoned her over.

"Class is due to begin," he said as she arrived at his side. "Haven't got time to talk now, but afterwards, okay?"

"Sure." Did he mean talk to just her or everyone? Although people took their own sweet time leaving, the social was meant to happen in the half hour leading up to class, so maybe it *was* just her he was talking about. Her cheeks surely glowed at the thought. Did he notice? she wondered. Probably not.

He turned from her, addressed the class, and everyone took their seats on the scattered cushions, the sound of the ensuing voices as everyone sang and mimed their way through songs such as 'Wheels on the Bus' and 'Morning Town' enough to drown out any screams from babies offended by the noise rather than enjoying it. A good class. Fun. Any tension there was dissolving into laughter. It had taken courage to come here today after Lou's snub, but it had also been the right thing to do.

She sang, and Jamie made noises and jiggled his body, loving the commotion. Whatever happened between her and these other women, she'd have to keep coming for his sake, not be put off by a bunch of cliquey mothers. Maybe, just maybe, someone new would turn up, someone more like her, and they could pal up.

With the session over, no one lingered. Ben ensured it.

"Thank you, class. That was great. Really uplifting! I have to rush back to the church for a meeting – about the future of the church, actually, so I'm sorry, but I must hurry you." He adopted what he clearly hoped was a hangdog look. "And there's me thinking life as a vicar would be a cushy number. Even one that presides over relatively empty pews. I'm run off my feet!"

His comment – slightly barbed, Ava thought, *accusatory* – didn't meet with the laughter she'd expected. In fact, there were some who did indeed look sheepish, not hanging around at all, as if they couldn't wait to leave.

Some *did* smile, though, still trying to garner approval.

Ava shook her head at the thoughts careering through her head, such nonsense at times. What should *she* do, though? Go, as he'd just asked, disregard what he'd said earlier about them having time for a chat? Of course she should. He was simply being polite before, perhaps even a little absent-minded. As disappointed as she felt by that – and it was *deep* disappointment – she'd scoop Jamie up and return home, fetch Jed and walk him. After that, she'd make some lunch, hope that Jamie had a nap so that she could have one too, looking forward to snuggling up with Jed on the sofa downstairs. After that...well, she'd try not to count down the hours until Paul returned. The afternoons could be so long.

"Ava? Ava. Shall we have that catch-up I mentioned?"

It was Ben, coming over to her as she wrestled with

Jamie to put his coat on. Swinging round to face him, she knew she was blushing again.

"Ben! Hi! I thought you were busy, you know, with church business?"

As the hall emptied, he leant in conspiratorially. "A white lie," he said, then quickly crossed himself. "May God forgive me."

What a character Ben was! A nice man. Not as hard to get to know as the others, keen, in fact, to extend the hand of friendship. *A vicar*, she reminded herself. Concerned for her. And, therefore, it wasn't friendship, not exactly. She was more of a duty, not a churchgoer but still a member of his parish.

Even so, she'd take it. The help he wanted to give.

"Oh right, great, well…I'm free if you are," she said, trying her best to sound casual. "It's not quite Jamie's nap time yet. If it ever is," she added wryly.

"Brilliant. Do you mind if we go to the church, actually, rather than stay here? Despite the heating, the hall's chilly this morning."

To illustrate his point, he hugged himself and made a *brrrr* sound. She hadn't noticed it was particularly cold, but he was right; with everyone's departure it had *grown* cold. A shiver ran through her too as she followed him when he turned, waiting patiently in the foyer whilst he produced a set of keys and locked up.

As they stepped outside onto the path, the heavens opened. It was as though someone had stuck a pin in a water-filled balloon, biblical even.

"Shit!" Ava said as the first raindrops hit her, then immediately clapped a hand over her mouth. "Sorry! I didn't mean to swear."

Ben was clearly amused. "Don't worry about it. As saintly as I look, I'm just a vicar. I even swear too, you know, on occasion."

Mocking. But *gently* mocking. Teasing her.

"Come on, quick," he continued. "Don't let Jamie get wet."

The three of them on the stone path, they dashed towards the church, Ava slipping slightly, the moss that covered a fair few of the slabs proving somewhat lethal. Despite holding on to the pram, she would have fallen if not for Ben, who, with lightning speed, reached out and steadied her. *There when I need him. Always.* It was such a vivid thought, technicolour, exploding in her mind and, in recent months, usually reserved solely for Jed. How could it be that a stranger – for that's what he was still – could be there for her? He was, though. He seemed to be. Mostly present in her thoughts, admitted, this man who showed such understanding.

They reached the church porch, none of them overly wet due to how quickly they'd run, the hood of Jamie's pram pulled low and thus protecting him. Ava was breathless, though, having to lean against the wall, caught between trying to steady her breathing and laughing. She'd experienced euphoria before thanks to Ben. Now it was something else as extreme: exhilaration. He was leaning against a chunk of wall too, a raindrop running down his nose to hang precariously off the end of it. When she gestured to it, it made them laugh harder.

"Come on, let's get inside," he said, brandishing the keys once again. "How's the little fellow doing?"

Ava peeked inside the pram. "He's asleep."

"Not one for drama, then?"

"Not unless it's three o'clock in the morning. He creates enough then."

As they ventured inside, she wrinkled her nose. The church had a fusty smell, which she'd smelt on Ben already, the result of lingering incense, perhaps, frankincense and myrrh.

Ben continued to chat. "You take it in turns, do you, the nighttime shenanigans?"

Ava shook her head, "No, not really. Paul needs his sleep. He has to leave early every morning. He commutes to London. Looking after Jamie's my job."

"Correct," he said, a reply which surprised her, made her raise her eyebrows a little as she parked Jamie in the aisle and took a seat in one of the pews at the back of the church, where Ben had already seated himself. Before she could ask what he meant, he explained, perhaps having noted her confusion. "What I mean is that you're right, looking after a child *is* a job, a twenty-four-hour, seven-days-a-week job, and yet so many don't see it that way. If you're not paid for a job, there seems to be very little respect. And yet child-rearing, producing sound individuals, *balanced* individuals to carry the beacon between generations, is the most important job in the world, surely? Too many are left to run feral, and, well…problems occur because of it. *Far-reaching* problems." He shook his head as if in despair about it. "I don't know, it's a strange world we live in sometimes. How much we get wrong."

Ava could only nod her head at his words. She'd thought along the exact same lines. Motherhood was a labour of love; it was indeed the worthiest job of all, and yet all too often you were dismissed because of it. Paul was guilty of that to a degree. He might not have come right out and said it, but she knew he thought that what he did – earnt a wage, basically – should take precedence. And it *was* important. They needed money to live just like everyone else, and so of course she attached importance to it. So why couldn't he afford her the same courtesy? It was their child she was raising, for God's sake!

For God's sake... She might have only thought the words, but she was in a church, the one place you shouldn't take His name in vain.

Not Catholic nor a Protestant, one of the increasing number who lived life *without* religion, she nonetheless lifted her hand and made the sign of the cross. Why, she had no idea. Did she honestly think she'd be struck by lightning?

Ben watched her do it, and his expression darkened, *considerably*, if only briefly.

"Ben?" she said. "Sorry, have I offended you? I wasn't taking the mick or anything. I was just...well, I don't know what I was doing, actually. It just felt...right."

"Offended me? No, no, no." The smile was back on his face, wider than ever. He had good teeth, was handsome, very. But that smell that clung to him...the smell of the church. Not his fault, though. The church was his work place.

"Are you okay?" she checked further.

He shivered. Understandably. It *was* cold in here, despite him suggesting earlier it was warmer than the hall. It wasn't. Perhaps *that's* what concerned him, the fact it was so chilly. Briefly, she looked around her. It was a church, an ordinary church with stone walls, an altar up front, and rows and rows of pews. The windows were large but plain. Not a church that had been heavily invested in, like those with stained glass and intricate carvings everywhere, memorials on the wall or paving the aisle, honouring those who could afford to be buried within sight of God – the favoured. Instead, this was a very ordinary place. Neglected, even. A layer of dust over everything.

"So there aren't many that come here nowadays?" she asked, feeling sorry because of that suddenly, when before she'd never given it a second thought.

Ben nodded, somewhat ruefully. "Did you read that report in the news recently?" When she said she hadn't, he went on to enlighten her. "For the first time in recorded history, over half of England say they've no religion."

As well as feeling sorry for him, guilt – an old friend, lately – reared up too.

"Sadly," he continued, "this church, along with many others, isn't packed on a Sunday, let alone any other time of week. Weddings, funerals, even baptisms can now all take place elsewhere. In truth, more attend the music class than here."

"I'm sorry about that," Ava replied. "That must be tough."

He shrugged. "We have to keep going. Such is the nature of the work we do. You don't give up." He turned to her, those eyes of his more intense than ever, black in the gloom that shrouded them. "You never know when the tide will turn."

She shivered again. The way he'd said it – *You never know when the tide will turn* – was with such passion, such…belief. Unmarried, she'd already discerned that about him from no ring on his finger, but he was a man wedded, indeed, to his profession.

"You know, Ben…I'm sorry I'm not a churchgoer. I've never really thought about it before. My family aren't churchgoers either. But…I do feel bad about it."

"Devotion is important," Ben replied simply. "It can shape a life. Give meaning."

"Oh, absolutely. I can see that must be true. It gives people something to live for, you know, when sometimes it's hard to find a reason for anything. But then…it's also responsible for such a lot of harm, down the ages, you know? A lot of death."

"*Man* is responsible for that," Ben insisted. "With their interpretation of religion."

"Right. Okay. Yes. Yes, I suppose that's true, too."

He nodded again, as if satisfied with such a paltry answer, then turned to face the altar. She was relieved he was satisfied, felt woefully under-equipped to enter into further discussion about it, a discussion that, given how passionate he felt, could become heated. Religion played no part in her life, and, in truth, she wasn't a fan because she *did* hold it responsible for so much wrongdoing. Yet here was Ben, coming at it from an entirely different angle, enlightening her indeed. Men like him were nothing less than warriors in this day and age, a new respect blooming.

From continuing to gaze at him somewhat surreptitiously, she faced the altar too. Both of them silent, Jamie still thankfully asleep.

It was an opportunity for what they'd said to sink in. Ava also wondered how she felt being here. At peace? Churches were intended to be peaceful places, so that's how you were *supposed* to feel. But was it true?

There was so much gloom, in the corners, accumulating,

and the place definitely had an air of desertion about it, as if no one had set foot in there for a century, let alone recent years, they the only congregation there'd ever been. Tilting her head, she studied the ceiling. A plain church but not decrepit, not exactly. All churches, those you entered on a country walk, perhaps, just out of curiosity, *pretty* churches, prettier than this one, all seemed in need of repair these days, requesting you don't just have a snoop around but leave a contribution. Funny, really, how people came to a place such as this to worship. If she'd ever felt remotely spiritual, it was when she was outside – on a country walk, surrounded by rolling hills, or standing in front of a stormy ocean, amazed by the power of the crashing waves. *That's* when she was reminded of just how magical this world was. Country and beach walks were something she didn't do enough of; having a pram to push around limited you, as did long winter months.

Lost in thought, it took a moment to register Ben had moved his arm and put it around her shoulders, subsequently drawing her closer, albeit just an inch or two.

She inhaled. Was it okay for him to do this? Was it…against protocol?

What protocol, exactly?

Instead, she continued to sit there silently, staring ahead, as did Ben, breathing calmly and evenly. Nothing wrong with what they were doing. It was a gesture of friendship. Something she wanted. *Desperately* wanted. Was it…? Could it be…desperation had a smell too?

She was *happy* sitting there with Ben. Her spine continuing to tingle. If only she could still the mind as well as the body, but it was going into overdrive.

Aside from wondering whether desperation could be

obvious, she thought about Lou and Jenna too, why they hadn't been at class and why everyone had been acting more subdued today. Growing bored with the class already? Once the warmer weather came, swapping it for something else entirely? She wouldn't. No way. She'd remain loyal.

Her mind kept on whirring. *Poor Ben. People will drop out of music class just like they've dropped out of coming to mass. God, it's cold in here! It's freezing. So...unwelcoming. Not his fault, though. He's doing his best. A warrior, as I've said. As lonely as me, in his own way. As much in need of friendship.*

Poor, poor Ben.

Not only did that thought linger longest, it obliterated all else, causing her eventually to lay her head on his shoulder.

Chapter Ten

Lou had been knocked off her bicycle whilst travelling to work and injured. As for Jenna, she'd suffered some kind of family trauma. That was why they hadn't been at the previous week's music class and wouldn't be attending in the near future either. No one had told Ava this was the case; she'd gleaned it from snatches of conversation around her.

Again, Ava almost hadn't come to class. Guilt nagged at her about what had happened in the church, the way she and Ben had sat so intimately together. Eventually, Ben had removed his arm, almost as quickly as he'd put it there, then stood up, as had Ava, who'd subsequently muttered she had to leave because she had a dog to walk. Ben had simply nodded and let her go. Despite any confusion about his abruptness, she'd floated home again.

It was wonderful to feel something other than a mix of panic, terror, paranoia, and numbness. Something...good. She'd tripped through the subsequent week lightheartedly. Paul must have noticed, although he hadn't actually commented despite how well she'd looked after him, conjuring more home-cooked meals and keeping the house so clean it gleamed. Jamie had been responding well to her mood, though, not crying as much, the pair of them getting more sleep. As for Jed, well...he hadn't growled at her again. That seemed to be a one-off, which she was thankful for, but, like the women at the music class post-Lou and Jenna, he was subdued, spending much of his time either staring at her, as if suspicious where this good mood had sprung from, or out the patio doors, into the garden – the far right corner.

"What is it, boy?" she'd asked him several times. "What do you think you can see? There's nothing out there, you know. Just squirrels and foxes."

He'd woof in response and maintain his position.

She mustn't linger after this morning's class but get back to Jed. Both she and Jamie had managed a lie-in this morning, and the dog had stubbornly refused to do his business in the garden. He needed a proper walk; it wasn't fair otherwise. Ben wanted her to stay, though. Had approached her again.

"Fancy a chat?"

"I can't," she said, explaining why.

"Oh, of course. That's a shame, but I totally understand."

Trouble was, she'd waited all week for this, to see him, and, by some miracle, Jamie had gone back to sleep after the class despite their lie-in.

Ben remained where he was, looking at her. A plea in his eyes? *Please stay.*

"Perhaps…perhaps a quick chat would be nice," she conceded. "And then I'll have to dash off, see to Jed."

"Jed is the dog's name, is it?"

Ava nodded. "Yes, didn't I just mention that?"

"Don't think so. What kind of dog is he?"

"A black Labrador. We got him from our local rescue centre."

"Nice. How old?"

"Not sure, actually. We think about five or six. He's a really good dog, the best. You'll have to meet him." Even as she said it, she wondered why. What was so important about Ben meeting Jed? Funny also because he knew her dog's name now, but not her husband's. He'd never asked about Paul, and she'd offered no information, both pretending he didn't exist, perhaps. As for Paul...he knew nothing about the vicar either. And she found herself keen to keep it that way. Paul had his work, and she had this, whatever 'this' was. *The only thing that makes you feel good.*

Stifling that thought before it could sprout wings, she spoke again. "So, shall we go back to the church? Do you have an office there or something, with a kettle? Maybe even some more biscuits? The ones here are all gone. I never got a chance to have one. I'm starving."

He was the one nodding now. "I do indeed! Let's go."

Private. Cagey. That's what this 'thing' was, the way they were acting, even, waiting for everyone else to leave before they did. But it also felt right, timely, *innocent* still. He was a friend, that was all, when she needed one. It could easily be misconstrued, though, she admitted that. They could hardly rush off together to the Brew Box, where everyone seemed to head after class. In fact, she'd heard three of the mothers planning to go there, to discuss further 'what happened'. They were guilty of being secretive too, hugging Lou's unfortunate accident and Jenna's family trauma to themselves, not willing to share the news with outsiders, not even mentioning it to Ben, or if they had, they'd done so before she'd arrived. Let them go, for she also had plans. *Teacher's pet.* If they knew, that's what some of them would say. Lou and Jenna would.

Again, they hurried along the stone path, not just covered in moss but an abundance of weeds, poking through various cracks. Ava also glanced at a selection of headstones on either side of her, wondering, as she always did, about the lives of those that now lay buried deep, their entire histories reduced to nothing but a name, a date, and an epitaph. Had they led happy lives? *Blessed* lives? Not everyone, of course. It simply didn't work that way. People experienced all kinds of emotions; like her, they could swing from one to another. Heartbreak? Tragedy? *Fear*?

At the church, the old oak door creaked as he pushed at it. Had it done that before, protested as loudly? She couldn't remember, only her own breathless excitement. Before following him in, something else registered: the cobwebs strewn in all corners of the porch, black and stringy, their architects lurking just out of sight.

Once inside, there was that familiar smell, what she considered to be faded incense, the light that filtered through the windows containing a thousand dust motes. The place needed a thorough clean. Could the church not afford it? The coffers empty? What about volunteers? Those that loved the church and all it stood for and so would gladly give their time to help. Perhaps *she* could volunteer. A crazy thought considering she had a young baby to look after, but...if her mother could look after Jamie for a couple of hours once a week, she could make a dent, spruce it up, make it somewhere inviting rather than hostile. Hostile? She almost ground to a halt. How could a holy place be hostile? Despite dust and dirt, it was *still* a place of worship.

"This way," Ben said, noticing she'd faltered. "The vestry's at the far end."

He hurried down the aisle, head down and – surprisingly – one hand lifted, clutching at the front of his jacket. A confident man, but now he appeared a little...nervous. Was the clandestine nature of their meeting playing on his mind as much as hers? Nerves were getting the better of her too. She wondered if she should speak up instead of blindly following him, tell him she couldn't make Jed wait any longer for his walk, that he'd be pining for her, howling the house down, most likely, and then what would the neighbours say if they happened to be home? Thinking of Jed conjured him, in her mind, at least – the trust in his eyes and, lately, a wariness too. She felt a longing for him, one that surpassed her longing for Ben, her inner voice demanding she turn around and go home. *Now!* As it screamed at her, she noticed again the shadows in the corners and just how *weak* the light was.

They were shadows that...writhed. The more she stared at them, the more she was sure of it. There was just something so *alive* about them. As if they were desperate to extricate themselves, break free. Then what? What would happen if they did? Would they lunge at her too? Attack? Shadows were everywhere. And not just here in this church; one had followed her home that day from the café, her heart bursting with terror because of it. One had also lurked behind the door in her dream, a dream she'd thankfully woken from before it appeared. Also, what exactly did Jed stare at in the garden? What could he see there that she couldn't? A hard stare. Sometimes she couldn't distract him, not even with a treat, which stunned her because Jed *loved* treats. Who or what did he think was coming for them?

More movement. In a distant alcove. *Real* movement.

Something there. And it was indeed writhing. Something unnatural, awkward, tortured even. In so much pain it needed to inflict pain too, for that was the only balm it knew. Nonsense! All of it, her inner voice screeching at her this time: *You're mad for thinking such things! You need help. Lots and lots of help!* But it was swamped because, right now, fear wanted to infect her further.

Not just movement but sound. Something scraping against the stone of the floor. Not solely courtesy of what was in the alcove, the *thing,* but from movement all around her, from shadows at her back that had also broken free and were now creeping up on her. When they reached her, they'd drag her back with them into the shadows, and not just her, but Jamie.

And finally, there was that smell. She now detected an underlying sweetness to it. Not something that made it more bearable but the very opposite. The smell of rot, a lump of meat with flies buzzing around it, maggots burrowing. Just as they'd burrow their way inside her when she was captured, inside her baby too.

The shadows, the scraping, and a smell straight out of the charnel house, all of it was overwhelming, the *fear* was. If shadows were behind and in front of her, they couldn't flee.

Oh, Jamie! What a terrible fate he'd encounter. She didn't deserve guardianship of his soul. Unable to look after him, she could only do this: lead him headlong into ruin. *Bad mother! Incompetent! Incapable! You wondered what 'this' was. It's punishment for the way you are, the hopeless being motherhood's turned you into.*

She heard a yelp. Whose? Her own or Jamie's, awake at last? Soon he'd be screaming. And she'd be screaming too.

The shadows also, but in triumph.

So much darkness in this church and so much loneliness too.

That was the thought that struck her hardest at the end.

There's so much loneliness here.

* * *

"There now, there now, take it easy. You feeling better? You sure? Come on, Ava, look at me, straight into my eyes. You do look better, more…focused. You gave me such a fright! I thought…I don't know what I thought, to be honest. Did you have breakfast this morning? I remember you said you were starving. You didn't? Okay, that could be the reason you fainted. I know you don't want a biscuit just yet, but in a moment try again. Meanwhile, sip this. I've put sugar in it, two heaped spoons. That's what you need, an energy boost. Shit. I think I'm shaking as much as you! No, don't fret about Jamie. He's fine. Slept through it all."

Ben was hurling a flurry of words at her, pressing a cup of tea into her hands also, the warmth of it trying to penetrate what was icy cold. Her last memory was hurrying down the aisle after him, with Jamie in his pram. No…scrub that. Her last memory was of shadows, trying to break loose from corners as cobwebby as the porch. Shadows intent on savaging her, *punishing* her, for being the way she was, useless at everything but particularly her new role in life as a mother, for becoming…distracted. By him. Ben.

Setting the tea down on a long, somewhat rickety table beside her, noticing the mug had a chip on the rim and old drip marks on the outside, she stood up.

"I should leave," she began, intending to do just that, grab the pram and go, head home to Jed. The thought, though, of returning down that long, long aisle… Noon had long since passed, it was almost one, but the sky on her way to the church had been grey, like all days were lately, with no hint of blue at all. It could have got darker still since, everywhere just so damned gloomy, in the church and out there too.

Her legs wouldn't support her. She not so much as sat back down in the chair but crashed into it, Ben there again, rushing to support her.

"You need to eat," he insisted, his eyes burrowing into hers just like she'd thought the maggots would. "Please don't hate me for saying this, but you're so…thin."

Thin? Was he being serious? She was still concerned about having retained her baby weight. Then again, she avoided looking at herself in the mirror too much, couldn't recognise the person she saw. Someone…haunted? Her appetite *wasn't* up to much, she supposed, so lately perhaps a few pounds *had* dropped off. When she sat down to dinner with Paul in the evening, he'd finish everything on his plate, whereas she tended to toy with her food, pushing it round and round the plate. Not that Paul ever commented or mentioned any weight loss. But here was Ben, doing exactly that, brave enough to broach such a sensitive subject.

"Ava, what happened back there in the church? Did you…see something?"

He still had his hands on her, encircling the top of her arms. His grip…tightening?

"What do you mean?"

"It's just, when I heard you yell, I turned around. *Immediately* turned around. And the look in your eyes just before you fainted, you seemed...shocked."

"Shocked?"

Ben nodded avidly. "Did you see something?"

Should she do it, confess? *I did see something. Shadows that moved. And it's not the first time either. I've no idea what they are or why I'm seeing them, and I'm scared, Ben, really, really scared. It's like something's lying in wait, wanting to harm me. That's the feeling I get.* No. She couldn't say that. He'd think her mad. Then again... *He's a vicar! He'll understand. He's perhaps the only one that will. Tell him! Tell him something's wrong with his church too. There's something here that's bad.*

"Ben," she said, and her gaze was just as intent as his. "Oh, Ben." How eager he appeared, so eager that she had to swallow. He knew, didn't he? What was here? That could be why he'd hurried down the aisle the way he had, why he was suddenly nervous. What if...what if he were the one in danger and not her? Oh, these thoughts! They were senseless. She was tired, and she was hungry. All she wanted was to go home. But would she find safety there? Once the shadows encroached and darkness took hold, were they everywhere you looked?

This stuff...it was unspeakable. No way she'd confide in anyone about it, least of all Ben. If she'd read him wrong, she risked alienating him. Her only friend. She was overwhelmed again, by tears. She leant forward and threw her arms around Ben's neck, clung to him the way she clung to Jed, just wanting him to hold her.

So why, then, did he not immediately return her embrace, his hands having dropped from her arms but not so they could circle her waist. Why the hesitation?

Eventually, he did indeed hold her, but it was not the tight embrace she yearned for. Nor did he press her further about what had happened. *Mercifully*, perhaps.

Jamie was beginning to stir, a few snuffles that would likely turn into full-blown cries if she didn't tend to him quickly.

Ava detached herself, already mourning the loss of Ben's embrace, even if it had been offered reluctantly. *Just your imagination, Ava, and if not...there could be a thousand reasons. He's a vicar, remember. And you're a wife and mother.*

Her legs supporting her this time, she rose from the chair and made her way over to Jamie. Of course she'd be able to make it back down the aisle, but she'd ask Ben to escort her, just in case. Such a gloomy church. *Lonely.* That was her last thought before she'd fainted. The church needed an injection of energy, *people.*

Whilst tending to Jamie, she surveyed her surroundings properly. There was the chair she'd just been sitting on and the long, narrow table, on it a kettle, small selection of mugs, biscuit tin, bag of sugar slightly ripped at the side, some of it spilling out, and a bottle of milk that looked like it was curdling, making her glad she hadn't drunk her tea. The room had a window, narrow, rectangular, and set high in the wall, which made it feel like she was in a prison cell rather than a room in a church. Even though the light was on – a bare bulb, actually, hanging in the middle of the ceiling – it wasn't enough to combat a gloom that seemed to have penetrated everything, even her soul. There were also bin bags in a corner, two of them. Stuffed with what? she wondered. Something soft and squishy, so clothes, maybe? For charity? Lastly, her gaze rested on a cupboard as tall as it was wide. Its doors were closed, but it was possibly where sacred items were stored, ferried back and forth for mass.

Ben was a vicar, but this had echoes of a student den. He'd helped her, and now she had the sudden urge to help him, to tidy up, to *mother* him. Ironic, but...

Instead of going home or tending further to Jamie, who was settled enough, looking around too, blinking back tiredness, she headed to the table and shuffled things into a much neater order. Picking up the milk bottle, she sniffed at it.

"This needs chucking, Ben. It smells bad."

Before he could answer, she crossed over to the bin bags. Perhaps she could help him sift through the clothes – what was worth sending to charity and what wasn't – bring her car back at some point and take them to the shop for him.

As she reached out, Ben came up behind her, his hand enclosing her wrist.

"What are you doing?" he asked.

"Just helping out. Tidying. I could sort out these clothes, get rid of them for you. I just think this whole place could do with a bit of sprucing up, and I don't mind help—"

"Stop!" One word, but issued with such force she flinched.

"I'm just trying—"

"I don't need you to reorganise."

"But, Ben—"

"Jamie's crying."

"What?" He wasn't, which was why she'd taken advantage of the moment to do something good, to give back.

Ben's eyes, black, black eyes, were hypnotic. "Ava, you almost fainted. You need to go home, eat something, and rest as much as you can. Look after yourself, okay? Not me. I don't want you to touch anything more. I don't need that kind of help."

"Okay, all right. I'm sorry—"

He interrupted her a second time, but his voice had softened considerably. "Really, you need to go home. If you don't feel you can walk, I'll call you a cab."

She shook her head. "No, no, it's fine. The fresh air'll do me good." Air that she wanted to breathe deeply, *clean* air. "Would you…walk me down the aisle, though?"

The question broke any tension that had developed. Ben grinned. Suddenly and completely. A twinkle in his eyes also.

"I thought you were already married?"

Ava laughed too. "You know what I mean."

"Of course! Of course! I'll walk you home if you want me to. It's not as if it's far."

"It's half an hour actually, and there's no need. You're busy enough."

"Busy?" he repeated. "Of sorts. Come on, let me walk you down the aisle of my big old dusty, empty church, at least. Actually, that's what I'll be busy doing this afternoon. You've inspired me. Dusting!"

Again, Ava laughed. "Glad to hear it."

There was nothing – *nothing* – frightening about the return journey, not with Ben by her side instead of hurrying ahead as he'd done previously. Not that she glanced into any far corners, just kept gazing straight ahead.

Jamie started yelling about halfway home, hungry, most likely. And Ava's mind continued to cogitate. What a strange visit it had been, although what she'd expected from it, she didn't know. Didn't want to probe too deeply into it either. One thing, though, what Ben had said, kept repeating in her mind: *I don't need that kind of help.*

A counter-thought too: *What kind of help* do *you need, then?*

Chapter Eleven

"Paul! Wow! I don't know what to say."

"You like surprises, right? You used to."

"Yeah, kind of, but—"

"So, there you go, no more work for me this week. I've booked you, me, and Jamie a couple of nights away in an Airbnb in the countryside."

"It's Thursday tomorrow, Paul."

"I know."

"But Thursday's music…" Ava's voice trailed off.

So what if it was music class, that's what he'd say. And part of her wouldn't blame him for such a response. But it had come to mean so much to Ava, this gathering at which she'd found an ally. One she still wanted to give back to, to help as he'd helped her.

As had so quickly become the norm, she'd spent all week looking forward to seeing Ben, wondering if she should broach the subject of volunteering at the church a second time. If she did it tactfully rather than act like she had, wading in without even checking if it was okay, surely he'd think it a good idea too? Although he'd pretended otherwise, it was *exactly* the type of help he needed. With that in mind, she'd spoken to her mother about the possibility of looking after Jamie just for two or three hours a week, which was part of the reason she was keen to talk to Ben. But now that plan, as vague as it was, had been scuppered. She wasn't going to music class; she was going away instead.

"Paul, I'm not sure when you booked it—"

"Only this afternoon. At work."

"Well, I wish you'd told me this afternoon or, better still, *beforehand*. I could have...I don't know... It would have been nice to have had some time to prepare myself mentally as well as practically. There's a lot of planning involved with a baby."

"Ava," Paul patiently replied, "nowhere in England is too far from the shops. If we forget anything essential, I can always drive to get it."

Of course he could; she knew that. "We'll need to take the breathing monitor."

"Still?"

"Yes, of course still! I'm not going anywhere without it."

"Okay, if you insist, but I think we've got beyond relying on it, don't you? There's never going to be a repeat episode of what happened. You really do fret too much." His expression softened. "Ava, look, if you're worried about packing, I'll help you, okay? This is our first break away together as a family of three. It's going to be epic!"

They were in the living room, the log fire aglow and the curtains closed, although Jed remained on his bed by the patio doors, his ears pricked as usual, either listening in to their conversation or alert to something outside. Jamie was upstairs in bed. They'd had dinner and were now relaxing, the time fast approaching nine o'clock.

Paul frowned as he laid a hand on her. "Ava? You don't seem overly happy about the surprise. Or the fact Jamie's coming with us. It seems to be a bit of a problem."

"I'm fine. It's just…I don't get why you waited so long to tell me."

Paul shrugged. "To be fair, I wasn't actually going to tell you until the morning. I really did want it to be one big surprise. But then I've been thinking…we'd want to leave as early as possible, make the most of it, so, yeah, you'd need more notice than that. I tried to get the cottage for the weekend, by the way, but it's booked from Saturday to Saturday, so had to make do with Thursday and Friday nights only. Wait till you see it, though, Ava, and before you ask, I'm not showing you the details beforehand, but it's idyllic, surrounded by trees."

"Idyllic?" she queried. Fair enough, but was it also family-friendly? Somewhere with baby gates and fireguards, that kind of thing? Because that's what an idyll would need to include, at least in the near future.

Concealing a sigh, she asked how far the cottage was.

"Not far, about seventy miles. I just thought it'd be nice to have a change of scene."

"Okay. And what about Jed?"

"Huh?"

"Are dogs allowed at the cottage?"

His blank expression told her he had no idea.

She sighed loudly this time. "What the hell do you think we're going to do about Jed?"

"I—"

"Honestly, Paul, I can't believe you! It's more evidence you just don't think. Send me details of the cottage, right now. *I'll* check if they allow dogs."

"Shit, Ava! You're not excited in the least, are you? I can't win with you, can't do right for doing wrong."

He climbed to his feet, such an abrupt movement.

"Paul—" she began, a little chastised, but he was on a roll, wouldn't let her speak.

"You know what? I'll cancel the cottage, okay?"

"Oh, for God's sake. Don't be so dram—"

He lifted a hand – *dramatically* – and waved it in the air. "No, it's fine. I'll cancel it. Probably too late to get our money back, but who cares? You've made it quite clear you're *horrified* by the thought of us going away as a family, so what's the point?"

She stood too. Even Jed got to his feet, focused solely on them now.

"Just because I mentioned the dog—"

"You're never happy, do you know that? You're always tired, stressed—"

"I am happy! I have been!"

"Really? I haven't bloody noticed!"

She was stunned, then wondered why she should be. He truly didn't notice a thing when it came to her. Even so, she tried to appease him. "You're right, I'm tired—"

Again, he interrupted. "Thing is, I'm sodding well tired too! I work hard for this family, long, long hours. I can't help that, not if we want to live a decent life, do the best by Jamie. I also need a bit of a break. Has that ever crossed your mind? Like I said, a change of bloody scene." In such a temper, but he strove to curb it, not for her sake but Jamie's, perhaps, in case he woke him. "It'll be nice, Ava, our first holiday together. I'll make sure it is. I *want* you to be happy, the way you used to be. For us all to be happy. And so, yeah, this was something I wanted to surprise you with. I remember you used to love being whisked away at the drop of a hat."

She'd lowered her voice too. "Things are different now,

that's all I'm saying. I need a little time to plan if Jamie's coming."

Another explosion from Paul. "*If* he's coming? *If?* Why do you keep saying 'if?'"

"Paul!" Ava couldn't help but screech back, Jed whining but not moving, keeping his distance. Wisely so. God, they had to calm down! "Just…don't keep raising your voice, okay? It's hard to settle Jamie if he wakes. And it *will* be me that settles him. Not you. Never." Another dig, but she couldn't resist.

He sighed, shook his head, just so pained. "How many times, Ava? I have to sleep. My job isn't easy. You know it isn't. I have to be able to focus the next day."

"Motherhood is also work," she countered. "*Hard* work." Ben had said so, and Ben was right. "I mean it. If Jamie wakes up…"

"If Jamie wakes up, what?"

Then no way she'd be going anywhere early. He could stick his holiday!

She had to turn away, fetch a breather, her eyes focused solely on Jed. Try also to keep in mind one thing: Paul *thought* he was doing something nice for her, for them as a family. Jed wagged his tail, as if encouraging that thought. She chanced a weak smile at him. *Okay, boy. All right. Have it your way.*

Facing Paul again, she relaxed her jaw. "I'm grateful for what you've done, really. And I'd like us to have a nice time too. You've offered to help me pack, which is kind. Count on the fact I'll be taking you up on it, but not tonight. It's just too late, and I simply don't have the energy or inclination. But, yeah, early in the morning we'll do it. I just…I'd like you to remember how different things are now. That surprises can add to the stress."

Not just angry, he was *wounded*. "You resent looking after Jamie, don't you?"

Ava knew he'd say this, had prepared herself for it during the time-out she'd just taken, a weariness in her voice when she answered him. "Oh, Paul, Paul, Paul. No, I don't resent looking after Jamie, not at all. But one thing I will say, that I've tried to tell you before, is it's not always an easy ride, especially when they're so young, so demanding. You know what? I'm sorry I can't be one of these dewy-eyed mothers, always gushing about it, full of loving smiles, the kind of woman you also see in those shit mother-and-baby magazines that in my ignorance I used to lap up, glowing like they'd stood next to a nuclear reactor or something. It simply isn't the truth. *I'm* the truth. Tired, grumpy, frazzled old me, with my hair all over the place, no makeup, and wearing clothes covered in the food Jamie throws at me. The real fucking deal. It's exhausting, okay? But I live in hope it'll get less exhausting. And…and…" *For fuck's sake, breathe, Ava!* "Let's not ruin this before it's even begun. I'm glad we're going away, that Jamie's coming. The cottage sounds amazing. Now I've got my head around it, I'm…excited. Jed's coming too, though. Forget any ideas you may have had about dropping him off at your parents' or mine, okay?"

"Okay, fine. So…let me get this straight. You don't want me to cancel it?"

"No! I've just said. I just need a bit more notice next time. Jamie needs so much paraphernalia for a trip to the park, so for two days away it'll prove interesting."

"*If* there's a next time."

"Oh, Paul, really, stop with the dramatics. Ping me the

details so I can check—"

Paul had turned, though, whilst she was in mid-sentence, leaving the room and heading to bed. As Ava stood there staring after him, Jed approached her warily, unnerved by the raised voices, just as Jamie would have been had he woken.

"It's all right," she told him. "Don't worry. We're going away for a few days. That'll be fun, won't it? Going somewhere different. And yeah, right, like we'd ever leave you, eh?"

As Jed trotted happily back to his bed by the patio doors, Ava followed in Paul's wake.

A change of scene might be just the tonic they needed. And it didn't matter if the cottage wasn't family-friendly; Jamie was rolling around on his playmat but nowhere near crawling yet. No need to remotely concern herself about things like that. As for music class, it wasn't going anywhere. It'd be there the following week. Ben would.

Why, oh why, couldn't she have just smiled when Paul had made his grand announcement, flung her arms around his neck and *thanked* him? Why make the fuss she had? No wonder he felt he couldn't do right by her. It was true.

Paul *could* be spontaneous, and Ava used to love that about him, how he would indeed whisk her off on a whim, meeting her from work on a Friday, and off they'd go into the wild blue yonder. Heady times, romantic. It was different now, but she should welcome the change, not mourn it. The prospect of their first family holiday, as daunting as it seemed, Ava knowing she'd pack everything, *including* the kitchen sink – was nothing to fear. It was another step in the right direction. A chance to forge precious memories. When she climbed into bed beside

Paul, she'd reach out, give him a hug. They'd barely even done that since Jamie's birth. And yet she'd hugged Ben readily, clung like a limpet.

Ben, whom she wouldn't see this week and couldn't get a message to either to explain why. What would he think when she was a no-show? Would he be upset? Presume she wasn't coming back? That he'd done something wrong? Overstepped the mark after all and upset her?

At the top of the stairs, she headed to the bathroom first rather than the bedroom, staring at her reflection in the mirror, despairing of herself, of everything she did.

This was *not* a time to be concerned about Ben. She'd argued with her husband, effectively thrown his surprise trip back in his face, his admittance, no matter how disguised, that he knew something was wrong between them and was trying to do something about it. She had to meet him halfway.

Briefly she closed her eyes, still not liking what she saw, the frazzled woman she'd described, as strange to her as she was to everyone else. Even Paul.

She'd *definitely* reach out tonight, force a reconciliation. Tell him morning couldn't come soon enough so the adventure could begin.

Music class could wait. Ben could.

Her friend and ally.

Paul was too, not the enemy.

Finally entering the bedroom after checking in on Jamie, any chance of smoothing things over fell apart. Paul, in true Paul fashion, was asleep already.

* * *

If the family break had started badly, it got worse.

Jed was allowed to come, but Paul remained disgruntled about it, sulking even, barely saying a word on the journey there except for when another motorist cut him up. He then shouted so loudly that he startled Jamie, who, after throwing his hands wide, burst into tears and refused to be placated. Thank God it was only seventy miles to the cottage; any further and Ava felt as if her head might explode.

The cottage, though, was undeniably lovely, set on the edge of a huge woodland, complete with thatched roof and timber frame. A rural idyll indeed.

As Paul parked on a small driveway, Ava almost leapt from the car, needing to put some space between her and Jamie's continual screaming. The sky was blue – a good sign, she told herself, no longer that perennial shade of grey. And even a hint of warmth in the air. All too quickly, though, Paul was by her side with Jamie in his arms, while Jed was still in the car, as if Paul refused to have anything to do with him. No matter. *She'd* see to him, and to hell with Paul for being so stubborn.

"You like it?" he said, and she nodded.

"It's very nice. The weather's great too."

"Yeah, yeah, we're lucky. Come on, let's get inside," he said, moving forwards.

"Fine. I'll get the dog, shall I?"

As he marched off, she was sure he muttered, "Whatever."

The name of the cottage was Holly Springs. Picture-postcard perfect. On the outside. Inside, not so much. It was dark – *gloomy* – with low ceilings, heavy beams, and deep-set windows, the somewhat rusted diamond leading resembling prison bars. Her nose wrinkled when she entered, detecting damp, and some of the furniture, although antique, was shabby.

Even Paul's face fell when he closed the door behind them, *imprisoned* them, clearly not expecting what he was presented with either, the photos on the website artfully taken and therefore misleading. In his arms, Jamie continued to fuss, his cheeks glowing red.

"Great," she muttered, despite feeling just a tiny bit sorry for Paul, at how his efforts had been rewarded. "To add to it all, Jamie's teething."

He heard her well enough. "To add to it all?" he echoed on a deep breath.

Jed had much the same reaction as them. Once released from the car, he'd bounded happily towards the house, but as soon as he entered, he ground to a halt. In the cramped confines of the hallway, he sniffed the air and then actually tried to backtrack, coming up against the closed door. With Paul still holding Jamie, Ava reached down to reassure him, although right now she was in dire need of reassurance herself, longing to return home, where there were at least twenty-first-century comforts. Thank God it was only for two nights!

Handing Jamie over to her, Paul returned outside to unpack the car. After setting up the travel cot in their bedroom rather than the spare one, at Ava's insistence, complete with breathing monitor and a range of cuddly toys Jamie loved, he then suggested they go for a walk. As it'd be difficult to tackle woodland terrain with the pram, Paul had brought the sling. Jamie, though, wasn't as small as he used to be, and so the walk for Paul proved arduous, with him constantly complaining about back pain. Only

Jed was happy. He was busy running in every direction, sniffing and marking the territory, laying claim to it. It really was beautiful countryside, trees no longer wintry skeletons but bursting into leafy life, clumps of daffodils at the base of them a cheery yellow. It was scenery to feed the soul, so when Paul suggested they turn back barely twenty minutes into the walk, Ava was dismayed.

"You can't keep going any longer?"

He tried; he really did. They carried on for another ten minutes, delving deeper into the trees on a narrow pathway, but Jamie wasn't making it easy for him. He was currently arching his back and grizzling, clearly not impressed with the sling either.

Paul ground to a halt. "I'm sorry. We have to go back."

At the cottage, Jamie was swiftly handed back to Ava, Paul heading into the living room to build a fire in the grate, one that had to be goaded into life. Whilst the thought of an open fire appealed – and, thankfully, there was a fireguard, so they could lay Jamie on his playmat – Ava couldn't help but think the cottage would remain damp and gloomy, as gloomy as their respective moods, as the church last week, like their home, even, filled with shadows.

Immediately she reprimanded herself. *Don't harp on about shadows. About stupid stuff like that. Show some appreciation. Paul's trying to make this special.*

Their past escapes had been far more exotic than this, to cities such as Porto, Seville, Valencia, Paris, and Rome. And always, *always*, they'd had a fantastic time. A *loving* time, cementing their relationship further, all the way to marriage vows. To this, to becoming parents. Times changed, of course, circumstances did. *But for the better,*

Ava. For the better. Even so, would they ever holiday again, just the two of them? Snatch a cheeky weekend away? Even if they did, if grandparents looked after Jamie when he was older, and Jed too, would they spend their time feeling guilty, unable to let go, counting down the hours to their return?

Flames in the grate at last leapt high, Paul throwing himself back onto the sofa, then bitterly complaining when his head hit the back of it, how hard it was. He claimed he was exhausted too, and certainly he looked the part right now. Defeated, even, this man who by his own profession could no longer do right by her.

Tears pricked her eyes to see how worn he was. As she swayed Jamie from side to side, as Jed looked from her to Paul and back again, she made a promise, albeit a silent one. They had two nights here. They would enjoy them.

No matter what it took.

Chapter Twelve

With Jamie settled in bed, Ava freshened up, then returned downstairs to where Paul was still gazing at the fire, a glass of red wine in his hand, half full.

Jed was with him, stretched out in front of the grate, snoozing. He wasn't allowed upstairs, not even in this house. When he'd tried to follow her, Paul had stopped him. A shame, as she'd felt slightly nervous upstairs even with Jamie for company. The cottage was somehow more claustrophobic up there, passing a series of dark and unfamiliar empty rooms as she'd hurried down the landing, each tugging at her imagination. If Jed had been with her, she wouldn't have hurried as much or, once in the main bedroom, so quickly shut the door.

And now Jamie was alone up there, which she felt bad about. They had the monitor, though. If anything went wrong, they'd know about it. Even so, she'd sleep so much better tonight if Paul just relaxed his rules, if all four of them pulled together.

No doubt about it, the living room as she entered it was cosier than before, thanks to the open fire, more tolerable than elsewhere in the cottage, all those empty rooms remaining cold. Would it be too cold upstairs for Jamie? The heating was on and the weather outside far more clement than it had been of late, but somehow in here such thick, thick walls hugged the cold to them. As she sat on the sofa next to Paul – the first time she had that day, as she'd been so busy seeing to Jamie – she found it every bit as hard as he'd complained about, the cushion beneath her lumpy too. She leant forward and picked up a glass of red from the coffee table, already poured, and took a mouthful.

"Paul, does it say anywhere in the paperwork dogs can't come upstairs?" Her tone was deliberately neutral, no challenge in it.

Not taking his eyes from the open fire, as if mesmerised by it, Paul shrugged. "Ava, can we just not? All I want to do is relax, okay?"

If she clutched the stem of the glass any harder, it'd break. No point in pursuing the matter, not if they wanted to have a nice time. And Jed was okay, more than okay, completely relaxed. For now, anyway.

"Jamie asleep?" he asked.

"Uh-huh."

"Good, drink your wine." He indicated his glass. "I've brought a few bottles, so there's plenty more where this came from."

Plenty more for you, perhaps, Ava thought. It wasn't as if both of them could get raging drunk, not with Jamie to look after, which was why she tried only to sip this time as she lifted the glass to her mouth and tasted its beguiling richness.

The evening passed, and they had dinner, just a couple of boxed pizzas heated in the oven, the fire proving even more soporific after they'd eaten. Like Jed, both of them dozed in front of it, Ava almost completely under when a scream from Jamie dragged her back to the surface. She woke with a jolt, Jed immediately sitting up too. Paul woke, but not fully, rubbed his eyes and asked if everything was okay.

"It's Jamie," she told him. "He's awake."

"Oh, okay. Do you want me…" His voice trailed off as he yawned.

"It's okay," Ava said. "I'll see to him." No point in dithering; she'd need to act fast if she wanted to make sure he returned swiftly into the arms of Morpheus.

As she rose, emitting a groan due to stiff limbs, Jed rose too to follow her.

She stayed him with her hand. "You can't, I'm afraid. Stay here. I'll be okay."

Such a good boy, so obedient, he nonetheless followed her to the door of the living room and stood within its frame as she padded towards the stairs.

This place! Even after flicking the randomly arranged light switches both downstairs and up, never really knowing which ones did what, the resulting light was lame, energy-saving bulbs, perhaps, the early kind that never really worked, responsible.

On the landing, she turned right, towards the main bedroom, with two other bedrooms behind her and a cramped bathroom with an ancient avocado-green suite. A strange place… She must have thought that a dozen times since being there, this cottage on the edge of the woods, three hundred years old or more. So old-fashioned with some mod cons, but the bare minimum. She'd have to look up reviews when she got a chance, see if anyone else found it as strange and as unsettling as she did.

Entering the bedroom, Jamie was grizzling still, his arms outstretched. In the darkness, she rushed over and picked him up, rocking him gently in her arms, and only then returned to the light switch, flicked that one too. They remained in the dark.

What the hell?

She tried a second time, but not before a creak sounded from behind her.

"Jed," she called out. "Is that you? Paul?"

When no answer came, she tried the light again. That did the trick. Still jiggling Jamie, she looked down at the floor. Of course the wooden floorboards in this place would creak, settling for the night. Likely there'd be an entire symphony of noises later, so no need to be startled by what was only natural. The floorboards weren't white like hers at home but stained the darkest of browns, and gnarly. There were gaps between them too, spiders no doubt hunkering beneath, getting ready to emerge as the night grew deeper, to start roaming the rooms, hunting for sustenance. A thought that made her shiver.

After closing the bedroom door, she decided she'd lie down with Jamie on the bed, snuggle him back to sleep. In order to do that, though, to create the right ambience, she'd have to turn the main light off again and switch on one of the bedside lamps.

Anxiety. There it was, lurking beneath the surface as much as any spider. She didn't want to turn off the main light, because to do so would allow the gloom to regather, shadows appearing in all corners, and *they'd* make the floorboards creak.

Of all the places Paul could have surprised her with, it had to be somewhere like this! What was wrong with a Premier Inn in a lively city such as Canterbury or Oxford? An uncomplicated modern hotel, not something...decayed.

Paul had described it as 'idyllic', but he'd only done so because that was the word used in the blurb on the Airbnb site. A word as deceiving as the photos. She had a hunch it was an inheritance, from grandparents to grandchildren. And, wanting to make the property work for them fast, they'd rented it out to holidaymakers like Paul who were gullible enough to believe such a flowery description.

Remaining by the light switch, Ava rocked Jamie, who was quieter, as her eyes travelled to the bed they'd be sleeping in tonight. It was a big old bedstead with a metal frame that looked hundreds of years old too. Okay, the mattress would be new, possibly, hopefully, but what if...what if...the previous owner had *died* in this room? In that very bed? The grandfather or grandmother. They might have left it to family members, but they wouldn't want this, an array of strangers coming and going. No, no, no, they wouldn't be keen at all.

She thought Jamie was settling, but, as if he knew the direction Mama's thoughts were heading, he let out a scream so ear-piercing she was surprised the glass in the windows remained intact. *Mean* windows, that's what they were, as if whoever had lived there – and was now long dead – shunned the light, encouraging darkness instead.

Ava left the main light on as she ventured further into the room, trying again to calm Jamie. "Come on, now, everything's okay. Really. We're not here for long."

Aside from a bed and a wardrobe, there was a dressing table in the bedroom, a chunky piece of furniture, also stained brown. On top of it was a freestanding mirror, angled so she was able to catch her reflection. It *was* her. Of course it was. This harried young woman. Pale and gaunt. Bags under her eyes you could carry home a week's worth of shopping in.

Again, Jamie screamed, startling Ava so much this time, she almost lost her grip. Terrified further by that notion, she clutched him harder than before. Why did he struggle so much? All the time, he fussed and cried and fought her. Yes, he was teething, she knew that, knew too that it must be painful, but nothing seemed to appease him. Surely, Paul had woken fully by now. The living room was just below the bedroom. He could take a turn at soothing Jamie. No work for a few days, so no excuse not to help. This was supposed to be *their* holiday, not just his!

Resentment was like anxiety: always there, her mood becoming blacker as she paced and paced, Jamie drawing no comfort from her, and little wonder when she had so little to give. Like this cottage, she was filled with the wrong kind of things, stuff which needed to be weeded out, but for now was rooted in place. She was in trouble. And yet no one could or would help her. Not here at this cottage. The only person willing was seventy miles away.

Damn Paul for snatching the opportunity to see Ben from her today! If Ben were the one with her, he'd have rushed up the stairs and taken Jamie already, not held on to some outmoded view it was women's work. No way she'd have more children; she couldn't go through this again, feeling so lonely and angry.

Up and down, up and down she paced, wearing a path into floorboards already worn enough. The light above her also began to flicker. Probably because she was stomping not walking. That bed...that mirror... She once more caught sight of herself, the skin on her face stretched tight over bones. She must stop grinding her teeth! She'd wear them away too, into stumps.

Another creak from outside. Paul on his way after all? Someone *was* approaching the bedroom but taking their own sweet time about it.

"Paul?" she repeated. "Is that you?"

When there was no reply, she decided she'd head over to the door and yank it open. After handing Jamie over to Paul, she wouldn't hang around; she'd head downstairs and make herself a cup of tea, her throat as dry as parchment.

Another creak, footsteps, they had to be. Her hand was on the door handle but hesitating. How come Paul was taking so long? The corridor wasn't that long!

Or...like her, was he unsure suddenly? Afraid? Even Jamie had stiffened. It was bloody cold upstairs! As if what little warmth the heating afforded had been suddenly claimed elsewhere. If she breathed out, she was certain she'd see a plume of mist. She couldn't breathe, though, or move a muscle.

PAUL!

This time, it was a silent plea. Earlier, she'd felt unwelcome in the house, that she didn't belong. So who did? Whose territory were they trespassing on? Such an old cottage with so much history. A lot of life had played out there, every kind of emotion experienced, deposited like dust into the fabric. The good, the bad, the happy and sad. *Angry* emotions similar to her own, a *rage* that had somehow kept alive what was dead.

No way she'd open the door. It wasn't Paul out there. He had no intention of helping her, helping *them*, his wife and son.

Instead, Ava took a step back, and another, still barely breathing. This was like the dream she'd had, almost exactly, something on the other side of the door that mustn't be given entry, or gazed upon, even, by someone as small as her.

Once more, she drew parallel with the mirror. If she tore her gaze from the door and looked into it, what would she see this time? Not herself – horror enough – but something even worse. *More darkness.* That was the answer that formed in her mind. *Because that's what you've become. What you attract. The blessed have fallen.*

She didn't want to know what was on the other side of the door or what was in the mirror, and yet her body was turning to the mirror, *forcing* her round.

Ava clutched Jamie closer, shielded his gaze, at least. He yelled in protest, but it was a tired yell, his fists reaching up to rub at his eyes.

Still, she turned, for there was no escape from what was there, the rot that had set in.

Tears were in her eyes, but they failed to blind her, conspiring with whatever hell had unleashed, forcing her to witness fully her terrible transition.

She was unworthy. Unfit. Insane.

Her face, when she next saw it, would confirm it.

Paul!

Another silent cry.

Paul, please! You have to help us.

No use. Anger flared again, something that would distort her further.

Another cry from Jamie, and it was pitiful.

"JED!" At last, she found her voice, Jamie flinching in her arms, but she didn't care. She had to scream, couldn't connect with what was in the mirror, the truth too hard to bear. "JED," she screamed a second time, at the very moment the door flew open. She whipped back round. Couldn't breathe.

It was not a spectre that had entered, something intent on wreaking revenge for their intrusion, or a shadow version of herself – existing in the mirror, beyond the door, and all around her – but Jed, having heard her when Paul hadn't, responded when he didn't.

He bounded towards her, jumped up, but gently, his wet nose nuzzling both her and Jamie as if to make sure they were all right, his pink tongue lapping.

"Oh, Jed," Ava said, hugging him with her free arm, breathing him in, the chill in the air immediately easing, the rage that had been there too, her own and someone else's. Incredibly, miraculously, she found she was laughing! More than that, and despite Jed's affections, Jamie had closed his eyes, and was falling asleep on her shoulder.

There'd been nothing behind the door. The creaking was Jed, only Jed. And in the mirror just a tired woman who also needed to sleep, for hours, days, weeks.

With the dog back on four feet, Ava gently lowered Jamie in the cot and covered him with sheets and blankets. As snug as a bug in a rug, that was the saying.

Walking over to the mirror, she only half glanced into it, saw just herself, a reflection she didn't particularly like but which wasn't ghoulish. Nonetheless, she turned the mirror over and shoved it back against the wall so it couldn't right itself.

Jed had headed out the room, and so she followed him all the way downstairs, clenching her jaw, grinding her teeth, but also trying not to.

She entered the living room, the flames in the grate

having died down to embers.

Paul had been awake when she'd left the room, albeit barely, but now he was asleep again, spark out. And the bottle before him, which had still had wine in it when she'd left, was now completely empty. He'd woken, let her go upstairs alone to tend to Jamie, maybe heard her calling, but carried on drinking instead. Then he'd slept some more, passed out. Left her to it, just like he always did. Well, she wouldn't wake him, she refused to, despite the awkward angle he'd adopted in sleep, a cricked neck guaranteed. Good. She hoped it ached and ached tomorrow, along with his back after carrying Jamie in a sling he'd grown too big for.

No way, though, she'd return to the bedroom alone.

She eyed Jed, who was eyeing her right back, and wagging his tail.

"To hell with his rules, eh?" she said. "And the owner's rules too."

She'd lied to Paul when she'd said she'd checked earlier that morning and that dogs were allowed. They weren't. To hell with everyone. "Come on, boy," she continued, signalling for Jed to follow her, which he did without hesitation. "It's you, me, and Jamie tonight. *Just* us."

Chapter Thirteen

Paul had booked two nights. Ava, however, insisted they leave after the first one. She could not spend another evening in that cottage. End of.

Paul was disappointed and upset, but also resigned. In pain too, just as she'd predicted, his neck sore, his back, and his head from too much alcohol. If he was looking for sympathy, though, he was out of luck. He'd slept on the sofa *all* night, Ava both angry about that and relieved. More relieved, actually, because it meant Jed could stay with her, and because he had, she'd slept surprisingly well, as had Jamie. But what sort of family holiday was this if Paul could technically abandon them like that? If memories were being forged, they weren't particularly good ones.

Besides, it rained the next day, even hailed at one point, the cottage just too damp and uncomfortable a place to hang around in. Best to quit while they were ahead.

The journey home was quieter than the journey there, no nasty road rage to mix things up a bit. Back in Heathfield, Paul drove right past the church, *quickly* drove past it, didn't even glance its way. But why would he? It was where she took Jamie to his music class, but what did Paul truly care about that? What *value* did he place on it? *She* looked, though, even if fleetingly, wondering if she'd spot Ben, head down and hurrying somewhere. No such luck.

A short while later and they were back at the house; another couple of hours and everything was back in its rightful place as if they'd never left. Jed took up residence by the patio doors, and Ava played with Jamie on his playmat, helping him to roll over, encouraging him to crawl, tickling his tummy, trying to make him laugh, sometimes succeeding, sometimes he grew irritable instead. As for Paul, he headed to the quiet of the kitchen with his laptop, deciding not to 'waste the day', as he put it, and get on with some work.

He ended up working all weekend because it continued to rain on and off, the weather not exactly conducive to days out anywhere. But at least they were home, they had modern, familiar comforts, and time was passing, no matter how slowly.

Regarding the failure of their first family holiday, not another word was said.

* * *

Ava was ill. Jamie was too. Both with colds. Thankfully, Jamie recovered far quicker than Ava, but she continued to feel rotten, her joints aching, her nose streaming, and her head feeling like a samba band was rehearsing nonstop in there. On days when she wanted nothing more than to lie in bed, she couldn't. She still had Jamie and Jed to see to, both growing increasingly restless at being kept indoors. Jed was mostly having to make do with forays into the garden, always heading to the far edge, she noticed, where the wall marked the boundary of the garden, beyond that a disused, narrow alley choked with weeds. Sometimes he'd sit and stare, other times he'd bark and bark. Worried about the neighbours, Ava had to keep calling him back, even though her throat was on fire and her voice hoarse.

"Jed, for God's sake, there's no one there. Stop it."

Despite her words, though, she'd be craning her neck, checking...

Her cold meant she missed another week of music class, or, more accurately, another week of Ben. He'd definitely be thinking she'd deserted him by now. If only she could let him know that wasn't the case. But since returning from the cottage and getting ill, she'd had even less energy than usual. It was as though she'd become unplugged from the main circuit. It was all she could do to get herself and Jamie out of bed in the morning, come downstairs, and lie on the sofa, shows such as *Peppa Pig* and *Hey Duggee* on a loop.

Hell. That's what it was like sometimes. Having to wade through each day until Paul came home, then insisting he take over because she was ready to collapse. He obliged, but in a subdued manner, no yells of laughter coming from the bathroom as he and Jamie splashed about, no litany of bedtime tales, just one or two.

Was he depressed? she wondered. Whatever had afflicted her now afflicting him, spreading like it was some kind of illness, a disease? No need to worry about him catching a mere cold, not when they were at risk from something far darker.

Once Jamie was in bed, Paul would return downstairs to make dinner. He'd eat his, and she'd push hers away after barely a mouthful, no conversation ensuing.

Not just depressed, was he resentful too? So many

unspoken words hung in the air between them. *His* this time, not hers. *Hey, Ava*, he'd say if he were brave enough, *I've been working all day, in case you didn't know, in case I hadn't drummed it into your thick skull hard enough. I shouldn't have to be doing everything when I get home too. I mean, are you sure you're ill, or are you just milking it? Because I don't know. I honestly don't know anything anymore, especially who the hell it is you've turned into.* He'd get up, go to bed, but she'd continue lying on the sofa, ushering Jed onto it as soon as Paul disappeared, holding on to him as tight as he'd let her. "If I didn't have you..." she'd whisper into his fur. *And Ben. What then?*

She got better, gradually, but looked awful, even more gaunt than before, her cheeks hollow, her skin grey. She still had so little energy, but today, Thursday, she'd make it to the hall for music class. No way she'd miss it a third week running.

She forced herself to get up extra early, knowing it'd require more time and effort than usual to get herself and Jamie ready. She let Jed out into the garden whilst she bolstered herself with coffee, watching again as he ran to that area of wall.

"Jed," she called out, "why do you keep barking at thin air? You're a strange dog, you know that? Perhaps that's why we get along so well."

She'd meant it as a joke, but there was no accompanying smile. He came back inside eventually, and she locked the doors behind him, told him to stay in his bed while she went out, Jed whining at that, barking still, as usual not wanting to be left alone. As bad as she felt about it, nothing was going to stand in her way.

As she and Jamie made their way to the church, she had

to wonder: Had she ever craved anybody's company as much as Ben's? Felt such an urgent need for it?

If she had, she couldn't remember, not even with Paul when they'd first met.

What a feeling this was. Both disconcerting and exciting.

In less than half an hour, she'd be at the church hall. Ben would greet her, make a point of it, lead the class, then collar her whilst the others were leaving. They might then stay in the hall talking or hurry to the church, to the privacy of the vestry, and, with Jamie hopefully asleep, they'd technically be alone.

Her spine tingled, just like it had when she and Ben had first met, such a strange sensation, something she only experienced when with him or thinking about him.

Her heart was racing too. Her skin felt slick.

She craved like an addict might, in need of a fix.

In the end, she got to the church in less time than predicted.

Twenty minutes was all it took.

Chapter Fourteen

Ben would be the first person she saw when she entered the hall; that's what Ava had expected. But he wasn't. Her gaze fell first on someone else. Someone who prevented her from hurrying forwards to his side, eager to explain her two-week hiatus. It was Sarah from the café, there with her baby, Leo. She stood in amongst the other women, at ease with them, chatting and smiling. Just as she wasn't a stranger to Ava, she wasn't a stranger to them either, but part of the group, accepted.

Something else Ava noticed: as she arrived, the energy changed. Heads turned and looked towards her – *teacher's pet* – laugher seemed to stop. *Her* head turned, Sarah's, and their eyes met. Ava had the advantage of surprise here, Sarah on the back foot. She could see how her eyes widened, her...dismay? *Hold your head up high*, Ava told herself as she forced herself onwards. *You've every right to be here.* Where was Ben? Never had she longed for him more, and the protection he offered.

With the gap closing between them, Sarah stepped forward too, still with uncertainty in her eyes, unsure how Ava would react, but apparently brave enough to give it a try. In her arms, Leo was serene. Always so bloody serene.

They were almost in front of each other, at the point they'd have to say something. Should Ava just dismiss what had happened that other day? Truth was, she wasn't even sure what *had* happened now; it had somehow got all jumbled in her mind. Perhaps Sarah would insist on dismissing it again, just waving away how her dog had reacted. Together they could, what…laugh it off? Brush it under the carpet? Alternatively, Ava could about-turn, even now, walk out and never return. Still see Ben but in other situations. *At the church.* They could meet there without pretence, without all this, the other women. No one liked her here except for Ben, and in that moment, she hated them all for it, for making her feel so excluded. There was self-hatred too because perhaps the truth was, she'd excluded herself. She'd done so because she couldn't dredge up, like they could, some insistent gaiety, bursts of false laughter and false interest, talking about babies and nothing else, discussing everything right down to the minutia. Oh, this hatred! Could Sarah see it in her face? *Smile, Ava, don't scowl.*

Before either said anything, Ben appeared. At last. And instead of confident and assured, *the star of the show*, he seemed slightly flustered. With something that could have been a scowl on *his* face, he looked from Sarah to Ava but then resumed his trademark grin. "There you are!" he said to Ava. "We've missed you."

We? Another white lie. He could hardly say in front of everyone *he* had missed her. *As much as I've missed you, Ben?*

His smile fading just a little, he gestured towards Sarah. "You know each other?"

"No," Ava said just as Sarah spoke too, answering entirely differently that, yes, they had met before.

"Oh. Right," Ben replied. "Well, as I say, welcome back,

135

Ava. Look, let's catch up afterwards, shall we? Class is about to start. Meanwhile, I'll leave you two to chat."

He turned away, walked towards the box that held the instruments, and unpacked them. Meanwhile, in front of her, Sarah waited expectantly.

"I...um...didn't know you came here, to the music class," Ava said at last, her voice catching slightly, forcing her to cough to clear her throat.

"A friend told me about it, Heidi. This is my first time."

"Ah, right, yes, Heidi. So, you know people here already?"

"Yes. Yes, I do. A couple of them. How long have you been coming?"

"I've only been a few times. Not during the last couple of weeks, I've been busy, but ordinarily I try to come along. Jamie loves it."

"They're a nice bunch, aren't they? The girls. Really friendly."

Friendly? Ava stiffened. Maybe even raised an eyebrow. "Yes," she responded.

"Shame about Lou, though. And Jenna."

"Lou and Jenna? Oh, yes."

"Did you know them?"

"No. Barely. I mean, I'd spoken to Lou." To a disinterested Lou, a Lou who hadn't bothered to hide her disinterest either, who'd left her stranded, returning to Jenna's side, the pair then proceeding to laugh at her, *secretively* laugh, their gaze continually catching Ava's, finding something about her oh so amusing.

Sarah was nodding now, leaning in also to plant a kiss on her baby's cheek, who basked in his mother's affection. Something about that gesture, how natural it was, almost absent-minded, bit deep with Ava. Did she ever kiss her own baby that way, that invisible bond tugging you in their direction all the time, growing stronger and stronger? She couldn't say she did. Every gesture – if not forced, exactly – she was all too aware of.

"Terrible about the accident," Sarah continued. "You heard about it, I suppose?"

"I heard something about it," Ava admitted.

"Oh, right? I'd have thought Ben would have made some kind of formal announcement, being as he's a vicar. She works part-time, you see, Lou. Cycles to work. A car ran into her, a hit-and-run, basically. She got mown down, run right off the road. Police found out later that the car was stolen. They don't think it was an accident but that someone did it deliberately, someone who knew her. She's broken both an arm and a leg."

"Shit! Really?"

"Uh-huh. As for Jenna—"

"That was some sort of family trauma, wasn't it?"

"That's putting it lightly. It was Jenna's mother. She's eighty-two, a very active eighty-two. She was mugged when walking home from the grocers."

"My God!" breathed Ava. "In Heathfield?"

"Yep."

"Who does that kind of thing?"

"Someone local," Sarah said. "Again, that's what the police think. Possibly even the same person. Who knows? What I do know is we all need to be more vigilant from now on. Something bad has come to town."

Ava flinched. "Something bad?"

"Yeah. Um…Ava, are you all right?"

"I'm just… I'm shocked, that's all. Poor Lou. And poor

Jenna's mum."

"She's an amazing woman. Apparently, she's making a full recovery. Says she won't let it stop her from getting out and about. But, yeah, whoever he is, he's a piece of shit."

"And neither got a look at their attacker?"

Sarah shook her head. "Nope. Both said the same: it was a man dressed head to toe in black. Nothing distinguishable about him. Like a shadow, you know?"

"A shadow?"

"Yeah. Look, I'm sorry. What I've said has clearly upset you. And little wonder. We all feel that way, well...most of us, at any rate." Whatever she meant by that, she didn't elaborate. "Do you want to come outside, and get some fresh air?"

Fresh air? She'd *love* some. But before she could answer, Sarah started speaking again. "Also, I just want to say that I'm sorry about what happened when we first met. To be honest, I'm not actually sure what *did* happen, but whatever it was, it's water under the bridge. It was just unfortunate, that's all. Now, come on, let's go—"

A clap as loud as thunder reverberated.

A voice boomed also.

"Okay, ladies. We really must start class. Sarah. Ava. Care to join us?"

* * *

Sarah tried to hang around after class, to catch Ava's gaze, even approaching her as she dressed Jamie. Ben, though, reached Ava first, started wiggling his fingers at Jamie, making him laugh, *uproariously*, in fact, Ava unable to stop herself from laughing too, loving the sound of it, wanting to hear that and only that. Wanting Ben.

Someone called out Sarah's name, Heidi, perhaps, and so she stopped hovering and turned to go, Ava relieved about that. She'd been the bearer of bad news today, but she'd also been nice to her, apologised for what had happened. Could they be friends after all? The natural mother and the challenged one? She was still so unsure.

The last of the stragglers had gone, and Jamie was tiring, rubbing at his eyes. It was time to place him in his pram and let him sleep.

After doing that, she turned back to Ben – and was taken aback to see not the goofy smile of earlier when he'd been playing with Jamie but a frown.

"You do know that woman, then?" he asked. "Sarah?"

"Well…not exactly. I met her once, in the park, then went for a coffee with her." The same coffee shop some of them were no doubt heading towards now, the clique. "As well as babies the same age, we've both got black Labradors. Like I said, we had a chat, but…we didn't particularly gel."

"You didn't?" He seemed to ponder that point. "Look, if she makes you feel uncomfortable in any way—"

"Oh God, no! I'm sure she won't." Blushing, she added, "Sorry about the God reference."

Whatever tension there'd been, which had occurred out of the blue, broke. "Don't worry. At least you're acknowledging Him. It counts for something. Seriously, though, if you feel uncomfortable about anything or anyone, let me know, okay? Whatever you do, don't let it put you off coming here."

"It won't."

"But you haven't been in a couple of weeks. Why?"

How forthright he was being, cutting straight to the chase. Of course he'd notice if she wasn't there, but there was a gravitas in his voice, not just concern but fear almost. Of what? Never seeing her again? Would it matter that much?

"Family issues," she said at last, wondering just how far to go into detail about them, the holiday break that had gone so wrong. "And illness. Jamie got a cold, and then I caught it, but with me it really took hold, became more like flu."

"You do look peaky."

Ava lifted her hand, gently rubbed at the skin on her cheek. "Oh. Do I?"

Immediately, Ben was contrite. "Sorry! I didn't mean it like that, as an insult. It's just...are you sure you're okay? That you've recovered fully? Would you like to sit down?"

"Here?" Ava said. "Or in the church?"

Not an innocent question, and Ben knew it every bit as much as she did. Jamie was in his pram and had indeed fallen asleep, a magical effect of the music class. And now there was this, something else that was magic: Ben's presence. Would they even make it as far as the church?

She'd taken a step towards him, and he'd mirrored her, the pull between them like a magnet, impossible to resist. Thoughts of anyone other than him faded from her mind. In his company, she wasn't a wife or a mother and failing at both, she was a woman. Just that. And he wasn't a vicar, a man who'd sworn allegiance to an invisible overseer. He was just a man. One whom she wanted to reach out and touch her. What they were doing was wrong. His God, if He was truly looking down, would condemn them, but she didn't care. She'd done everything right in life, all the things expected of a person, and look where it had got her.

Ben was the only one who made her feel she was worth something, who perhaps saw the darkness in her and dispelled it.

He was so close, the warmth of his breath brushing her cheek. She was giddy with excitement, breathless. If his arms didn't come out soon, she'd take the lead.

"Sorry, am I disturbing something?"

It wasn't a godlike voice that demanded to know what they were about. It was Sarah, having returned to the hall, her eyes on stalks at what she'd encountered.

"Sarah!" Ava gasped, her stomach lurching, making her feel nauseous.

"Sarah," Ben managed more evenly. How smoothly he moved away from Ava, quickly, but not quick enough.

Thank God the pram was close. Ava reached for it, seeking to steady herself and, at the same time, get her breathing under control. How remarkable Ben was! He walked towards Sarah almost leisurely. His walk more of a swagger, actually.

Ava blinked as she tried again to get to grips with the situation. Sarah looked...angry. Because of them? Because of what they'd almost done? Why had she come back into the hall anyway? Had she forgotten something? A scarf or some other item of clothing? She'd hovered around Ava before. Could she still be trying to make peace between them?

But Ava was *not* the reason Sarah had returned. Quickly she realised that. Ben was.

"Sarah," he said again, convivially. "Is there something I can help you with?"

If Ava was nonplussed by his manner, Sarah seemed to

be too, her cheeks red, marring that peaches-and-cream complexion.

"It's just…" she began, but her voice faded away.

"Just what?" Ben prompted.

"I…" She shifted her gaze to Ava. "I genuinely didn't realise you'd still be here."

Ava opened her mouth to formulate an answer, but Ben beat her to it.

"We were talking," he told her.

"Talking?" The hint of mockery – of disbelief – in Sarah's voice was crystal clear, but she didn't challenge it further. "Right. I see."

"Sarah, anything you have to say," Ben continued, "you can say to me in front of Ava. Now, what's wrong? Did you enjoy the class or…not?"

"You're a vicar," Sarah answered.

"Well…yes," replied Ben, still with a hint of amusement.

"Our local vicar."

"Right again," he said.

"You don't wear a collar."

"Not a necessity nowadays, more of a choice."

"You're very hands-on."

"That's right, I am. I try to be."

A deep breath, and then she said it, what Ava felt to be the crux of the matter. "You know what happened to Lou recently, and Jenna's mother, don't you?"

Ben nodded. "Yes. Yes, I do. And it's very sad. I've been praying for them."

"As our local 'hands-on' vicar, aren't you supposed to visit them as well?"

There was a beat of silence, one that weighed heavily.

"I would like to visit them," he replied, his voice slightly tight now.

Sarah raised an eyebrow. "So why haven't you? On the table, next to the kettle, I noticed there's a sheet of paper for class members to write their contact details."

"Correct, there is," Ben replied. "But, again, it's voluntary. Lou, for example, has written her mobile number but not her address. And, actually, the number's wrong. She may have mixed one or two digits, easy to do when you're distracted by a baby."

"Jenna wrote her number *and* her address. What's more, some people here know Lou and Jenna outside of class. You could have asked them for Lou's address."

"Sarah," Ben said, "as a vicar, I have many matters to preside over, many projects other than this. Of course I'm happy to visit Lou, Jenna, and Jenna's mother if they'd like me to. They are, however, not the only members of my parish. Nor the only ones in need. I also have it on good authority both are making good recoveries, happily, and so I thought if I was to visit, I'd do so when both are indeed on the mend. And...forgive me if I'm wrong, but do any of them attend church? Certainly, I haven't seen Lou or Jenna at mass, none of the music class, yourself included."

"Actually," Sarah retaliated, "I did try to come to church recently. It was closed!"

"When was this?" Ben asked, frowning.

"Um...about two to three months back."

"When I was ill?"

"I don't know!" Sarah almost shouted.

"It must have been," Ben returned calmly. "I *was* ill back then, with Covid. Did you not see a notice on the door explaining? A vicar I might be, infallible I am not."

"I just don't understand. Why aren't you…investigating?"

"Investigating?" he queried, his head to one side.

"What happened to them were criminal acts!"

"And I'm a vicar, as you've taken pains to point out, not a member of the police force. I'm very sorry, Sarah, but that kind of thing really is outside my jurisdiction." He heaved a sigh. "Look, I'm really not sure what you're trying to get at here. Are you accusing me of something? Some kind of neglect or misconduct?"

As he asked the question, Ava moved forward. She wondered also what Sarah was trying to get at, was as indignant. What had happened to Lou and Jenna's mother was terrible, truly, but as Ben had just said, he was involved with a lot of people in the community, his parish. He wasn't responsible for everyone!

She came to a halt behind him almost like a sentinel, a second-in-command, not caring now what Sarah might have thought earlier, wanting to signal that she agreed with Ben, was one hundred percent on his side. *He's a good man.*

Ben turned his head to look briefly at her, Ava feeling weak again when she saw the gratefulness in his eyes, cementing their bond further.

If Sarah had been surprised by them before, she looked that way again. Horrified, even? Ava didn't care. This woman was a busybody. She'd tried to interfere in Ava's life and was now doing the same with Ben.

Ben turned back to Sarah, waited patiently for her to answer the question he'd just posed. When she didn't, he prompted her. "Are you accusing me of misconduct?"

"No," Sarah said at last, although dully. "Of course

not." Ava, at least, was relieved she'd backed down, clearly her head was stuffed with stupid notions too. "I just think you should pay them a visit, that's all. A member of your music class and another member's mother, a frail old lady that's been hurt. I can give you their addresses."

"And you think they'd appreciate it?"

"Yes. Yes, I do."

"Then I'll make arrangements. Certainly. And apologise for my delay in visiting before, although, as I've said, I've kept them in my prayers."

"Right. Well...good," Sarah said, her gaze shifting from Ben to Ava and back, Ava knowing full well that she wanted to ask another question, this busybody: *What's going on between you two?* She didn't, but what she did ask was if Ava was planning on leaving too, as they could do so together.

"You go ahead," Ava told her before gesturing behind her at musical instruments still lying within the circle of cushions. "I'm going to help clean up."

"Right," Sarah repeated. "I'll leave you to it, then, I suppose."

"See you next week?" Ben asked.

"Yes," Sarah answered. "Maybe."

"And at church?"

God, how she blushed! "I...I'll have to see. Ava, are you sure you don't want to come with me now? A few of us are meeting at the Brew Box. They've gone ahead, obviously, taken Leo with them, but there'll still be plenty of time for a catch-up. You really are very welcome. Maybe come after you've helped tidy."

"See you next week," Ava said, turning from her.

Chapter Fifteen

Paul and Ava tried again. He'd booked another night away
– one he was fully conversant about with her beforehand –
and this time, at his insistence, not hers, it was to be only
them, no Jamie or Jed. And thankfully it wasn't on a
Thursday but a Saturday night, Ava's mum coming to stay
whilst they were away.

She hadn't wanted to go. Had felt…guilty about going.
Guilty too about seeing Paul so excited at the prospect of
some alone time together. *You're a bitch, Ava. A real cow.*
Just a few days before the announcement, she'd almost
kissed another man. Had *wanted* to, so very much. But all
Paul wanted to do was kiss her, which he would on this
night away together, becoming intimate once again. It was
to be a night *designed* for intimacy. That's how he'd see it.
And perhaps…perhaps he was right. It was what they
needed, restoring something between them that recent
months had eroded.

The hotel he'd booked in the Ashdown Forest was
gorgeous. In complete contrast to Holly Springs, it was a
modern boutique hotel with a bar and highly rated
restaurant attached. Airy inside, it was also warm and
inviting. In a place such as this, there were no shadows
gathering in corners, no smell of damp or neglect. It was
buzzing, people having coffee in the lounge, eating, and

drinking wine, staff hurrying back and forth, tending to guests' needs.

"Paul," she said when they were shown to their room, the walls a duck-egg blue, offset by bright yellow furnishings, "you've outdone yourself."

"So, you approve?" he said, an element of sarcasm in his voice, which she ignored.

The night away was make or break. And she prayed for the former. It was Paul with whom she'd built a family, that she'd fallen in love with years before, pledged herself to in front of friends and family – not at a church altar, admitted, but in the beautiful surroundings of a manor house, the gardens immaculate. Her heart had burst with hope as she'd stood in the drawing room with him, wearing a traditional full-length white gown. A naïve woman back then, who thought the world was easy and relationships too.

In the hotel room, she turned to him. There'd be too much pressure if sex was left until later, too much…anticipation building throughout the evening. If they got it out of the way now, it might pave the way for something less frenzied later, more loving.

On a deep breath, she approached him, reached up to stroke his face, then kissed him.

A familiar kiss, and because of that, there was comfort in it, an element of warmth that spread throughout her. Their kiss deepened, and his arms came around her, pulling her closer still. Soon, they began undressing each other and themselves as they inched their way closer to the bed. Already Paul was hard; she could feel the bulge of him against her thigh, *desiring* her despite what she felt: undesirable.

On the bed, he was just so eager, the pair of them dispensing with foreplay and Ava pulling him into her, sealing the deal: *We can make this work.*

A bolt of pain, sudden and unexpected, pulled her from the ecstasy. Paul was driving so hard it was becoming uncomfortable. She clung to him, but any personal enjoyment continued to recede. Instead, she stiffened, let go of her grip on him, but Paul didn't notice.

At first, she talked down her resentment. *Don't make a fuss. Just let him do what he has to. Suffer. Endure.* Then she decided she couldn't.

"Paul," she said and then, when he didn't respond, "PAUL!"

"Huh? What? You okay?"

"Actually, no. I'm not. Paul, can you stop? Can we…try again later?"

"For real?"

"For real?" She tried so hard to keep the anger out of her voice as, somewhat incredulously, she repeated his words. She knew this was what he'd brought her here for – the hotel a glorified knocking shop – but she needed gentleness. This was the first time they'd been intimate since the birth; she couldn't even contemplate doing this before now, the trauma was still so fresh. Of course, sex would have to happen at some point, here or at home. A marriage was not built on friendship alone – theirs wasn't. But his eagerness was exactly what she'd feared.

"It's okay, I've come," were Paul's next words as he rolled off her.

"Right," she whispered, clenching her jaw. "Good."

After a few moments, Paul turned to her and drew her close. Horror rose in her. Did he want her again, so soon, and after what she'd just said?

"Paul—"

"It's okay. It's fine. I'm done, believe me. How come...you wanted to stop?"

The shape of him was familiar too as he moulded himself into her side. They'd spend hours doing this in that dim and distant past, cuddling, all through the night sometimes, nights that were now something else entirely: unrecognisable.

This was better. *Much* better. She felt herself relaxing into him. Relishing this, whereas before... There was tonight to get through yet. And sex *would* happen again later, after dinner and a few drinks, but she'd make him go slower, consider her more. She'd explain why she'd stopped him. Not now, though. Right now, she closed her eyes and drifted towards sleep.

* * *

"Paul! What are you doing?"

"Playing a little footsie."

"Your foot's going a little higher than mine right now. And...you've kicked your shoe off. Paul! This is a busy dining room. People will see!"

"Makes it more fun, then, doesn't it? Oh, come on, you loved this in the old days!"

The old days. She pondered what he'd just said, a choice of words that showed he lamented, probably as much as she did, the changes in their relationship. *Temporary* changes. Changes for the better. They could be. They *should* be.

She shut down her careering mind, focused solely on

Paul and how playful he was being. No longer tired, stressed, or plain bewildered, he looked happy tonight, and because he was happy, he looked younger also, his hazel eyes glittering.

Both of them had fallen asleep earlier, not just her, although she'd been the first to wake, pushing him gently off and padding over to the window. The sun had been setting, leaving in its wake an orange glow on the horizon. The hotel really was beautifully located, surrounded by so much greenery. Spring was there in all its glory, and then would come summer, longer days with more warmth, *easier* days. Surely?

After Paul had woken, they'd got themselves ready for dinner, sipping at ice-cold champagne ordered on room service, the bubbles going straight to Ava's head, making her feel giddy in the lift down to the dining room as she leant into Paul again.

And now this. Flirtation. His foot going higher still, grazing her thigh, and a miracle happening because of it. Desire. For him, Paul. A breathless, heady thing. Inside her all along. The same level of desire he'd felt earlier, maybe even exceeding it.

The waiter arrived with their starter, Paul keeping his foot in place as it was served. Thank God for the oversized tablecloth! White and starchy and protective.

This was going to be a good night, relief about that making Ava giddier still. They'd hurry their way through dinner, delicious though it was, and go back upstairs, order another bottle of champagne.

Laughter filled the air as they returned to their room, smooching in the lift while it sped upwards, having to jump apart when it stopped in between floors and another, older couple got in, their expressions bemused when Ava stifled giggles as she smoothed down her dress and her hair, all the while Paul nudging her to stop, also struggling to keep a straight face.

As they approached their room, so did room service, a second bottle of champagne on ice handed over and a pair of fresh glasses.

Back inside their room, Paul popped the cork and poured the fizz, Ava draining hers quickly, loving how bubbly it made her feel, how *willing*.

Like before, she closed the gap between them, her arms reaching up around his neck, Paul lowering his head to hers.

"I'll go gently," he whispered into her ear.

"At first," she whispered back, knowing the effect such a comment would have.

Nothing else mattered. Not in that moment, in that room. The world comprising solely of them, two people in love who just needed a little time and space to find a way back to each other. Who, from now on, would go from strength to strength. That's what she thought as he tore at the dress she wore, entirely swept up by the promise of more pleasure to come, not registering the muffled sound of her mobile when it rang.

Paul was the one who remarked on it, stopping halfway through removing his shirt. "Is that your mobile?"

Ava frowned as she listened. "Shit. I think it is."

"Shit," Paul echoed, and then he added, "We can leave it, you know."

And she was tempted. So tempted. This was the first time in so long she'd felt like the old Ava, and she wanted it to continue.

Shrugging her dress back on, she shook her head. "We'd better get it. Jamie…"

"Sure. Sure," Paul said, trying to conceal his disappointment too.

As she strode towards her bag, her mobile buried deep within it, she continued talking. "Maybe he's woken and Mum just wants a bit of reassurance he'll settle. She knows he tends to wake, although…not so much lately." Digging the phone out, she chanced a smile back at Paul. "Maybe we really are turning a corner here."

The caller ID showed it was indeed Carol, Ava already planning the advice she'd dispense: *Walk him up and down, and give him some more milk if he wants it. The bottles are in the fridge, made up. Warm them first, thirty seconds in the microwave. Test it, though, on the back of your hand; make sure it's not too hot. He'll settle. Honestly, he will.* But even if he didn't, would one sleepless night really be the end of the world? Ava had had so many. Couldn't she be spared just the one?

"Mum!" she said, hoping there was no slur in her voice. "Is everything—"

"Ava! Oh, thank God! Someone's out there. In the garden. On the prowl."

Not only was there immense agitation in her mother's voice, Ava could hear Jed in the background, howling, barking, and growling, the commotion pulling her all the way into sobriety. Paul must have heard it too, as he hurried over.

"Is everything all right with Jamie?" he asked, trying to grab the phone from her in his panic, but Ava avoided his reach, kept hold of it herself.

"Mum, calm down," she said instead. "What's

happening? Who's in the garden? Is Jamie all right? Mum, try to get Jed to quieten down."

As she spoke, Paul reached for the phone again, but Ava shot him a look that stopped him in his tracks. "Mum?" she repeated, putting the phone on loud speaker. "What's going on?"

Her mother's voice had reduced to a whisper, such a quiver in it.

"Jamie's asleep upstairs, and I was just sitting here, watching TV, when I sensed it more than saw it, some kind of movement in the garden. I got up to look, and...there's someone out there, Ava! A man. It has to be. Staring. But he's in the shadows. In so much darkness, it's hard to make him out, exactly. What does he want? What could he possibly want?"

"Mum, Mum, where exactly is he? In the far corner by the wall?"

"Yes!" Carol hissed the word at her. "That's exactly where!"

The very space Jed had stared at so insistently for weeks and weeks now. Had he foreseen this? But how? Another thought occurred, one that froze her blood further: Had he foreseen it because it had happened before? This man, whoever he was, it wasn't his first time standing and staring. There were curtains at the windows, but Ava didn't always pull them at night. But if he'd been there before, Jed wouldn't have just stared; he'd do as he was doing now.

"Have you called the police?" Paul asked, his hands balled into tight fists. "You've phoned us, but surely you've let the police know as well?"

Carol faltered. "I...I haven't, not yet."

"Fuck's sake," Paul said. "It's the police you need. I'll bloody call them!"

"Mum, the patio doors are locked, aren't they?"

"Yes. Yes. Of course."

"If you have to run…" Ava's mind was busy calculating. If the man had a crowbar or something, he could smash through the glass and open the door that way. Her mother wouldn't have time to run upstairs and get Jamie out of there to safety.

Realising this, her legs gave way, and she half fell onto the armchair where her bag was. "Shit! Shit! Shit!" she said, too scared to even cry. Meanwhile, Paul had retrieved his own mobile, punching numbers onto the screen.

Shock overwhelmed her. Fear did. How could this be happening? A dream evening had turned into a waking nightmare, and so quickly. They should never have gone away! She blamed Paul. She blamed herself. Carol for agreeing to it. She should be at home with Jamie, protecting him, not having sex in a hotel room in the countryside. The one saving grace was it was sex with her husband, at least, not him, not Ben. *Oh, Ben!* Would he be able to get to them sooner and help? She didn't have his phone number, though. So far, he hadn't given it to her.

"I've closed the curtains. I've closed the curtains."

It was her mother talking. Paul was too, into his phone. He'd got through to the police and was giving details of the incident and their address.

"Mum—"

"He's still out there, though. He's come closer. He's standing behind the door now. I can…it sounds insane…but, Ava, I can *feel* him there."

With Jed still going crazy in the background, Ava started

sobbing at last, fear for her mother and child going into overdrive. Paul rushed back to her side and this time succeeded in taking the phone from her.

"Carol," he said. "The police are on their way, okay? Hold tight. Just...hold tight."

"The dog...the dog's no deterrent," Ava mumbled through her tears. "He would be. To most people. Why not this one? Paul, who is it behind the door?"

"It's okay, it's okay," he said, reaching for her, trying to hold her, but she was in no mood for solace, not this time. Guilt had got a stronghold, isolating her again. *This is no one's fault but mine!* Paul had taken her away because he felt he had to; he knew she was slipping away from him, from everyone. And, in her absence, her greatest fear had been made manifest, something *had* stepped out of the shadows, the something that Jed, in his own way, had tried to warn her about.

"Carol," said Paul again, "step away from the door, okay? Head to the front door and wait. The police will be there very, very soon. Get ready to let them in."

"Yes. Right. Okay. Oh, God, this man! He's so...sinister. So...determined. I can feel that too. It's like...he thinks he's invincible. He's not afraid of anyone."

"I'm sorry, Mum. I'm so sorry." All Ava could do was apologise over and over. "The police are coming. And...and Jed will protect you meanwhile. Do as Paul says, step away from the door, but don't leave Jamie, will you? Please, please don't leave him."

There was a whine from Jed, several, all in succession, every bit as desperate as Carol's voice. Other than that, there was silence. Was her mother doing as they'd asked? And no way she'd abandon Jamie; she'd defend him to the end.

A bang made them both jump.

"That must be the police!" Paul yelled. "Answer the door, Carol. Quickly! Let them in. Carol? What's happening? What are you doing?"

The doorbell was ringing too.

"Mum, what are you doing! It's the police. Let them in!"

Why was Jed continuing to whine rather than bark? Why was Carol saying nothing? "Mum, let the police in!"

The sound of footsteps now. Someone running and Jed howling in outright fear.

"It's okay, it's okay! The police are there, Mum. Answer the fucking door!"

The phone cut out.

Chapter Sixteen

Those ensuing moments of lost contact were not filled with fear and panic but a bewilderment so strong it was impossible to speak. To react, even. Ava continued to sit there on the arm of the chair, Paul also statue-like by her side.

The police were there. The police were there.

Her thoughts, at least, were active enough, going around and around in her head. *They were there!* Weren't they? It *had* been them knocking at the door? Knights in blue uniform, coming to save the occupants of that innocuous terraced house in Heathfield from some kind of comic-book villain, swathed in black.

There'd been footsteps. Someone running. Whose footsteps?

Why had Carol gone so quiet at the end?

How could a dog sound so scared?

What if it had been *his* footsteps they'd heard? The shadow man's? Somehow he'd entered the house although they'd heard no glass being smashed, Carol mistaken about the patio doors being locked. Or he could have doubled round to the front door, *pretending* to be the police, seeking entrance that way?

Was he indeed invincible?

The sound of her mobile ringing sprang them from the

silence that had entrapped them. Quickly, she answered it.

"Ava Kent? Is this you?"

A male voice, curt and demanding.

"Yes. Yes, it is. Who are you? What's happening? Jamie…my mum…"

"They're fine, absolutely fine. This is PC Ray Adams. I'm here with several of my colleagues. Everyone's fine at the house. There are no signs of a break-in."

Ava was incredulous. "No sign? My mother saw someone in our garden! Have you sent officers round to the alleyway behind the garden? There must be signs of something if he was there. Footprints in the mud or whatever."

Again, there was that curt, almost tired voice. "Of course we've searched the back of the property and the vicinity thoroughly. As I say, so far, no sign of anyone."

Anger flared. "My mother isn't lying! She didn't imagine this. Someone was there. Jed doesn't bark like that for nothing either!"

"Jed?" the officer questioned.

"The dog!" Ava yelled.

As he'd done earlier, Paul took the phone from her. "Officer, I'm so sorry," he said, adding to Ava's fury. How dare he apologise for the way she was reacting! "I see," he continued. "That's great there's no sign of a break-in. It is dark out there, I agree. I'll install a security light, I think. We were due home tomorrow, that's correct, but we'll leave tonight, now, in fact, grab a taxi as I've been drinking. Someone's happy to stay with Carol until then? Great. Absolutely great. We're very grateful. And yes, we'll speak again in the morning, discuss more security measures. Really, thank you so much for your help."

He ended the call and started pulling on clothes. She had to do the same, not just sit there tight with anger when she should feel only relief. Disappointment was also trying to muscle its way in, something else that mustn't be entertained.

They'd had a chance tonight, a real opportunity to start over. She and Paul. To become as close as they used to be.

And it was ruined.

* * *

Paul doubted Carol. That much became evident in the following days. He even said as much at one point, words he muttered under his breath, but Ava still caught them: "Paranoid. There's no sign of anything."

It took all her strength not to react, to hit out, to *claw* at him. *My mother is not paranoid, and nor am I! There was someone out there, trying to get at us. Jed knew it too.* All those feelings she'd recently had for Paul, that desire, seemed such a distant memory. Ruined indeed. Crushed. Including any peace of mind she had regained.

They had security lights installed at the front and back of the house, and better locks were fitted as well. Paul also tried to get Ava not to worry, told her lightning rarely struck twice, and she wanted to believe him, made out she did. That she was fine. She would *not* have him tar her with the same brush as Carol. Condemn her for it.

Thursday came around again, time to see Ben. She'd head there early. *Very* early. Before anyone else got there. She'd tell him what had happened, how frightened she'd been and still was. He wouldn't condemn her but understand.

She hurried along to the church, the sky as grey as it had been in winter, any warmth gone from the air, another cold snap on its way, apparently, the beast from the east. She hoped he wouldn't mind her turning up so early. What was the difference between that and staying late, as she so often did? Would Sarah turn up today also? Such an odd woman with her unspoken accusations, trying to create drama.

Poor Jed hadn't wanted her going anywhere today without him. It'd been five days since the attempted break-in, and he was clearly still as shaky as she was. Paul would think that stupid as well, insisting a dog couldn't feel the same level of fear and anxiety as a human. Ava disagreed. Like her, Jed wouldn't forget what had happened, especially when he'd *sensed* it was going to. He'd likely remain on permanent alert for intruders from now on. Such an awful thing to happen, so damned frightening. She needed Ben and his special brand of comfort. She couldn't *survive* another day if she didn't see him. But Jed had stood in between her and the front door, not growling as such, not again, but definitely unhappy.

"Hey," she'd said, "I'm scared too, you know? Perhaps, though, we *are* being a bit silly. Break-ins happen. They're a sad fact of life. But we're safe now. We've taken precautions. No one's getting in here, I promise you. It's like Fort Knox. Jed, come on. Go back to your bed. I'll walk you soon. A long walk. Be good for me. Please."

Thankfully, Jed had returned to his bed, but he'd done so in a slow, somewhat pitiful manner with his tail between his legs. She wouldn't hang around after class, maybe not even stay for it. As long as she saw Ben beforehand, she'd be happy with that.

There was the church, its spire coming into view, and soon the grounds it stood in, the few headstones that were there, and the hall itself. A desolate place, really, if she were honest, despite being on holy ground, just so…unkempt, all of it, but a place where she'd found solace and hope nonetheless.

Almost there, Ben. I'm almost there.

He'd be setting up round about now, preparing to greet everyone. He'd be all alone in that vast hall, waiting to spread some joy, to communicate with those around him who refused to communicate on any other level, not quite his flock if they didn't attend mass, but there he was, reaching out anyway, having an impact, hands-on. She pictured his face as she entered, that easy grin of his and how quickly he'd close the gap between them. She envisioned falling into his arms too and whispering into his ear, 'Hold me, Ben, just hold me. Something dreadful almost happened.' A reference to the attempted burglary, *only* that, or something else besides? *I almost fell in love again with Paul, not you.* Back *in love.*

Such *cursed* thoughts. If lightning should strike, it would indeed find her as its target. But she didn't care. She was drowning. *Silently* drowning. Jed kept her afloat, but so did Ben.

As she approached the door of the hall, she noticed something. A sheet of paper pinned to it, its bottom edge flapping in a slight breeze that had developed. It was so quiet in the churchyard, *deathly* quiet. Not amused by that thought, she frowned instead. There was nothing funny about what was written on the sheet of paper: *Music class suspended until further notice.* Big, bold words. Unapologetic.

"What the…?"

Ben hadn't said anything about there being no music class this week, no music class…ever. And he'd had an opportunity. Last week after Sarah left, they'd been alone together again. Not for long, she had to admit. Ben, so calm and collected in the face of Sarah's outlandish behaviour, had then got a little flustered. She'd thought they might try a second time, lean in for that promised kiss. But, just as the intruder had ruined the moment between her and Paul, so Sarah had between her and Ben. He'd turned from her and begun clearing up. She'd tried to help, but he'd stopped her, just as he'd done when she'd started tidying in the vestry.

"Please," he'd said. "Leave it. I can manage."

And she hadn't argued; she'd left. And now there was this.

She turned from the hall to the church. If he wasn't here, he'd be there, a man of the cloth doing whatever it was vicars did.

With Jamie chattering happily away to himself, repeatedly batting at the various toys attached to the safety bar of the pram, she retraced her footsteps, then took the path towards the church. Whatever reason he'd had for pinning such a notice, there'd be an explanation soon enough.

Excitement bloomed in her chest, chasing away any worries and doubts.

Doubt?

There was that, certainly, concerning whether he'd even be at the church. The place just had such a deserted air about it. Not sacred but forsaken.

She could help with that, though. She would. Clearly,

Ben was a proud man as well as devoted, but also something of a martyr. He couldn't carry the burden alone.

Still on the approach to the church, she remembered not just a sense of desolation within its walls but the loneliness that clung to it and, by proxy, Ben. Ingrained. He was a man of faith in a sea of faithless. A hero. *Her* hero.

What she tried *not* to remember were the writhing shadows.

Sweeping into the porch, that nagging doubt didn't just cause her heart to sink, it fell right into her boots. There was another note. As blunt as the first one.

As mysterious.

Church closed.

Chapter Seventeen

Ava was frantic. She banged on the church door, convinced that, despite the notice, Ben was in there. She also tried to open the door, again and again, clutching at a big metal ring that constituted the handle and trying to turn it. It wouldn't budge. Stuck solid. Locked. When it should be open, as *all* churches should be. Ready to welcome the weary sinner.

She only stopped shouting and banging when Jamie began to cry, yet again tuning in to his mother's anxiety, feeding off it.

"It's okay, it's all right," she said, trying to soothe him. Secretly, though, she envied him. She wanted to scream as well. *Ben, where are you?*

He wasn't there, so maybe he was on a visit – to Lou, perhaps, as Sarah had demanded, or Jenna's mother. If not them, then he could've been called away on other urgent business. The note he'd pinned to the door was *just* a note. The church was closed, music class wasn't taking place, but perhaps only for this week?

And yet – as she turned back to stare at the note – it seemed so…final.

No choice but to return home and fulfil her promise of giving Jed a nice long walk.

Still, she hesitated, having to force herself and Jamie out

of the porch, away from church grounds, and back onto the streets. As she was walking, her legs leaden when so often on this route they'd felt light as air, an idea surfaced, which brought her to a grinding halt. What if Ben was ill? *Really* ill? Not at the church but wherever he lived – and she had no idea where, knew so little about him in a practical sense, she realised, not even his surname, only that he was Ben, the vicar, a kind and caring vicar. If he was ill – and he'd already had to close the church once in the past few months for that reason, as he'd told Sarah – did he have anyone to tend to him? Maybe just as she needed a friend, so did he. He needed *her*. Thinking this, she almost stamped her feet with frustration. *Where the hell are you?*

What if she stayed put, waited for the other music class attendees to arrive, Sarah et al? But what did they know about him? Nothing, she'd bet. No, she'd go home, while away the morning, come back later. Alone. Get her mother to look after Jamie for a little while, returning over the next few days until, at last, he showed up.

She immediately put that plan into action, leaving Jamie at her mum's – as Carol was still nervy about her daughter's house – before returning to the church that afternoon.

"Just be careful," Carol said, clutching at Ava. "I know the police found no evidence of an intruder, but my eyes didn't deceive me. Okay, all right, I didn't outright see him, but I told you, I sensed him well enough, how...creepy he was. Honestly, love, I know you've had those lights fitted and better locks, but I'm so worried about you there. Sometimes I can't sleep for thinking about it."

Despite the cold fear that remained in her too, Ava sought to channel Paul. "Mum, the incident's over. We mustn't keep dwelling on it. It's a blessing in disguise, in fact, because it made us reassess security and do something about it."

"True. Very true," Carol said, liking that angle, Ava could tell. "You're just going to the supermarket, are you?"

She nodded. "It's just nice to be able to do something even as mundane as that without having to cart Jamie around. I get so distracted."

How easily the lie came, and how quickly Carol bought it.

"Of course. Get something nice for your dinner. Treat Paul a bit."

"Treat Paul?" Ava tried not to accompany that remark with a caustic sigh. "Absolutely."

She'd driven to Carol's, so from there got back in the car and drove straight to the church, parking close to it. The notices on both doors were still there, and no matter how hard she banged on the doors, there was no answer.

Several times she returned over the next couple of days, always achieving the same result, a stalker herself. She even took Jed there, but the dog, displaying a previously undetected stubborn streak, refused point-blank to enter the churchyard. He pulled and pulled on his lead, dug his paws into the ground, and wouldn't give in. When she tried to insist, he growled, Ava having to reprimand him.

"You can stop that, Jed. Right now!"

He obeyed, switched to whining instead, sitting there on the pavement, nudging at her, indicating *he* wanted *her* to move, in the direction of home.

Church closed. It looked like Ben meant it. He'd gone.

Abandoned her.

As stubborn as her dog, she refused to believe that. She'd known him such a short time, but the connection they'd forged, their friendship, was real. He understood her in a way no one else did, the *new* Ava who struggled but didn't know why, who was vulnerable. And he didn't judge. And now here she was, trying not to judge either, or blame him for disappearing. *For reeling you in, Ava, then spitting you out.* There'd be a reason. A good one.

Back at home, whilst Jamie was having a nap, she drafted an email addressed to the Diocese of Chichester, no less, which as far as she could tell via research covered the whole of Sussex. In it, she explained the situation and asked for advice, signing it, *A Concerned Parishioner.* Twenty-four hours later, there was still no reply.

Paul noticed how preoccupied she was, Ava half amazed at that. Apart from that one night away which had been interrupted, she felt largely invisible to him. But several times he asked her if anything was the matter, badgered her to tell him, in fact. The answer she kept giving as Jed looked forlornly on: 'Nothing.'

Lies. All lies. A web she was weaving. And it was Thursday again. Immediately on waking, she checked her emails. Nothing.

If she didn't find answers soon, she'd burst! She'd drop by the hall this morning just in case, miraculously, the note had been removed and the doors flung open, Ben there with his wide smile, welcoming parents and babies, *her* in particular. If not, if the note remained in place, she'd go to that other place where mothers gathered, the Brew Box, try to find Sarah or anyone else who attended, and glean from them if they knew something she didn't.

Jamie was particularly irritable as they left home. He'd been awake during the night, teething, Ava tending to him and both greeting the dawn exhausted. They'd managed to grab around three hours' sleep since, but she was as bleary-eyed as him as they left a whining Jed and headed to the church.

Closed. As per usual. The café it would have to be.

"Jamie, come on, settle down." Ava too was whining as they made their way to the high street, able to hear in her own voice that usual weary plea.

The mothers might congregate in the Brew Box after music class, but would they do so instead of? She could only hope.

There were a few people on the high street, an old lady dragging a trolley bag behind her, a couple of younger women, and a teenage boy with his hood up and hands stuffed in his pockets. The café came into sight. Soon, she'd see them. A gaggle of women with babies in their arms or sleeping in their buggies, all glowing with contentment. None of them worrying like she was. None of them even remotely panicked.

She stopped just before the café and had to take a deep breath. Once again, waves of hot and cold washed over her. Anxiety in all its dubious glory.

She felt…on display standing there, watched. That same sensation she'd had hurrying from the coffee shop after meeting Sarah that first time. Was there someone following her on this occasion too? The same person who'd then trespassed on her property? The same because he had followed her…*all* the way home?

The darkness.

Nonsense! All nonsense! These thoughts would swamp

her if she didn't do something about them, *believe* they were nonsense. Although the urge was there to swing around, prove no one had her in their sights, she refrained, wouldn't give herself that dubious satisfaction.

On another deep breath, she moved forward.

She was right in what she'd surmised. Through a window, she could see a few of the mothers who attended the music class, looking very cosy huddled around a table, chatting. She could do this. Barge her way in. Ask where Sarah was and if she'd be joining them too. Also, if they knew anything about Ben. One of them might, so she had to try.

The familiar smell of coffee greeted her as she entered the café. Some heads looked up, but not theirs, the mothers that she recognised; they were too deep in conversation.

"Hello, come to join the throng?" asked an older woman serving behind the counter, eyeing the pram, perhaps a mother herself who knew the drill. "They're over there."

"Thanks," Ava said, steering that way.

The distance between them was only a few feet, but it was like crossing an ocean. Never before had she felt such a strong urge to turn and run – *You're not part of the club, and never will be* – but she kept on going because of Ben.

In front of them, she waited for someone to notice her.

Eventually, one of them looked up. Jo.

"Oh," she said. "Hello, Ava! Have you…um…come to join us?"

Ava nodded. "Just for a little while. Is that okay?"

"Sure," Jo said, nudging Christina beside her to make space.

Christina obliged, but there was more of a frown on her

face than a smile. It didn't matter, Ava decided. She'd interrupt a thousand times if it was for Ben.

"Have you ordered a coffee?" another of the women asked, Polly.

"Not yet," Ava answered.

"What would you like? I'll get it for you. I need a refill anyway."

"Oh. Thank you. An Americano, please, black."

"Coming right up," Polly said, rising from her seat and heading to the counter.

The brief silence that followed her departure was excruciating, and then everyone seemed to start talking at once.

"Your baby, Jamie, is that right? He's so sweet."

"Shame about the music class, isn't it? Although we never really spoke there."

"Do you live close by?"

Jo laughed at the sudden commotion. "Sorry," she said, and the smile on her face was genuine enough, "it's just…yeah, we haven't really got chatting before, have we? Always meant to, wondered if you'd come along to the café to join us after music class." Her expression grew more serious. "You never did, though."

"Does…does anyone know what's happened to Ben?" Ava blurted out without further preamble or pretence. Despite how nice these women were being, it was Ben who was her friend, and she needed to find out what had happened to him. "Why the music class is closed till further notice? The church too, apparently."

Polly was back, two cups of coffee in hand, which she placed on the table. She'd clearly heard the question Ava had posed, because it was her that answered.

"I'm not sure about the church," she said, resuming her seat. "I don't actually go there. Does anyone else?" The question was greeted by a few shakes of the head. "No, well," she continued, "there you go. As for the music class, I've no clue about that either. To be honest, that's not our main concern right now."

There was another brief silence, expressions growing more subdued, awkward even, with some tending to their babies and others staring into their coffees.

"Has something happened?" Ava asked, even more baffled.

"You haven't heard, then?" Jo asked.

"Heard what?"

"About Sarah," Christina answered.

Ava frowned. Why would she have heard about Sarah? Although it was Sarah she'd initially wanted to speak to, Sarah with her veiled accusations.

"She was attacked," Polly continued, her eyes suddenly welling with tears.

It took a moment to digest the news, and then Ava gasped. "When?"

"A few days ago. She'd gone out, told her husband she was meeting a friend, although it was none of us, so she was by herself. And...yeah. She got attacked."

"Badly?" Ava breathed.

"Bad enough that she's in hospital. I wish we could visit, but we can't. Her family have kind of closed ranks, the police too, of course. She's conscious, but only just. It was a blow to the back of her head she received, a *cowardly* blow, the bastard! No one has any idea who did it. Dave, her husband, told me when I snatched a few minutes with him on the phone that she managed to turn around and catch a glimpse of her attacker. It was a man, definitely a man, but no way to describe him other than he was dressed entirely in black. Some kind of balaclava pulled over his head, you know? So he was featureless. A bit like a shadow."

Ava didn't think she could be any more shocked by the news, but when Polly said that, she felt the colour drain from her face.

"Have you not read about it in the papers?" Christina asked, slightly incredulous.

Ava shook her head. "I don't really read the papers."

"Ava? Are you okay?" Jo asked, reaching out to rub at her arm.

"I...can't believe it," Ava admitted.

"I know, I know," Jo soothed. "It happened in broad daylight too. She didn't even have Murphy with her. That's her dog by the way. No one to protect her at all. Honestly, it's so sleepy around here, dull most of the time, you wouldn't think stuff like this could happen. But we've had a run of back luck lately, haven't we, what with Lou too and Jenna's mum." She breathed deep. "Actually, that's a point! I wonder if it's the same person?"

Christina shook her head. "Jenna's mum was mugged. Sarah was a knife attack."

"A knife attack? Shit!"

Again, Jo rubbed at Ava's arm. "I know. Totally horrendous."

"I thought you said a blow to the head?"

"Well, yeah, that *and* stabbed."

"But she's going to be all right? She's going to recover?"

"Physically she will. She was stabbed in the shoulder, so no vital organs damaged, thankfully," Christina replied

172

before tapping at her head. "In here, though, who knows?"

"I'm so sorry. It's just…" Should she tell them about the intruder at her own house? A man, a shadow, who'd been spying on her. For some reason the words wouldn't come. This was about Sarah, not her. There might have been an intruder, but she'd come to no harm. All it would do was terrify them further. "We need to be so careful," she said instead. "Until whoever's committing these crimes is caught."

"Amen to that," Polly said before coaxing Ava to have a sip of coffee. "It'll make you feel better. Sarah *will* be all right, Dave said so, but of course she's in a state of shock too, and, yeah, I really do think she'll be scarred by it on several levels."

"*All* of us," Jo said, and Christina agreed, nodding her head avidly. "Never mind about throwing away the key when they catch him, I hope they string him up!"

"Where was she, exactly, when this happened?" Ava asked, struggling to piece it all together. The nearby park tended to be busy, even in winter, with dog walkers, teenagers, and mothers like herself. The answer when it came stole her breath.

"Not far from me, actually," Polly told her. "Sarah lives in the street behind me, Hampton Road. Do you know it?"

"Hampton Road?" Ava mused. "Where's that?"

"By the church," Polly answered. "It's just by the church."

Chapter Eighteen

Another day passed. Another day without Ben. Ava retreated further inside herself, unable to stop such a perilous journey. She was confused. Lonelier than ever. *Where was Ben? Who'd attacked Sarah? Lou and Jenna's mother too?* Her own family had also been a potential target. She mustn't forget that.

Suspicions formed. *Crazy* suspicions. If she voiced them, would it make her seem crazy too, more than she already felt? Worse still, would she be guilty of more betrayal? Of hanging the wrong man? A *decent* man. He was. He *had* to be.

Living with Paul, she was all too aware of his frustration with her but, for now, was powerless to change it. She even felt disconnected from Jamie, seeing to his needs, providing for him, but in ways more perfunctory than ever. As for Jed – he tried to reach her. He stayed by her side, kept jumping up, his paws either side of her shoulders as if trying to hug her. He nudged her too with his wet nose, over and over. *Come back, come back*, the message.

Such a sweet dog. And if anyone could reach her, it'd be him. But she was embroiled. That's what it seemed like. Obsessed with the mystery of Ben.

She had to find him. The diocesan still hadn't replied to her email, and so she'd resent it, marked urgent. Had also swung by the church and church hall time and time again. Both remained closed, with those wretched notes on the doors.

This morning, her mother arrived. It was just after ten, but Ava and Jamie had been up for hours already, the baby having slept in the night but awake at six, Ava subsequently pushing herself out of bed and bringing him downstairs for feeding. The TV was on as he drained his bottle, but if Sarah had been mentioned on local news, she wasn't anymore. A few days had passed, and it was onto other things. Ava switched from staring at the TV to staring out at the garden, at the low wall like Jed used to, imagining an intruder there bold enough to strike even in daylight.

Paul had woken too, got dressed, and left for work, then Carol turned up, still nervous about being there but deciding enough was enough; she wouldn't be intimidated anymore. As far as Ava could tell, she didn't know about Sarah either – another who avoided the news – and Ava, for now, decided not to enlighten her.

"Oh, look at him!" Carol said happily enough, taking Jamie from her and planting a big kiss on his cheek. "He changes every day. Oh, darling, darling, what an angel you are! That's it, that's right, big smiles for Granny. I love your smiles."

Carol was so good with Jamie, so loving. Ava should have felt warmed by such a display, basking in it – others would, Polly, Jo, Christina, and the rest. Those that hadn't lost themselves like she had, strayed from the path.

As they headed towards the kitchen, Jed also wanted in on the love fest, jumping up at Carol. Once in there, Ava quickly closed the lid of her laptop, which was beside

Paul's on the table, open because she'd been checking emails again, then switched on the kettle. Carol, sitting at the table and still hugging Jamie, eyed her.

"Didn't get much sleep last night?"

Ava shrugged, had to stifle a yawn. "It's fine. I got enough."

After making the tea, she handed a mug to Carol.

"Thank you," her mother said, taking a sip. "Oh, that's lovely, much needed. It's cold out there today, colder than it should be for April. But you know what they say, don't you, 'ne'er cast a clout till May is out,' or something like that." After another sip, she added, "What do you want to do today? If you're tired, love, why not just head back upstairs?" From being all smiles and enthusiasm, Carol grew more serious. "You know...I'm worried about you. We *all* are, Dad and Paul too. You really don't seem yourself. Take advantage of my being here and top up on your sleep. Tell you what, why don't I come round a bit more often? As often as I can anyway."

Ava, who by now was also sitting at the table, looked up. "Sorry? You're all concerned about me? Paul too? Since when?"

"Well, lately especially. Even more so after the break-in."

"Have you...have you been talking to Paul about me?"

"No! Of course not," Carol denied, but Ava could tell it was a lie. Her mother wasn't like her, so good at concealing things.

"What's Paul been saying? Come on, Mum, out with it. What's he told you that he can't possibly tell me, because one thing's for sure, he's barely said anything to me about being concerned, sod all. All he wants is reassurance nothing's changed."

Her mother dared to reach across. "Of course everything's changed! Having a baby changes life beyond all recognition. He knows that perfectly well."

"Okay, all right. So come on, what's he been saying?"

Carol took a deep breath. "Darling," she said, "are you depressed? There's no shame in admitting it. Postnatal depression is something that affects a lot of women. But it helps to talk, to admit you're finding things tough instead of just...carrying on."

"I have admitted it! I've told Paul already I don't find it a walk in the park, and using those exact words!"

"It's not, though. Every mother knows that! Lack of sleep is really debilitating."

Ava sighed. So her mother wanted a heart-to-heart. The kind a mother and daughter should have, that Paul had possibly put her up to. She was close to her mum, but they rarely talked like this. Before Jamie, there'd simply been no need.

Carol shifted in her seat, uncomfortable, clearly. Perhaps as uncomfortable as Ava herself felt, Jamie thankfully oblivious, snuggling into his grandmother. Even if words wanted to tumble from her mouth concerning how she'd been feeling since having Jamie, the whole sorry shebang, going back to the trauma of the birth itself – that certainty she was dying and Jamie was too, the bleak place she'd found herself in, akin to hell – they didn't, but remained stuck in her throat. Carol would never be able to deal with it. She'd brush it all under the carpet, pretend it wasn't as big a deal as Ava thought. Just as you'd say to a child, she'd say, 'There, there, it's going to be all right,' adding, most likely, that a problem shared was a problem halved. She'd then run back to Paul and tell him all, even if Ava asked her not to. Paul would be horrified, *secretly* and perhaps justifiably, not equipped to deal with it either. She had postnatal depression? Possibly. She could read up about it, she supposed, try to understand how to deal with it, but by herself. Or she could just find Ben, in whose company she always felt so much better, normal, *understood*. One thing she knew, she had no chance of feeling better if she *didn't* find him.

Rather than show her anger, she changed tack.

"I'm fine. Really. I just...I really miss a bit of 'me' time, that's all. Getting out there, doing something on my own, even if it is just a trip to the supermarket. If you can come around more often, that's great. You know how much we love seeing you. But...rather than looking after Jamie whilst I take a nap, could I just head out instead for some fresh air? Just for an hour or two, that's plenty. I'm fine, Mum. Honestly. If I can just grab some time alone to be me again, that'd be perfect."

There was relief on Carol's face. *Predictable* relief that Ava had banked on.

"Go on," Carol said, gracing her with the indulgent smile she normally reserved for Jamie, "grab your coat and go. I'll keep the home fires burning."

Ava didn't need asking twice. She hurried from the kitchen to the hallway and shunted on her coat. Jed reached the door before she could, wagging his tail and barking excitedly. *I'm coming with you!*

On hearing the commotion, Carol appeared. "Everything all right?"

Ava's heart sank as she continued to stare at Jed. There were times he'd tried to bar her way recently as she was leaving the house without him. Now he was demanding she take him with her. Just a dog, but did he know where she hurried off to? Could he *smell* the church on her with that sensitive nose of his? A place he'd refused to set foot in, she reminded herself.

She didn't want to take him along, but she didn't want to alienate Carol either, put her off visiting if Jed rather than Jamie was a pain in the proverbial.

The lead was hanging on the coatrack, and so she grabbed it and attached it to his collar. "I'll take him, I think," she explained. "Give him a good run in the park."

"Just be careful out there," Carol reiterated. "Keep your wits about you."

"I will," Ava promised. "I plan to."

On opening the door, she found it was raining – hard.

Carol screwed up her nose. "Oh dear. Looks like some 'me' time will have to wait."

No. No way. Ava was as desperate a creature as Jed. She *had* to go to the church, try and try again, because the strange thing was, she was beginning to doubt Ben's existence, thinking him a figment of her imagination, forgetting him, even, her one and only friend. She also wanted to prove something else: he *wasn't* hiding.

From what, Ava? From what?

No answer to that, not yet.

She pulled up the hood of her coat. "We'll be fine. Jed loves playing in puddles."

Carol continued to protest, but Ava dashed forward, Jed matching her in haste, the pair of them practically running from the house towards what, she didn't know, but a mystery, definitely that. Rain that was indeed too cold for spring beat down upon them, hammering like tiny fists.

Despite being dressed adequately, she was chilled to the bone.

They hurried onwards away from home, a sanctuary, although one that someone had tried to violate. And because of that violation, she knew something else too: there was *nowhere* safe in this small town where she lived.

Not unless she got some answers.

As the church spire came into view, then the church itself, Jed didn't pull back on his lead this time or dig in his heels. If anything, he raced ahead of her, knowing exactly their destination. Like her, not just desperate but determined.

* * *

As Ava had done many times before recently, *countless* times, she stood on the edge of church grounds and observed. Why were some churches so austere? she wondered. Built from huge slabs of grey stone, lofty buildings, grand. Were they designed to make you feel small? Insignificant, and therefore in need of leadership? A place to worship a deity, to craft a faith, to bow down to love *and* fear.

Was she fearful standing there? Yes. She was. Was she hopeful? Strangely, just as she'd thought hope was dwindling, it returned with a vengeance.

The church hall was also in front of her, and the burial grounds, stones that commemorated the insignificant, those who craved to be remembered. A final wish.

No one went to church anymore. No one she knew. *She* didn't.

And yet here she was, constantly at its door, begging for

entry.

Jed gave a mighty tug, forcing Ava to step forwards onto the path. She could see the note was still pinned to the hall door, the rain having made the ink run, some words illegible.

Nothing made sense here. The church and the grounds were unkempt, she'd already noted that, but her previous thought about no one going to church anymore wasn't quite true. People did. Some. But did they come *here*? She didn't even know the name of the church, for there was no board. Which saint was it dedicated to? Perhaps it was Mary, the mother of Jesus, the ultimate female icon. *Forsaken ground*, was another recurring thought. Surreal. Could it be she'd not only imagined Ben but also coming here all those times? Her mind could conjure so much, so why not that? *She* was the great creator, Ava Kent, not God. Creating Ben.

This latest escapade was as ridiculous as the previous ones. She should just go. Turn around. Of course Ben had existed, but he'd now vanished. She should forget all about him. Focus on nothing but her own life, learning to love all the changes that had been wrought.

To feel *good enough* for them.

She was lucky. So very lucky.

Yet she continued to stand there, feeling as bleak and as drab as the sky, as grey as the stones the church had been built from. As abandoned.

Turn around. Go.

The words presented themselves in her mind, big and bold.

GO!

She stared down at Jed, who was staring back at her with

his deep brown eyes. Another funny thing: he looked as confused as she felt, as if he didn't know what to do either. He was pulling on his lead in the church's direction but whining about it.

Ava stroked the top of his head. "What a pair we are," she muttered, forcing a smile. "Doesn't matter, though. We'll get through it. We have each other, eh?"

He gave another tug on the lead, yanked it clean out of her hand this time. Jed was running towards the church, his mind made up at last. He was *flying*.

"Jed?"

She broke into a run too, following him, catching a hint of something in the porch as she drew closer. Movement! Some kind of movement! A figure, she was sure of it, but one that quickly retreated, the church doors subsequently closing, banged shut.

Ben. It had to be. He hadn't disappeared. He was in the church and perhaps had been all along. That room he'd taken her to, the vestry, a vision of it came to mind, of the bin bags stuffed with something soft – clothes? She'd presumed they were for charity, donated by parishioners, but what if they belonged to him? And the wardrobe against the far wall, what did that contain? More clothes, more bedding? A sleeping bag, even, or some kind of put-you-up? Did Ben…*live* there? In the church? Why? Vicars didn't do that, were given separate accommodation nearby. *Who are you, Ben? Who exactly are you?* She had to find out.

Jed reached the church doors. He was flinging himself at them, snarling.

What the hell? "Jed? Jed, stop that. What's wrong?"

He was acting…insane. She wanted to reach out and forcibly stop him, but she was frightened. What if he turned around, turned on *her*? He wouldn't do that, would he? Her gentle dog? But who could she trust here? Could she even trust herself? What she was doing, was it also insane? If Ben was sleeping at the church, then he'd ignored her every time she'd come calling, didn't want contact. He'd made that clear enough. Why pursue the matter so relentlessly?

She couldn't help herself, started calling his name instead of Jed's.

"Ben! Ben! It's me, it's Ava. I know you're in there. I saw you."

Sure he wouldn't hear her over the noise Jed was making, she reached out and grabbed Jed's collar and jerked it. "For God's sake, pipe down, will you?" Contrary to her fears, Jed didn't bite her, but his agitation ensured she had to hold on tight to control him. "Jed," she screamed again. "I said, quiet! Let me deal with this. Ben! Ben, I'm sorry about the dog, but listen to me, please. I know you're in there. I saw the door open and close. I don't understand what's going on. Is something wrong, Ben? If I can help you, I will. I *want* to help. Whatever it is you need, I'm here, okay? Listen to me. Please."

Nothing from inside. No door creaking open. No face appearing in the crack.

Jed had at last quieted, as if he was waiting too.

"Ben, are you there?"

The only response was from the crows in the trees above them, a sudden burst of cawing that sounded dire, almost like a warning.

"I won't abandon you, Ben," Ava continued. "You were there for me. You understood me when I didn't even understand myself. Whatever's happened..." An image of

Sarah lying in blood, just like she herself had once, tried to push its way to the front of her mind – a *created* image. It had nothing to do with Ben. Nor those other attacks. It couldn't! "Whatever's happened, I will try to understand too. I'll go now, but I'll be back. Don't keep shutting me out."

As she backed away, Jed tried to resist, snarled again, a parting shot. Ava remained firm, though, yanking on his lead again, holding it firm. When she came next time – because, true to her word, she would – she'd leave Jed at home with Carol, no matter how much he played up. A dog she knew nothing about – that reminder flashed too – that Iris at the rescue centre knew nothing about, who'd suddenly appeared just like Ben had disappeared, a *dangerous* dog.

He saved your life! And Jamie's! How can he be dangerous?

And yet it was only Ben she could think about. The mystery that *enshrined* him.

She'd got a fair distance from the church, was at the beginning of her road, both she and Jed as sullen as the day, when her phone pinged. Ava sighed heavily. Was it her mother, checking up on her? Perhaps Jamie was kicking up, and she'd had enough, wanted out. Everyone loved a baby when it was smiling. Everyone wanted to hand it back when the tears started. Even Carol.

With resignation and weariness, she dug her phone from her pocket, noted the No Caller ID. Having been thankfully silent on the journey home, Jed barked as she hurried to open the text, excitement causing her stomach to lurch. It was from Ben. He had her number, of course! When she'd first joined the music class, there was a sheet of paper to jot down your details – entirely optional, as

Ben had pointed out to Sarah. It was just there on the table, next to the tea and coffee and biscuits. She hadn't written her address, just her name, Jamie's name, and her mobile number. *Absent-mindedly* written it. But now she was so grateful she had.

He was texting, reaching out, listening when she'd said she'd try to understand.

Ava, I do need to see you. Alone. Something's happened. Something bad. Really need to speak. Come back. Tomorrow. Noon? Just you. No one else. No dog.

She couldn't type her reply quickly enough:

I'll see you tomorrow at noon. No dog, I promise. Just me.

Chapter Nineteen

Despite what Carol had said to her daughter about being readily available, her face was a picture when Ava told her she needed her again, the very next day. At noon.

"But, darling…it's just… Look, I can do tomorrow morning for about an hour, but I'm planning a work Zoom meeting after that."

"Can't you do that here?" Ava countered.

"Not if Jamie needs attention!"

"But, Mum." She tried hard not to sound like a demanding, petulant child. "I…look, you're right, I haven't been coping great recently." She was jiggling Jamie – a contented Jamie, she had to admit, probably still basking in the attention his grandmother had showered him with, a proper one-to-one. "And…well, my time earlier, alone, has really helped. It's like…I don't know, the best medicine." She found she was blinking back tears, then wondered if she should just let them fall; they'd add to the authenticity of what she was saying. "Sometimes, Mum, sometimes I feel like I can't get through the day. I don't know why, I just…dread the night falling for some reason, the darkness, and the nearer it gets to sundown, the more agitated I become. Don't look like that, so shocked. I always cope. I do. But just getting out today, having time to think, to *breathe*, I feel so much better because of it, bolstered. I just need an hour. And it's better at noon than in the morning. It kind of breaks the day up a bit more." When Carol still hesitated, she added, "I need this, Mum. I wouldn't ask, would never burden you, you know that. It's just...please."

There it was, the petulance, no way to suppress it.

"For goodness' sake, you're not a burden!" Carol flapped. "Okay, all right. Leave it with me. I'll see what I can do about rearranging things."

Later, that evening, Ava had to fend off Paul, who was perfectly aware Carol had been there today and kept asking how the visit went, *innocently* asking rather than letting on that it had been planned between them both.

"Fine," was the only answer she was prepared to give him.

They were together on the sofa, doing the usual thing, watching some TV once Jamie was asleep, but with Ava finding any excuse to leave the room – checking on Jamie, making tea, washing the dishes, and always taking her phone with her just in case Ben messaged again, wondering too: Should she message him?

Even though her fingers hovered over the phone's keypad, she refrained. They had their plan, one she'd move heaven or high water to fulfil.

The morning arrived after another fitful night, at least on Ava's part. Jamie had slept soundly, the Calpol she'd given him before bedtime for his teething doing the trick. Paul left for work, but not before checking with Ava again if all was okay.

"Yes! Of course!" she told him, her voice tight, which she immediately felt bad about. The concern in his eyes was genuine. God, if he knew the full story, he'd be so *disappointed* in her, not just about Ben but also how hard she was struggling with what should come naturally: motherhood. She'd find out what was wrong with Ben and then find her own feet, lay all this to rest in time. Somehow. Someway. Prove to herself that Ben was who she thought he was, help him if he needed help, give back, and then move on. If the church was to remain closed and he moved to another parish elsewhere, that'd be for the best.

Waving Paul goodbye on the doorstep and smiling widely – the *perfect* wife – she noticed it was another dull day, clouds hanging so low they threatened to suffocate. Oh, for sunnier climes! For the chill to relinquish its lingering grip. *Soon*, she told herself as she stepped back and shut the door, turning to go upstairs when there was that familiar ping, a message coming through on her phone.

Ben! was her immediate thought. It wasn't, though; it was from Carol.

Sorry, darling, I really hate to let you down, but I'm actually not feeling well. I got up this morning, thought I'd see how I went, but getting worse by the hour. I really hope it's not the dreaded Covid. First time for me if it is! I won't be able to come today, maybe not for a few days, but as soon as I can, I will. I know how important it is for you to have time out. So glad you've opened up to me about everything. It'll all be better from now on, I promise. Going back to bed now, will call later.

Ava could only stare at the phone. Her mum was cancelling?

Bitch!

The force with which that word entered her mind

shocked Ava so much, she almost threw the phone from her. Yes, her mum was cancelling, but because she was ill, not because she was a bitch! Where did Ava get off calling anyone that? She'd never have done such a thing before... *Before what?* It was a question demanding an answer, but one she refused to give.

As she reached the landing, Jamie was starting to howl. Jed, knowing that Paul had left, that Ava was a soft touch and wouldn't reprimand him, was upstairs too, hovering at Jamie's bedroom door, more intent on getting in there and seeing to him than she was. Pushing the door open, she allowed him entry. He ran to the bed and jumped up, resting his front paws against the bars of the cot, and immediately Jamie stopped crying. Taking advantage of the reprieve, Ava texted too, not her mother but Ben:

I can't make it, not today. Sorry! Childcare fallen through.

The response came with breathtaking speed:

You promised!

He was right, she had, but this morning, promises were being made and broken.

I'd have to bring Jamie.

Where was the harm? She'd been in his company plenty of times with Jamie.

Again, an instant reply:

No! Come alone! I've told you, something bad's happened!

Dread seized her as her fingers worked furiously:

What has? Hang on, I'll phone you.

Another lightning response:

Don't! Texting best. When we speak, better if face-to-face.

Ben, I'm worried. You're alone at the church, aren't you? If not, if it's a problem, I can call the police. In fact, I'll do it. I'll call them. Right now. V worried.

Don't. I mean it! You don't understand the situation.
Then tell me! Are you alone?
Hard to explain.
Who could possibly be with you? God?!

It was a joke. A feeble one. Not meant to be laughed at, not really, so when his reply came through, she was beyond confused.

Something like that.

With Jed still keeping Jamie amused, she headed over to the window and looked down onto an empty garden, the far corner in particular. She then adjusted her gaze to stare at the phone again. What on earth could she say next?

Her phone pinged again. If she was at a loss, Ben wasn't.

When can you come? Need you soon.

He *needed* her. An undeniable thrill at those words. But she was needed at home too.

Ava, please!

She wrote back:

I'll try. Mum's ill. Husband at work. Evenings are difficult. Find someone else to look after the baby.

The baby's name was Jamie. Ben knew that well enough. Why be so impersonal?

Ava! Please!

She frowned. Who else could she ask? There was no one. Certainly not anyone from the music class, those she hadn't integrated with, had refused to.

Sarah's in hospital. She was attacked.

Why she wrote that, she didn't know. Sarah's situation, Lou's, Jenna's mother, and now Ben's, was it all linked? Linked also with the intruder that had tried to break into her home? With the shadows she saw everywhere? *Especially* in the church.

The reply wasn't so immediate this time, although it eventually came through:

I know.

Jed was on four feet again, a bark alerting her to that fact, making her swing round to look at him, at deep brown eyes that were…accusatory?

Ignoring him, she felt tears sting her own eyes as she typed the next words:

Is it you, Ben? Are you the attacker?

No barking, no whining, there was just silence, heavy, heavy silence, as heavy as the weight inside her, a heart filled with terror.

Ben?

You don't understand. I need your help. Get here soon.

Chapter Twenty

A cat on a hot tin roof. Ava knew exactly what that saying meant, couldn't settle, couldn't focus, couldn't do anything except think about Ben and what he'd said.

She'd had her suspicions about him since his disappearance, and then she'd dismissed them. The Ben she knew was kind, gentle, and compassionate. He'd seen beyond the façade, knew she was in distress and tried to help – never any judgement on his behalf, just concern and love. The latter was a notion that wouldn't shift. Ben was in love with her. Wouldn't hurt her. But was she in love with him?

The day waned, the evening came, and Paul arrived home. No sooner had he entered the house than he did that thing Jed had taken to doing, staring at her when he thought she wouldn't notice, scrutinising her, trying to see through the façade too.

It wasn't as if she wanted to keep lying to him; something in her was desperate to tell him everything that was going on. But what would his reaction be? She couldn't help but think he'd go mad, maybe even accuse her of putting Jamie in danger because she'd been alone with Ben, suggest, even, that she was having an affair.

"You're in love with him, aren't you? You've probably even slept with him!"

She could hear the shrillness in his voice. And what would her answer be?

"I haven't slept with him, Paul. I haven't even kissed him. But do I love him? I just don't know. No. Yes. Maybe. If anything…I'm more confused than ever!"

In this scenario, she'd watch as Paul's expression hardened, the way it did when he was angry, and she'd hate him for it. It would surge in her, that hatred, become a tidal wave, unstoppable, destroying everything in its wake, all that had gone before. And so easily. Fragile. Not just her, but her entire world. Hanging in the balance by a thread. She wanted to run into Paul's arms; she also wanted to scream at him to stop staring, to ask *her* what the matter was, rather than her mother, and be prepared for the answer. If only he'd force a confession from her! Because no matter how many times she imagined telling him, she knew she'd struggle. There was a ridge of silence between them. Growing wider.

In this house, she had no connection, not to Paul, to Jamie, not even to Jed anymore, who was the last bastion. She was isolated, cut adrift, waiting, waiting, waiting for that precious 'me' time which would become 'their' time, hers and Ben's.

Carol felt even worse the next day. Ava had called and asked if her dad could have Jamie instead. He loved Jamie as much as her mother did, but, as Carol said, he was trying to run a business and couldn't just drop everything.

"Besides," Carol continued, coughing a little, but it seemed forced to Ava, as if trying to ram the fact down her throat that she was ill, "he's feeling a bit under the weather too."

Paul went to work again, Paul came home again, stared

at her again. The texts from Ben continued but only checking when she could come, that it had to be soon.

Another night passed, a week gone already since she'd first found the church closed.

Paul was later than usual, having gone to the pub with some colleagues – *just for one or two*, he'd said when he'd texted her. He hadn't asked if it'd be okay or said something like 'Would you rather I come home instead? Perhaps, you've had a hard day and could do with a break yourself. You could even meet one of your old work friends. It's about time, isn't it? Head out to Eastbourne with them.' Oh no, nobody had to ask permission for going anywhere except her; they could do what they liked, whilst she…she was *trapped*. And it *had* been a hard day, raining, making the prospect of a walk and some fresh air unpleasant, Jamie screaming, likely because he was as bored as her, nothing keeping him entertained, and Ben texting – *Will it be today? Time's running out. It has to be soon.* And Jed, staring, staring, staring.

After the pub when Paul returned, Ava was at fever pitch.

"You know what," she screamed at him, "you can just fuck off, Paul! I can't even get an hour or two off in the day, not one measly hour. Just to go for a walk, Paul, a *walk*, or a coffee. I'm fed up with it. I've had enough."

A whirlwind, that's what she was, all the fury and frustration, the fear, the bewilderment, guilt, loathing, and confusion exploding. If her ranting woke Jamie, if it frightened Jed, so be it. No longer stuck in her throat, the words wanted release.

"You asked my mother if I was okay, not me. You don't have the guts to have a proper conversation with me about how I'm feeling, because you know you won't like what I have to say. You want a perfect home to return to after a hard day's work at your oh-so-important job, a wife straight out of Stepford, a baby that alternates between smiling and sleeping, your dinner on the table, a wine glass filled, and no sodding complaints."

Paul had no chance to reply as she continued. "I nearly died having Jamie! *He* could have died because, as usual, you weren't around, not for hours afterwards. A stranger had to help me. And you've no idea what it's been like since. You just don't care, not really, not enough. Everything's about you, your job, your promotion, and how you have to focus. You never help with Jamie during the night, not even on the weekends or that joke of a holiday we went on. You just sleep through whilst he screams and screams. You take what you need, always. Maybe there's some that would consider me selfish too, but, Paul, you take the piss. The fact there might be something wrong with me baffles you. But you know full well there is – *that's* why you organised those nights away, so ask me about it, Paul! Me! Not my mother. You think you're there for us, but you're not. You even work at weekends on your bloody laptop. I'm tired, and I'm struggling. Nothing's perfect. We're certainly not. You and me are fucked."

Such a burst of anger, so many accusations, yet no reply was forthcoming. What there was, was screaming. Jamie had indeed woken, and Jed was chasing his tail like he did when excited or frightened. Other than that, silence. *Paul's* silence.

He turned from her, marched from the living room and headed upstairs. The fact he'd done that rather than retaliate was worse somehow. She should go after him or go to Jamie, at least, pick him up and comfort him. *Say you're sorry.* Of course she was! For all of it. But above all, right now, for meeting Paul in the first place.

She *couldn't* go upstairs. He wouldn't want her there. Besides, Jamie was quiet again, likely because Paul had gone to him, was soothing him, their poor baby boy.

Her whole body caved, and she slumped down onto the sofa. Didn't just sit but lay on it, her entire body trembling, staring not out the patio doors at the darkness and the shadows but at nothing, into thin air. He switched the hallway light off, another sign he didn't want her to follow. The path to redemption closed. *Stay away from me, Ava. Stay down there, you…madwoman. Just keep away.*

More alone than ever. That's what she was. Her phone remaining silent too, not even a text from Ben. No matter. She wanted to sleep. Just sleep. Enter the void and forget she existed. Just for a while. A nudge at her knee told her Jed was with her still, would stand guard no matter what. Even so, she drifted. Oblivion in reach.

Morning arrived, as morning always did, a flurry of activity pulling her from the deepest sleep she'd had in a long while. Pushing herself upwards, every bone ached, and her head thumped, the sleep deep, perhaps, but not restorative.

She looked towards the source of activity: the hallway.

"Paul?" she called out. "What is it? What's going on?"

Rising from the sofa to check, she saw he was up and dressed, Jamie too, held in his arms. She frowned. Were they going for a walk? What time was it?

She checked her watch. Just past nine. Why wasn't Paul at work?

Tentatively, she approached him. "What are you doing, Paul?"

She saw what else was in the hallway: a holdall and a rucksack, packed full.

"Paul? Paul! What's going on? Why have you got packed bags with you?"

His face was as pinched as it had been last night.

"Paul?" Her voice was lower this time, practically a whisper.

"We're leaving," he finally answered. "Jamie and I. We're clearly a burden to you, you hate us being here, hate…being a mum, so…we're leaving. Which, you know, you should be glad about. Bloody ecstatic, in fact. You're going to have a ton of 'me' time. Which, let's face it, is the only thing you crave. It's certainly not motherhood."

"Paul—" she repeated, but it was his turn to rant now.

"You've been texting someone. Oh yeah, that's right, you think I'm a fool, don't you? An idiot. That I wouldn't notice how you sneak off all the fucking time, especially in the last few days, always texting. If I should happen to come into the room and you're texting or you're reading your texts, or whatever it is you bloody do, you hide your phone, try to conceal it, look like butter wouldn't melt. But I've got it. I have. The reason you—" he gestured wildly around him "—*hate* this, what we have. It's because of someone else, isn't it?"

"Someone else?" All she could do was repeat what he'd said, neither confirm nor deny it. When she found her voice again, it was small, whiny, totally obvious that she was lying. "It's not what you think. You don't understand." Words Ben himself had said to her. "Look, you can't just leave, take my baby from me!" And yet isn't this what she'd wanted? Freedom? And Ben too.

She marched closer, vaguely aware Jed was at her heels.

"You cannot take Jamie! I won't let you. He's mine."

"You know what?" Paul almost sneered. "Despite you trying to pretend otherwise, he's mine too. Look at you. For God's sake, Ava, just fucking take a cold, hard look at yourself, how you are. I don't even recognise you anymore."

One hand shot upwards to smooth at her hair. She knew she looked dishevelled from her night on the sofa. Is that what he meant? Or was his meaning deeper?

"You're not taking him!" she repeated.

"You can't stop me," he countered. "We're going to my parents', just for a few days. Days in which you can sort yourself out. If you are seeing another man, if that is the case—" his voice broke, but quickly he recovered himself "—then…then you'll have to choose." A sob escaped him, which shocked her. "Ava, we have so much! We *do* have perfection! I know it isn't easy, adjusting to life with a young baby. I know I work long hours too and that…perhaps you haven't made any friends yet with other mums, but it'll happen. Besides that music class you go to, look for other things, swimming classes, maybe. Jamie would love that. Perhaps we could take him swimming together on the weekends. We don't need a class, anything formal. I won't work weekends, okay? I'll make a point of it. That company will suck the life out of me if I let them. If I never get promoted, so be it. It'll likely only mean more work if I do and not a lot of extra pay." All positive things he was saying, but then his eyes suddenly narrowed. "The music class, is that where you met him? This man you're texting? Is he, like…another dad or something?

Single or married?"

"NO!" Ava burst out. "There isn't anyone else. I mean, look at me. I look like shit. You've as good as said it. Who'd fancy me?" She reached out, tried to tug at Jamie. "You're not going! Stay here. Be a man, for fuck's sake, Paul. Stay and sort this situation out, or at least leave Jamie." Jamie, who'd begun crying again, feeding off the situation again. A child growing up in a warring home, who'd be left scarred by it.

Ava dropped her hand, stopped tugging at him, began to cry also. Paul was right; this was no place for Jamie. Not right now. She *did* have to sort herself out. Sort Ben out too. Go to him, yes, but only to tell him he needed to find help from some other source than her. If she couldn't help herself or her family, she couldn't help anyone. And here was Paul, giving her the opportunity to do just that. Afterwards…well, afterwards, it'd be fine. It'd have to be. They could have that fresh start.

"Ava." Paul was crying too. The three of them, standing in the hallway of their brand-new family home, which was drenched in suffering rather than happiness. Jed was still behind her, and it was like he was crying too, emitting a few whines and the occasional yelp.

She stepped back, away from Paul's reach – because if he reached out, if his hand touched hers, she'd crumble, all resolve gone.

"Go," she said, and although he had seemed so determined about doing just that, he now looked stunned by her command. "Go, because you're right. I do have things to sort out, things I'll discuss with you, but later. I need a day, a couple of days at most, but I'll sort it. I promise. Go, but come back, okay? Promise me that much."

"I will, Ava. You know I will."

After whispering, "Sorry," to both Paul and Jamie, she and Jed turned, and together they walked back into the living room, waiting for Paul to open the door, to load the car with bags and Jamie, and then for it not to slam shut but softly close.

Chapter Twenty-One

Ben, I'm coming. I'll be with you soon.

A thumbs-up emoji was the response Ava got. That was it. Nothing more. And yet it had taken her hours to summon up the courage to say that. Hours of sitting with Jed in the living room, in the dark with the curtains drawn.

She'd sat there dry-eyed but no longer numb. A sea of emotions churned inside her. She was certain that if she opened her mouth in a wail, they'd erupt, every one, pour from her, filling the room from floor to ceiling, drowning her completely this time. And so, for now, they must be kept contained. Until what? Maybe after she'd seen Ben and explained she had to put her family first, encouraged him to seek help from the police and not her, insist on it, that sea of emotions would calm. It would do so because she'd done the right thing. Finally.

She had to stir herself, get washed and dressed, head there soon, as it was already getting dark outside. And yet the cover of darkness was what she'd waited for, seeking the furtiveness of it, the secrecy, which was so much a part of her life now.

Paul had accused her of seeing another man, come right out and said it just like she'd thought he might, and yet she'd meant it when she'd questioned who'd want her as she was now, someone with no shine left. Did Ben truly want her? Someone like him who was handsome and charismatic? She couldn't deny it, though; if Sarah hadn't interrupted them in the hall, they would have kissed. And, certainly, they'd embraced. There *were* feelings between them, but ones that confused her, left her feeling no longer elated but more wretched than ever. She'd betrayed her family. If she continued to do so, she'd lose everything. She had to help heal them, her own soul too, a soul that was tarnished. By motherhood? How could that be?

She forced herself to her feet. Jed, who'd been sitting serenely by her side, allowing her to cling to him the desperate way she did, not flinching at all, also sprang into action. It was as though he were *dancing* in front of her, not a happy dance, though, one born of agitation, not wanting her to move, encouraging her to sit down again, to stay. And she wanted to. She did. Every ounce of energy had deserted her. Perhaps…perhaps it'd be all right if she didn't go to the church and see Ben. Whatever trouble he was in, perhaps it was simply too big for her to deal with. If she texted him, explained, would he understand? This man whom she felt understood everything, who could see deep inside her, who *knew* her soul was tarnished. Because…his was too?

"Jed, stop it," she said, referring to his continuing antics, but it was half-hearted. She wanted to sleep. Just sleep until Paul and Jamie returned home. Pretend, even, it was a dream they'd left. That *all* of this was. Once she'd slept, she'd wake up her old normal self again, ready to embrace family life, to be like the other mothers she'd met, relishing the responsibility, holding close every precious second.

She was going to do it, sit back down, give in. *Sorry, Ben.* No way you could give to someone when you were running on empty.

Jed, as if sensing her intention, wagged his tail, *furiously* wagged it.

"Okay, okay," she said, about to add 'you win' when her phone pinged.

A message. From who? Paul or Ben?

Her heart thumped in her chest. Her mouth was dry. Jed was no longer dancing. He stood perfectly still. And stared.

As she stared back, she felt her eyelids flutter. Sleep doing its utmost to shut her down. She was so tired. Couldn't understand how you could *feel* this tired. Could sleep standing up if she had to.

The phone pinged again.

And again.

And again.

Despite aching with fatigue, she darted for it, sure that Jed would get to it first if she didn't, and would take it in his jaw and bite down, crushing it. A stupid certainty, and he didn't move, but he growled.

Ben, then. It was him.

His patience at an end.

The phone in her hand, she unlocked the screen.

They *were* from Ben. A whole series of texts.

No words and no emojis either. Each one simply a question mark.

* * *

Getting out of the house with a baby was bad enough, something Ava knew well enough. Usually, every time she tried to leave, he'd start screaming, hungry suddenly, or vomit or fill his nappy in a spectacular manner. Without him it should prove easier, but Jed had stepped into the breach. He just kept getting in the way, almost tripping her up on several occasions, jumping up at her too, barking, howling, even weeing on the floor at one point.

"Jed! What is wrong with you?"

Terrible behaviour, disturbed. Worse than he'd ever exhibited before; certainly, he had never messed in the house. *You haven't been out with him today, though. You haven't even let him into the garden. Again, this is your fault, not his.* True. She couldn't deny it. The garden would have to do, though; she couldn't waste more time, although the thought of opening the patio doors, of what lurked beyond them…

She *had* to let him out before she left. There was nothing out there.

Back in the living room, she crossed over to the patio doors and drew the curtains back, her stomach, predictably, lurching.

She wasn't being dramatic; an attacker *was* on the loose. Very possibly the same man that had been in her garden. Paul said lightning never struck twice. Not true. Sometimes it did. What if he was out there again and this time had disabled their security lights, smashed them, preparing for attack?

The patio doors were now open, but Jed hadn't bolted forwards as he usually did. He remained where he was on the threshold.

"Jed, go on," she encouraged. "Let's get this over and done with."

He stood his ground.

She raised her voice. "Jed! Go on! It's okay out there."

Still, he remained.

About to push him out if needs be, she half bent and then stopped. She'd heard a rustling, like someone treading on leaves who'd then, realising they'd made a sound and been heard, had abruptly come to a halt. She'd been focusing on Jed when she'd heard it, getting ready to push him from behind, and she noticed that he'd tensed as well, leaning his head to the side the way he did when listening intently.

Memories of the night her mother had phoned when she and Paul had been at the hotel returned with a vengeance. The certainty in Carol's voice there was an intruder out there, the fear that had ruined what might have otherwise been a night of healing. *Deliberately* ruined it? That's what it felt like, as if the intruder knew what was happening and refused to allow it, wanting to keep Ava where she was, in a position of isolation, only one real friend to her name: Ben. Such perfect, perfect timing. But Ben had had no idea about her weekend plans. She hadn't told him.

She shook her head. No sense in blaming anyone but herself. It was her and her alone who'd created this mess, by her refusal to admit how she was feeling, to accept also she might be suffering from depression, psychosis even.

She'd given birth, but during the process was impregnated again…with madness.

Another rustle. Unmistakable. Someone stepping closer? If that were so, the security lights would have registered such movement and floodlit the area. *Unless they've been disabled or smashed.* The latter easy enough to do, happening whilst she was upstairs showering and getting dressed. No reason to think she'd hear a thing, not over the rush of water. An attacker that had targeted her, along with Sarah, Lou, and Jenna's mother, the same someone who'd followed her home from the café that day. And now here he was, close again, spying, *knowing* she was alone.

Another rustle. A thud.

Why hadn't Jed sprung forward in full-on protection mode?

In the end, it was Ava who raced into the garden, roaring. Tonight was all about resolutions, one way or the other. Without them, she'd be stuck in hell.

The lights immediately came on, not disabled or smashed, causing Ava to skid to a halt and look wildly around her. What would he do, this attacker? *How* did he intend to hurt her? Was he brandishing a weapon of some sort? The same knife he'd stabbed Sarah with? "Come out, you bastard, wherever you are. I am *not* a victim."

There was no one there. At least not where he'd been last time, in the corner that Jed would stare at, where her mother insisted he'd been. A shadow. An imagining? Even her mother prone to them? The police had found no sign of an intruder, after all. Paranoia. Something inherited. *Hysteria*. The garden was empty but for a squirrel, which raced across the lawn as if fleeing the four horsemen of the apocalypse. The perpetrator? Who knew?

Something had prompted Jed at last, and he also raced into the garden, straight past her, making her heart pound again. What was he chasing?

The squirrel, of course. *Just* the squirrel. Who, further alarmed, flung itself at the nearest tree and climbed, Jed sliding to a stop just below it, barking and wagging his tail. *Come back down and play!* Whilst he continued to plead, she scanned the grounds again. It was a small garden, nowhere to hide, not really, the night creatures – tonight, at least – benign.

"Jed, do your business, then come back in. And hurry, because I have to go."

Realising he was on a hiding to nowhere, Jed gave up on the squirrel, headed into the bushes, then swiftly returned.

"Good boy, come on."

She turned towards the house, as did Jed. Initially. But then he stopped and turned back around, staring once more at the far corner.

"Oh, for goodness' sake…" she began, but her voice died out.

There was no one there. Lights still flooded the garden, and she could see perfectly well there wasn't, peering every bit as hard as he was. Still, Jed whined, he growled, his eyes fixed on the spot where someone *had* been. It wasn't hysteria, paranoia, or imagination. Unlike her daughter, Carol wasn't guilty of those things.

Even so, he wasn't there now.

And she had to meet Ben.

Who was in trouble.

Who'd reached out.

A charismatic man. Was she really his only friend?

The lights, on a timer, went out. There was darkness once more.

Jed flinched, *actually* flinched, then turned around as she started striding back to the house, following her at last, his body hunched and his tail between his legs.

No sooner was she over the threshold when messages started to flood through. Several of them, one after the other. Actual words. *Desperate* words.

All from Ben.

Where are you?
What's taking so long?
You said you'd come.
You promised.
I need you!
No more time.
IT HAS TO BE NOW!

Chapter Twenty-Two

Ava hurried along roads barely penetrated by the glow of streetlamps, the rain beginning to fall. Such a dark night. Lonely. She passed no one on her way, everyone, it seemed, doing the sensible thing and staying indoors. Perhaps it'd be busier on the high street, in the restaurants, but on the outskirts you'd be forgiven for thinking Heathfield was a ghost town, deserted.

It was cold too. She hadn't put on her own coat but Paul's, a jacket, really, and not very warm, but it was comforting nonetheless, the familiarity of it. She'd worn it as a reminder of him and what she had to do this night. Whose side she was really on.

She didn't want to see Ben, she realised, not any longer. Those last texts he'd sent were *crazy*. She was running through darkness to reach what? More darkness? Was Ben the attacker? The stalker? It was torture thinking such things!

He was right when she'd asked him outright whether he was the attacker and he'd replied, *You don't understand.* Would he understand when she ended it?

Another crazy thing was Jed when she'd left the house. Acting up again, worse than ever, hurling himself at the door so hard she'd feared he'd break his own bones. Howling too, refusing to be hushed. What the neighbours thought, she couldn't imagine.

Jed had done something else strange as she was trying to calm him. He'd run to the kitchen table where her laptop was, jumped up, and barked at it, over and over. Then, with Ava staring at him in absolute bewilderment, he'd jumped onto the table and nudged at the laptop with his nose, so hard he'd sent it crashing to the floor! She'd had to scream at him then, haul him down from there before picking up the laptop. What if he'd broken it? No time to open the lid and check, but she bloody hoped not. Paul would be furious. *She* was furious. What a fuss Jed had made when she'd placed it back on the table, as she'd shooed him out of the kitchen and closed the door to prevent him from doing anything like that again.

She loved that dog, she really did, felt that he'd picked her every bit as much as she'd picked him, the way he'd barked and barked at the rescue centre until she'd looked over, but rescue dogs, some of them had suffered trauma. And trauma, as she knew, could cause you to behave in bizarre ways. Perhaps – and this was another tortuous thought – she couldn't deal with him as well as a new baby. The combination was just too much, pushing her further over the edge. Right now, she was in freefall. What she was doing proved it: hurrying to a church at nightfall, a church no one ever seemed to go, that was dusty and tired, that smelled of neglect, meeting a man she thought she knew but really didn't, who was in some kind of trouble. Meeting him because she was *able* to. Her family had deserted her, and to hell with it being temporary; it was *still* abandonment. Crazy. Crazy. Crazy. All of it. A rollercoaster ride. To get back on track, she had to expunge Ben from her life, cut the cord that tethered them, but do so gently. A kind man. He was! Not someone capable of such cruelty – mugging an eighty-two-year-old woman, for God's sake! Stabbing Sarah. Driving a car into Lou. No. No way. He was *not* guilty of that. No way she could be fooled to that extent.

The tip of the church spire was visible as she continued to hurry, low clouds covering the rest, *concealing* it, this place to gather, to worship, that she'd not paid any attention to before she'd attended the music class in the church hall. A building that hid in plain sight. *Nobody* really noticing it. Symbolic of a past age, whose doors had finally closed. They'd open tonight, though. For her.

"Aargh!"

The paths in the churchyard weren't the only ones ill-maintained, so was the pavement beneath her feet. One slab jutting upwards, she tripped, hurtling forwards as if someone had delivered the mightiest of shoves. The lampposts turned out to be good for something after all, as grabbing on to one broke her fall, although her forehead smashed against its steely stem, every bit as painful as if she'd hit the floor.

"Shit! Shit! Shit!" She was blinking rapidly, seeing stars, panting hard too.

To add insult to injury, a wave of nausea overcame her, causing her to clamp a hand over her mouth, she was so certain she was going to vomit.

She reached up to touch her forehead. "Fuck!" It hurt. A lot. No doubt a huge bruise developing in the next couple of days that she'd have to find an explanation for. For now, though, it was of no matter. She straightened up, took a deep breath, and continued onwards until she swapped the pavement for the church path. A weed-ridden path, and the gravestones either side, what few there were, were not a way to be remembered after all, as forgotten about as the rest of the place.

A slippery path when wet, so she slowed down. No way she wanted to fall again. Could it be...was the church truly abandoned? Not sacred ground any longer but...there was a word for it, which she searched for...deconsecrated? Not entirely outlandish to think that. She'd seen no one go inside all the times she'd been there; it had only ever been her and Ben. She could have gone on a Sunday, she supposed, to see if there was a mass taking place, but she hadn't suspected before, only now.

The music class in the church hall was another matter. That *had* attracted people. It'd attracted her, with its glorious hope of meeting new people, new mothers, whom the class was specifically aimed at. One of various community projects that Ben was involved with, *directly* involved, despite what a busy workload he must have, a follow-on of a previous project created by another vicar, Moira something. Moira Lintern. That was it. She'd run the class previously, but Ben had taken over because it helped, he said, it forged a connection with a parish growing ever distant, a way to stay in touch. Such good intentions. You became a vicar because you were *filled* with good intentions, a desire to do good, to help those in need, everyone, no matter how damaged, to spread the word of God, of course, but finding new ways to do it, more subtle ways, preaching fire and brimstone no longer effective. It was *especially* the damaged you helped. Reaching out as Ben had, and in his hands a lifeline. He was a vicar. A man. Nothing else. She was *not* in danger tonight. Madder than ever.

But it still had to end.

And it would. She lifted a hand and almost caressed the sleeve of Paul's jacket. No way she'd waiver. Not even when she finally looked into Ben's eyes, so dark they were almost black. She'd separate fact from fantasy. At last. Be what she was born to be, what she *wanted* to be above all else: a good wife and a good mother.

But first, a good friend.

* * *

"Ben? Ben, are you there?"

The door was open. *He* must have opened it but then, strangely, retreated down the aisle into a darkness to which her eyes simply would not adjust.

Ben was just a man, and this was just a church, but the building she'd stepped into felt much bigger than before. Cathedral-like. Cavernous. Insignificance was certainly the feeling it inspired as she ventured further in, loath to shut those heavy oak doors behind her but doing so anyway. Sealing them in.

A church that was also a haven, not just for Ben presently but dozens of others too, hundreds, thousands. People would have hurried here on a Sunday, *twice* on that day for some, morning and evensong, would have got married, been christened, and had their funerals here, no other alternative when now there were so many.

Continuing to advance, she called Ben's name again, her voice no longer raised but hushed, the reverence of such a place insisting upon it. A modern church. But wasn't it often the case that churches were built on ground already considered holy? Ava didn't know when this particular church had been built, maybe a hundred years before, a hundred-and-fifty. So what had stood here in the eighteenth century? The seventeenth? The sixteenth? Beyond that, even? There were so many layers to peel back, each one hiding from the other.

But why was Ben hiding? Still.

"Ben, come on, where are you? Why don't you answer me?"

He'd wanted her to come, had been so insistent, and now this? Games?

She needed a light, wished she'd brought a torch with her. This place *had* lights. Could she backtrack, find them, and flood the place? Or was darkness the better option, the light something that would draw – for Ben, at least – unwanted attention?

Ava continued onwards, the sound her boots made every time they hit the ground producing a hollow sound that echoed. She looked to both sides and upwards. Nothing but darkness met her eyes. A holy place, so why was she feeling more afraid than ever? Ben was her friend. A man in trouble. Yet he hadn't denied he was the attacker when she'd asked. *You don't understand!*

She shouldn't have come. He was her friend and a vicar, but no man was divine.

A noise from behind her, not so much a creak as a shuffle.

Ava whipped round. "Ben?" she said again.

The darkness behind her resembled something of a shield wall, and therefore impossible to breach. She could try, though, start a retreat of her own, but for another idiotic notion: that if she did, it would swallow her up, and she'd wander in it forever, then.

She had her phone in her jacket pocket. She could cast a light from that. Glad of something practical to do, she reached into the right-hand pocket only to find that it was empty. Frowning, she tried the left pocket. Only her house key was in it.

"What the fuck?"

She *had* brought her phone with her. No way she'd leave it behind, it was her lifeline. But willing it into existence didn't work. It wasn't in the pockets of Paul's jacket, shallow pockets, she realised, not deep like the ones in her own coat, on a slant.

She was baffled, one hand reaching up to rub at her forehead, a bolt of pain reminding her not to do that, of the accident she'd had with the lamppost. Had the phone fallen from her pocket then? Tipped out of the pocket because it was shallow, gone flying too? And she'd never noticed, just hadn't thought to check.

"Damn it!" Paul's jacket was supposed to anchor her, help, not hinder. Not just a jacket, symbolic, but now cruelly so. Her phone was gone, it was out there somewhere on the street. Vanished. There'd be no light.

Her eyes *were* adjusting, though, as she took more steps forward, the pews and arched windows now varying shades of grey. Shadows. As she scanned her surrounds for signs of Ben, she could see them in corners, the multitude.

It was silent in the church, but her heart galloped, a thunderous sound that filled her ears. Not even halfway down the aisle, she was closer to the exit than the vestry. There was still time to turn around, take her chances with the shield wall, which would *not* swallow her whole, and flee from there, but – because of the shadows – she froze, remembering how sure she'd been last time she was here, just before fainting, *absolutely sure*, that those shadows could wrench themselves free, and start dragging themselves towards her.

Not a lover of horror films, Ava preferred comedy and romance, lighthearted stuff. It didn't matter, for her mind was filled with horror regardless. The shadows were approaching, not wisps but far more substantial. They had claws and jagged teeth, were starving things, desperate to feast. There'd be blood everywhere; she'd be covered in it. Her own blood again, just like that day when Jamie had been born.

Rather than them, something else assaulted her, although in its own way every bit as terrible. A smell. A stench. The odour of neglect, the air ripened with it. It was more pungent than it had ever been, rising like mist from the pews either side of her. If she breathed it in, it would choke her. She was so rigid she couldn't even lift her hands to cover her nose and mouth. An easy victim. That's what she was. Prey that couldn't fight back, could only succumb, surrendering to hell, not heaven, because she'd known hell these last few months.

And now it knew her.

Another shuffle, a scrape. Closer, but still behind her. Was it really the shadows creeping up on her, or Ben? Which should she be more afraid of?

Whatever the answer, there was nothing she could do about it. Whatever had entered her life recently, other than Jamie, had won. She was trapped indeed. Furthermore, she'd rushed into that trap of her own accord. Quite the fool.

Oh, Jamie! He was the good that had entered, a fractious baby, admittedly, but when he smiled, it should have lit something in her too! And why was he so unsettled? Because she was? Because that's what a baby did, fed off its mother, right down to the emotions.

She was unfit, unworthy, and, when tested, fickle. She kept calling Ben a friend, but of course she'd wanted more than that from him, had *fantasised* about it. She might have theorised everything was Paul's fault because he hid from the truth, but she had as well, shutting out those she was closest to for the sake of a stranger whom she now sought to oust from her life.

She was able to move her arms at last, but only to wrap them around herself, trying to form a barrier against the shadows, the shuffles, the scrapes, and the creaks that told her this was not an empty church but filled to the rafters, the smell that could only be associated with something *un*holy. Who could ever preside over a church like this? Someone…twisted? The diocese had never replied to her emails when she'd tried to play detective. If they had, tonight might have played out very differently. This wasn't their fault either, though, not in the end; it was still her own. For being such a faithful subject. So blindly devoted.

Someone *was* behind her. Waiting to spring.

Ava closed her eyes, the darkness behind her lids as vast and as deep as that which surrounded her. No need to worry about retracing her footsteps. She was lost, and had been for months and months.

I'm sorry. So sorry. Sorry. Sorry. Sorry.

She'd been the ungrateful recipient of the most wonderful gift, and this was her punishment. Whatever was going to happen to her in this abandoned church, she deserved it. Paul and Jamie would be better off without her. There might be grief on Paul's part initially, when he found there was no one to come back to, but with time it would fade. He'd meet someone else. Paul was a good-looking, hard-working, kind, and decent man, all the things she'd lost sight of. Whoever Paul chose, he'd do so wisely, not make the same mistake twice. If only their time in the hotel hadn't been interrupted. In the afterglow of lovemaking, she might have felt more able to speak about her feelings, and Paul, also relaxed, might have understood rather than criticised, got her the help she so clearly needed.

Postnatal depression. Ava had Googled it, found out how bad the condition could be. Hallucinations, delusion, manic moods, depression, anxiety, feeling confused and fearful were all symptoms. Symptoms she didn't want to believe of herself.

Was she hallucinating now, and there was no one creeping up on her? She was alone here but for Ben. Or supposed to be.

If Jed were here, Jed would know. He'd protect her, or seek to. He was the only one in her life that hadn't abandoned her; he had no guile, no agenda, only love and loyalty. Paul hadn't even considered taking him when he'd left. He was *her* dog. Always had been, always would be. If he were with her now, she'd feel braver, but Ben didn't want him either. And Jed, she reminded herself, didn't like it here, not one little bit.

Still with her eyes closed, her teeth chattered. Should there be this much ice in her veins? Yet another reason to have chosen a warmer coat. She should open her eyes, spin around – and run. Run fast. All the way home, to Jed, to safety.

Breath. Someone exhaling. *Scalding* breath, fetid,

grazing the side of her cheek. The ice in her veins crystallised. Someone was this close to her, and she hadn't known it? Was just…standing there? Inches away? Getting ready to do what? Attack her? This was ancient ground. Sacred ground. Once. Now it was given over to the profane.

If only it were hallucination! If only she'd done so much differently. *Never had Jamie.* No! She'd never regret that. But if she'd never had a baby, she'd never have gone to the music class, met Ben. Fate could be cruel too.

Tears spilled from her eyes and rolled down her cheeks. Whatever had happened since Jamie, she was glad she'd breathed life into him, that he'd survived her, both at birth and now. If – *if* – she ever left here, she'd seek help straightaway, present herself at the damned hospital if needs be, for both their sakes.

But for now, her mistakes had formed a web she was at the centre of.

Someone was reaching out for her, slowly, slowly, slowly. But once their claws sank deep, there'd be no more teasing. She'd be torn apart.

A touch! And it was as icy cold, as alien, as she'd expected.

She wasn't being embraced, however, but dragged forwards, deeper into hell.

"Hurry," a voice said, one she barely recognised as Ben's. "Quickly! We have to."

He had grabbed her, by both hands, Ava at last matching him step for step.

Chapter Twenty-Three

They reached safety, no matter how temporary – the room at the far end of the church, the vestry, where she'd been before.

No lights on anywhere in the church, but in the vestry was at least a lamp, which he switched on after shutting the door behind them and locking it. She'd stared at him when he'd done that and turned the key, feeling more wild-eyed than ever. What was out there that they needed protection from? Just a few feet away, behind the door.

The dim glow of the lamp reminded her of something pustular. *Everything* was poisonous here, so little wonder it was struggling. It provided enough light for her to see by, though, to once again take in her surroundings: the bin bags full of clothes, a wardrobe that was half open instead of shut, and what looked like food on a shelf in there, tinned goods of some sort, a plate, and some cutlery. On the table in front of her was another plate, the food congealing. There was a sleeping bag on the floor, a stained pillow at the head of it. Ben *was* staying there; this proved it. Ben, who was standing before her, his pallor grey – even in this light she could tell it was – and his shoulders hunched. She scanned him further. His hands were clutching at the side of his torso. Was that blood there? Whose? *Don't jump to conclusions, Ava!*

She strove to keep her voice steady. "What's happened to you? Are you…hurt?"

He shook his head, but as he did, he winced.

Ava quickly closed the gap between them. "You are. You're hurt! Where?" Her hands travelled to where he was clutching his side. "Let me see."

There was indeed a dark stain on his clothing and an iron-rich smell. *Dried* blood, it looked like, also congealed. Not just the smell of blood, there was the smell of *him* too, Ben. He clearly hadn't washed in days, Ava having to swallow.

She steeled herself, resolved not to step away. Not yet. Soon, though, or what sanity remained would slip even more. No doubt about it, this was a mad situation, something, once upon a time, she could never envisage becoming entangled in. For now, though, Ben was still her friend and, as yet, any suspicions unfounded.

She didn't step away, and Ben, perhaps seizing his opportunity, grateful for it, reached for her and dragged her closer, enfolding her in his arms. He was crying, at first quietly, but soon his shudders reverberated through her body too.

His arms were around her, but her own remained by her side. Ironic, because she'd dreamed of this, when they would touch again. And now it was all just part of the nightmare. She was going to end their relationship today; she'd already promised herself that much. Before she left here, and she would soon, she'd tell him: *I'm not the help you seek. If you know the attacker* – God forbid if it *was* him – *get proper help, call the police.* Something that she would also do when she was far, far away from here. Sarah was lying in a hospital bed, and somehow, someway, Ben was involved in her attack; no way she'd keep her suspicions to herself any longer. She might be mad, but she wasn't evil. Now, though, he needed her, perhaps more than she'd ever needed him, which was a revelation in itself, that she wasn't as lost as she'd thought she was, and, if not, then maybe there *was* a way back to who she used to be. A way back because she hadn't sunk as low as this. She could be a wife and mother again, living a normal life, in a normal house, in an unremarkable town. The love she shared with Paul and Jamie, though, there was nothing unremarkable about that. If she survived this night, she'd never again forget that.

If?

She had to end things, but end them carefully. *Oh, Paul!*

It was her husband's name she thought of but Ben's she whispered.

"Oh, Ben, Ben, poor Ben. Can you tell me what happened?"

Still his body shuddered, still he cried. She had in her arms a wounded animal, something vulnerable. If he stayed that way, she'd have nothing to fear.

It took effort, but she gently pushed him from her, tried not to feel further repulsed at the mixture of hot salty tears that trailed down his face and the sticky snot on his chin. She willed herself to get used to his smell, to the smell of everything there, desperate to know what had happened, but also desperate to get this moment over and done with. Fickle. That description of herself seemed yet more pertinent. This was a man she'd craved. Whom she'd thought had the kindest eyes, the sweetest touch, someone she was attuned with. And now? She couldn't *remember* feeling that way.

Having extricated herself from him, Ava steered him gently backwards into the wooden chair positioned by the table, both so rickety. As she did, she noticed something else: a notebook in amongst other items on the table, tattered around the edges, although it remained closed. Well used, and for some reason it fascinated her. What type of things would Ben write in a notebook? If only she could reach for it, open it. Would it give her the insight she needed?

Ben was sitting but still slumped forward, soft cries again audible as grief continued to pour from him. Ava knelt, took one of his hands in hers and then gently, with her other hand, lifted his head so she could look into his eyes. Perhaps therein lay the key to all this, his eyes, not the notebook. If she could look deep into them and indeed see grief, the grief of the world, which must weigh so heavily, it would confirm Ben as the compassionate man he'd portrayed. Also, that she wasn't such a fool. His eyes, though, were blurred by tears. If only the light were better in this room! Where she'd positioned him, he was still in so much shadow.

She must persevere. She wanted to leave this room and this church, but she wanted him to escort her. What was out there, what she'd experienced...never mind if it was imagination or not, it *still* had power. In an instant it could stop your heart from beating, leave you as cold as those in the graves outside.

Her heart quickened at the thought, and she mustn't let it, strive instead for calm.

"Who attacked you?" Different from her recent pleading, there was steel in her voice, an *insistence* on knowing. "It's a knife wound, isn't it? Someone came at you with a knife." And if that was so, then he *wasn't* the attacker but a victim too. "Ben, it looks like a bad wound, like it could be deep. You'll need medical attention. I'll take you to the hospital, okay? You can't stay here. Why...why would you?"

"Ava, it's all right, it's okay. It's not as deep as it looks. Just...painful."

Despite his reassurance, questions poured from her. "When did it happen? A while ago, as the blood's dry. Am I right? Have you any idea who did it? Did it happen here, in the church?" More terror in her veins. "Oh God, whoever did it hasn't got access to the church too, have they? They're not in here hiding? I heard shuffles out there, creaks. I thought..." Briefly she squeezed her eyes shut. "I thought someone was beside me, reaching out to grab me. I felt hot breath on my cheek, and then *you* grabbed me and yanked me away from them." Her voice rose, no calm in it at all. "What the hell is happening here?"

"What the hell..." he repeated, his tears drying, his voice far steadier than hers now with an element of something else in it too. Wonder? "What the hell indeed?"

Water. That's what he needed, Ava decided, reaching up to touch his forehead; the skin there was hot indeed.

She looked around, couldn't see any evidence of water, something like a plastic bottle that might still be half full. He must be dying of thirst.

There had to be a WC in the church; she'd find water there.

As she tried to stand up, he stopped her. "What's the matter? Where are you going?"

"To...to find you water. You're feverish. I don't want to go out there, but—"

He shook his head wildly. "No! No! No! Don't leave."

"Ben—"

"You *can't* leave. I waited for you. For so long."

His words, coming at her in short bursts, were nothing less than stricken. She had no idea how best to deal with him or what to do, felt more useless than ever. He needed water, and it could also clean his wound.

Despite his pleading, she tried to untangle her hands from his and rise. Still, he wouldn't let her, his voice a hiss this time.

"You can't go back out there again, Ava! You've made it this far, and I…" Whatever he was going to say, he evidently changed his mind. "You can't go out there alone."

Despite the sudden cramp developing in her thighs, Ava stayed kneeling, frantically trying to interpret his words: *You've made it this far.* Did he think she wouldn't? But if there was danger out there, *true* danger, why had he opened the door and then retreated, *deliberately* left her to negotiate it alone? And yet now he was protective of her.

"Ben…" she managed, having to rise because of the cramp, snatching her hands from his. This time, he allowed it. Stood too and faced her.

"I don't need water," he said. "I don't need anything but you."

His eyes remained in shadow, but his voice sounded genuine enough.

"Who stabbed you?" she asked again. "Answer me this time. You must have some idea. If you…if you continue to play games with me, I'll leave. I'll take my chances with whatever's out there – if, of course, there's anything at all."

Only silence met her questioning, but she would not be

the first to break it.

More seconds passed. *Only* seconds, but each one dragged. And yet, in such an ancient place, what did time matter? *We've got all night.* Another horrific thought. No one knew she was here. Not another soul.

She didn't break the silence, but she fervently hoped Ben would, because in it she was hearing other things. Another creak beyond the door, whatever it was getting ready to burst through, perhaps, like it tried to do in her dream and in the cottage, not content to wait on the other side anymore in constant shadow. Seeking the light, this *mockery* of a light.

There was a window in the room, but not one she could easily negotiate. Such a narrow strip of window, high up. *Sufficient*, she supposed, normally.

This was not a room to dwell in, merely a changing room, vicars disrobing of religious garments and donning their normal clothes. Where was Ben's formal clothing? she wondered, tearing her gaze from him to look around again. She'd never seen him in anything other than jeans, a shirt, and a jumper. A casual vicar. A vicar who eschewed formality because in modern days it wasn't needed; if anything, it was off-putting. *Hey, look, I'm one of you. I'm ordinary.* That's the impression Ben wanted to convey. Or so she'd presumed.

He was certainly scaring her now, the way he looked at her with those guarded eyes of his. She'd never loved him. For how could you love someone who concealed their true nature, who *enjoyed* deluding you?

"I'm sorry, Ben. I can't help you. And I am leaving. This very minute."

She turned, refusing to think of anything but escape,

believing in it, when she felt hands on her arms, spinning her back round.

How close his face was to her, his breath as rotten as that other thing out there.

"Something *has* happened here. Something…something…big! Explosive! Oh, Ava, Ava, Ava, thank you for coming. For keeping your promise. As soon as I saw you, I knew you were the one. Those others…you stood out. There was just…so much pain in you. So much fear. You and I have a connection. You know that, don't you? You accept that? I know you're married, I know you've got a baby, but, Ava, you *hate* having a family. It's us who are meant to be, you and me."

Words. Strange words. Words she had trouble making sense of. She hated having a family? Did he really think that? Was it true? After all, Paul had said something similar, had taken her baby from her. She didn't hate it! She loved it. But actions had clearly spoken louder than words. For both of them.

"Ava." Ben's voice dropped a notch now, became gentler. "Don't look so distraught. I know you're frightened still, confused by what you're feeling, everything that's taken place. But I'm what you need. We need each other. At first…I wondered if I could trust my judgement, trust *you*. No more wondering. The very fact that you're here tonight proves your trustworthiness. You've put me first, above all else. I was right. *Blessedly* right. We're the same. Soulmates. That's what you think too, isn't it? I know you do. I understand you, Ava, and you…you'll come to understand me."

She shook her head, slowly but decisively.

"Who attacked you?" Right now, that was all she wanted

to understand.

Ben briefly glanced down at his wound. "I'm fine. I've told you. It's just a flesh wound. You worry too much!"

How could he be so blithe about it? So...uncaring? This man who professed himself full of passion. "Tell me who hurt you, and who else is in the church. Because I won't fool myself further – someone else is here. It's *not* my imagination." She was wide awake now, when previously she'd been sleepwalking, the realisation of what she'd done and where she was hitting her. "How much danger are we in?"

He dropped his hands from her shoulders, but only so he could take her hands again. "I hate to see you this way, so upset. This wound...the attacker...there are other issues at stake of far greater importance." The look in his eyes was so earnest. "Ava, the pain in you is my pain. We mirror each other. For so long...I felt I didn't belong. That I was on the outside, looking in. Since...since forever, actually. It was like everyone belonged to someone except me, not even my own family, my...flesh and blood. They didn't want me, and I didn't want them either. You *make* your own family. That's what I've discovered with you. You don't have to see something to know it's there, not if you're finely attuned, if you can sense it. We're the same, and I've helped you to see that also. And so, we've grown closer."

There were lies *and* truth in what he'd said. God, if only she could think straight! If anything, her mind was becoming more clouded with confusion because it wasn't all delusional nonsense he was spouting. He *had* realised how lonely she was, been able to read her eyes well enough, her very soul, it felt like, and, although they'd been strangers to each other, he *knew* her when no one else did anymore, not Paul, her mother, or any of her friends all carrying on with their childless lives, leaving her far behind. She *had* felt she belonged with Ben; she'd craved his company, deliberately sought it out, was alone with him, a shiver running through her those times, *delicious* shivers, not the kind that wracked her now.

Despite the smell emanating from him, she had to breathe. Ben was acting in an odd manner, *frenzied*, but so far hadn't tried to harm her. She'd come here to end it tonight, their liaison or however it could be defined, but if she suddenly threw him from her, turned, and braved what was outside this room, how would he act then?

Caught between a rock and a hard place. The saying had never rung so true. Another came to mind: *Better the devil you know...* She was indeed better off in here with Ben, for now, at least — Ben, whose eyes, still guarded, were boring into hers.

"We're outcasts," he continued to insist, "me sailing this empty ship, and you with a world full of people but still alone. I want to be with you, and you want to be with me. Your presence is proof."

"No," she managed, her voice so low she barely heard it. She had to speak up, explain what had happened. "I didn't leave them. They left me. Paul's taken Jamie and gone to his mother's, just for a couple of nights, but...it was them who left me."

Just as sobs had burst from Ben, they burst from Ava. Uncontrollable. Loud. Her whole body shaking. It was hitting her, the magnitude of everything. Her husband had left her. Actually *left* her. Taken their baby and gone. And no matter that it was temporary, allegedly, he'd *still* done it, leaving her more alone and vulnerable than ever. Another thing, the worst thing: a part of her had been *pleased* he'd done it, because it had given her the chance to do this, race to the church to see Ben. Now here she was, just inches from him, his hands reaching up to cup her face, to quiet her tears.

Just before he leant in closer, he whispered something, his lips touching hers.

"Perfect," he said. "That's just perfect."

Chapter Twenty-Four

The kiss. She'd dreamed about it so many times. They'd almost kissed before, Ava and Ben, but had been disturbed by Sarah, marching in with her accusations and now lying in a hospital bed, having been attacked by someone, *knifed*.

A man in black.

A shadow.

Always a shadow.

And now the moment had arrived: she was being kissed by the man she'd longed for, who insisted they were soulmates, so alike. Paul knew nothing of the truth; all he'd had were his suspicions. But as Ben had said, you didn't need to see something to sense it – the ethos that religious faith itself was based on.

Perhaps Ben was right and she *did* belong with him. A couple of days, that's all Paul said they'd be gone for, but just because he was coming back didn't mean he'd stay, that what they'd had before would miraculously restore itself. If she hadn't come here but stayed home, worked things out on her own, counted her blessings instead of dwelling on all her failures, had faith in herself, she and Paul might have stood more of a chance. One thing was for certain: tonight was truly about make or break, not in a hotel room with her husband but in a church with the vicar.

The kiss... His lips were fuller than hers, covering her mouth entirely, his tongue like a serpent that probed. Such an intimate act, in some ways the *most* intimate.

And so far from what she'd imagined.

She *had* to kiss him back, find out if she'd thrown away everything for something. If not, Ben was right: she had no one by her side, not even him.

A *horrific* kiss. Everything about him was unclean. And still his tongue sought hers, trying to reach deeper still, stealing her breath but for all the wrong reasons.

Desperate to end it, she struggled in his arms, but his grip, already secure, tightened. She tried to yank her head back, but it was as if they'd fused, truly become a part of each other. If she pulled away now, forced it further, bits of her flesh would remain stuck to his, and she'd never be whole again.

Even so, she had to sever what bound them. She raised her arms and pushed them against his chest, made strange yelping noises with her mouth, trying to get him to release her. He ignored her. This man she'd trusted, whom you were *supposed* to trust. As people trusted doctors, nurses, the police, God even.

Perhaps he aimed to choke her? Death by kissing. The most ironic death to impose. She had to have air. Her fists were weakening, her legs too. One last-ditch attempt, and she'd put all her might behind it.

Ava brought her knee up and smashed it into that sensitive place between his legs, hoping it was *bloody* sensitive, that it'd do the trick.

Instantly, his hands released her, and his head fell back. From his mouth – now bereft of hers – came a high-pitched squeal as he crashed into the chair and desk behind him. The notebook that was on there flew off, landing at her feet.

She should seize the moment, the triumph, turn and open the door, get out of there, but the notebook was in front of her and so enticing.

Whilst Ben continued to cup himself, his entire face distorted by agony, she quickly bent to retrieve it. Such a well-used notebook, some pages turned down at the edges, ones of special significance, perhaps. She tore back the front cover to the first page with a turned-down corner. It contained handwritten notes. Hand-drawn signs. Strange signs, like nothing she'd seen before, one of them a circle within a circle, jagged rays emitting from the inner edge to the outer one. A *disconcerting* sign. She might not know what it was, but she didn't like it, was as repelled by it as she was by him. There was writing too, Latinisms.

Again, with haste, she turned more pages, saw something she easily recognised: a cross. Etched in black. *Inverted*. And not just one, several, *dozens*, on this and other pages. Sometimes just one covered a page, other times lots of smaller ones. If Ben's hand was responsible for this, he'd scored right through the paper, signalling anger behind such an action. Unbridled fury.

Ava could only stare. Mesmerised.

Ben was a vicar. Was this truly his book? Or someone he was protecting?

"Shit! Fuck! Crap! Ava, you bitch! Why'd you have to do that?"

Vicious words snapped her out of her trance. She looked up, noting not only his expression, which was still twisted, but also the distance between them, calculating all the while. She took a step back, just a tiny one, imperceptible, at least she hoped so, whilst he continued to stare at her, to ask again why she'd hurt him.

He wanted answers, but he'd given her none when she'd wanted them, only more mysteries to solve. "Whose is this book?" she asked.

"What book?" Such scorn in his voice, utter derision.

"This fucking book," she screamed, holding it up for him to see. "It's full of...shit. Inverted crosses. Other symbols. Words I can't understand. Is it yours, Ben? Because if it is, you're not a holy man. You are far from someone holy."

"You don't understand," he breathed. "I wanted you to. I hoped you would. But you're not special at all. Who I thought you were. You're as stupid as the rest."

The rest? What rest?

"Who attacked you, Ben? It's time for the truth. Is there someone out there? Do you have an accomplice? What do you intend to do with me?"

Incredibly, a smile played upon his face, and all traces of pain vanished. He looked beatific, *saintly*. And yet here was she thinking the opposite: he was demonic.

"An accomplice?" he murmured. "In a way, Ava." He laughed, a harsh, sudden sound that grated. "Except, for now, *I'm* the accomplice. The one that serves."

She was shivering again, so cold, as if his words alone could drain the life force from her, the bizarreness of them.

"You're not a vicar, are you?" she said. "You..." how she hated to say it, "*fooled* me." Remembering the music class, she added, "Fooled us all. But how? Why?"

"I knew Moira." He shrugged as he said it, so nonchalant. "Remember I told you about Moira? She was the last vicar here, who'd retired. As I say, I knew her, that much is true. I was one of her...pet projects, you could say. That's how she thought of me."

Without warning, something in his expression changed, became darker, so incredibly bitter. There was a change in his accent too, a slight twang she'd never noticed before or he'd concealed. A Northerner? Now that her eyes were wide open, she noticed something else. She'd thought him the same age as her, even a year or two older, mature, worldly wise. He wasn't. This man was *younger*. Why she'd perceived differently was down to street smarts, perhaps? No way he was any older than his mid-twenties. Revelation after revelation, heaps of them.

"She was one of those do-gooders, was Moira," Ben continued. "You know the type? Always going the extra mile to relieve the burdens of the troubled, thinking she could save them, bring them back to the light. Never really taking the time to consider that some of us don't actually like the light, prefer the darkness instead. That's where we feel most comfortable, most welcome, even, part of something at last, something raw, natural, that doesn't fucking pretend. Oh, Moira," he said, sighing. "How she loved the homeless! She invited them here to her church but also to her home, would even give us a bed for the night if the weather was particularly bad, if it was cold or raining. With me, though, she'd give a bed when the weather was perfectly fine. I was her pet project, like I say, one she was desperate to convert. I felt sorry for her. I let her think she was on the road to success. Ah, she wasn't so bad; she was what she set out to be, I guess. She was old, about to retire after a long, long service to her God. A bit sloppy too, or should that be...trusting? She'd often leave her keys lying around. Easy to grab hold of them, get duplicates. Thing is, it wasn't only her the church were retiring, but this church too, abandoning it, one of their own. It's like I said, hardly anyone bothers coming here nowadays, and so they can't afford to keep it running for a handful. It costs too much. They have to invest what money they have elsewhere, consolidate." Another harsh laugh. "Yeah, right. The church, broke? That's a laugh! They're the most corrupt institution on the planet. They have an obscene amount of wealth. This isn't sacred land, Ava, and it never has been. And where there's supposed to be light, there is definitely darkness, a *gathering* darkness. So many wait in the shadows. An entire legion."

"A legion?" Ava whispered, trying to take another small step backwards. "Did...did you hurt Moira?" At the prospect, her voice became a ragged whisper.

"Did I what?" Ben replied, also taking a small step forward, mirroring her again.

"You heard me. Did you hurt Moira?"

"Hurt her?"

Oh, how he was teasing her! Intent on prolonging the agony. "Did you? Tell me!"

He shook his head, still so amused. "No! She was a stupid, misguided old bat, but I didn't hurt her. Never got the chance. She moved, that was all – to Scotland, I think she said, to be with relatives. Knowing her, I don't reckon she's retired at all, is probably still running around interfering in everyone's lives. Such is her vocation."

"She sounds like a good woman," Ava said, catching the break in her voice and hating herself for it, for showing any sign of weakness.

"Goodness be damned," Ben said then with a sneer. "No, really. *Damn* it."

Another whisper from Ava. "I thought you were my friend."

How indignant he looked. "I was! I still could be! Oh, Ava, Ava, Ava, why don't you ever listen? We can still salvage something from this. Look, we can't stay here at this church. This was only ever temporary. We'll have to move, but there'll be other places like this, better, even. Opportunity is everywhere. You and me could have a wonderful life together, a life without restraint or boundaries, that's truly free. Ava, listen now, okay? Listen good. Everything you've been taught, turn it on its head. Have the courage to do that. There is no God! You only need look at the state of the world to realise that. All there is, is evil. So what can we do about it? People like us? *Mere* people? We can channel it, that's what. Bend it to suit our purpose. Harness it. Oh, look, look, I know this all seems really out there. But you have the ability to learn, I know it." So much excitement in his voice, but then he lowered it, developed an earnestness instead, outright awe. "You've tapped into the darkness, Ava. It's *attached* itself to you, just like it attached to me. We're so, so alike, but we're not like everyone else. Therein lies the beauty of it. Together, we're stronger. We'll move from here. Keep on moving. Keep learning how to master this thing. Become as powerful. As revered. If there's a God, it's Satan. He is the *only* God."

Mad.

Ben — if that was even his real name — was the most insane person she'd ever met. All this talk about Satan, that notebook, those symbols…and she'd been fooled by him, taken in completely and so easily. Because it was true, what he'd said? That the darkness in her matched the darkness in him? If he had his way, it soon would.

Sarah hadn't been fooled, though. She'd returned to the hall after music class and confronted him, *veiled* confrontations, admittedly, she'd trodden carefully, but the intimation was there: *What happened to Lou and Jenna's mother, you're involved.*

How Ava wanted to run from him, but escape wasn't immediately beyond the door; there was that long aisle to negotiate, then an empty churchyard, streets she'd have to run down, with no one on them. Freedom was as far off as her understanding.

Sarah might not have come right out and said it, but Ava did. "Lou and Jenna's mother, what happened to them, it was you."

"Lou and Jenna's mother?" Ben simply repeated.

"Ben! For fuck's sake, stop playing games! If this is ever going to work…"

Hope in his eyes! Plainly, she saw it. He believed she might succumb to his wishes. Therein lay her only chance.

"Ben," she continued to plead.

He shook his head. "Jenna's mother had nothing to do with me. It was just a…happy coincidence. Lou…well. That *was* more by design. Ava, I saw what they did to you in class, how they turned their backs on you. *Laughed* at you."

"But that's what you wanted, wasn't it? For me to have no one but you. Why punish Lou for that?"

Ava thought Ben couldn't surprise her further, but now a flicker of confusion replaced the hope in his eyes. "It's just…they thought they had the upper hand, looking on you as something lesser. As we know, nothing could be further from the truth. And so I planned, I plotted, and I prayed, out there, at the altar, an altar cleared of all relics except mine. Then news broke of Jenna's mother. A terrible thing to happen, causing such angst for the family! And a sign my God had listened. He made that happen. And so I had to show Him what I was capable of too. I needed to make sure Lou and her family suffered also, and so I stole a car, did the deed. You see, Ava? Do you see? My God doesn't turn his head from me when I pray, hide behind such pious sanctity. A hypocrite, that's what your God is. He says He cares, but He doesn't give two shits. He only wants those that blindly follow him, who don't dare to question, who *thank* him for failure and hardship, who are just so bloody grateful!"

Ava quickly held her hands up. "I never said I had a God, Ben. Come on, think about it. When have I ever said that?"

Such a dim light, but she could see well enough the spittle that had collected at the corners of his mouth, what a snarling beast he turned into whenever he talked about *his* God and the God whose church he was occupying. Because no matter what he thought he'd turned this place into – no matter that people had stopped beating a path to it in recent times, that the church itself was closing, its religious blessing removed and the land sold for some commercial enterprise, perhaps – it was *still* the rightful God's. He was the one who'd been worshipped here by the majority.

Her words had the effect she'd hoped, and he was calming. She was dealing with psychosis for certain, his.

Still, she inched her way to the door, wondering too what she'd face out there. An accomplice equally psychotic, as perhaps all three of them were? A hat trick.

He'd hurt Lou but not Jenna's mother. What about Sarah? It'd been such a terrible attack that could have proved fatal. Ava had to know what she was dealing with here – a potential murderer – ask him outright about her too, his confession complete. She couldn't keep her voice from trembling as she went ahead, hating the smile that crept over his face, wishing she could erase it, erase *him*, the devil incarnate.

"I couldn't wait for prayers of guidance with Sarah. She was another one who interfered. Think they always know better. So high and mighty. No. No way I could wait. I didn't want to. She had to be silenced."

"You're the man in black? The shadow?" Something occurred, more pieces of a scattered jigsaw sliding into place. "The man at my house, in the garden, spying, that was you as well." She frowned. "But how did you know where I live? Unless…was it you that followed me home that day from the café? Someone left, just before I did. It *was* you, wasn't it? You knew I didn't live far, you actually said that to me once, when you offered to walk me home after I'd fainted. You saw the altercation that took place between me and Sarah, realised then that I was struggling. It was only a day or so later the leaflet came through my door for the music class. Maybe Sarah got a leaflet too, but she didn't turn up, not straightaway, and by the time she did, she was on to you. Saw straightaway what no one else seemed to, that there was something…off about you, how strange it was for a vicar not to be concerned about what had happened to two members of his community. Not to give a flying fuck, basically. Pulling you up on it."

Ben was nodding. Nodding and smiling. Looking so damned proud of himself.

"Why a music class, though? Something so...innocuous?"

The roll of his eyes indicated how exasperated he was getting with her. "I've told you! Moira used to run a music class for new parents. She used to talk to me about it. Talk and talk and talk. Honestly, that woman, she loved the sound of her own voice. She'd talk about the vulnerability of new mothers, vulnerable because it was a time of transition. The class was a valuable tool in her arsenal, she said, because she could weed out those that were sinking and make a point of involving them further, introducing them, I suppose you could say, to the right people. It's that whole like-calling-to-like concept at play, a variation on it, a spin. She wanted to head off despair and depression, *isolation*, before it could take hold, thus saving them from entering a dark, dark place.

"And so, you know, after what happened in the café between you and that fucking woman, how...lost you seemed, how...distraught, so completely and utterly vulnerable, I thought I'd give it a go and take Moira at her word. The class had been disbanded, of course, when she left, but there were still leaflets in the church. I knew you'd come when I popped one through your letterbox, had seen already the desperation in your eyes, that need to belong. I *prayed* you would. Prayed too that the other attendees would be the right kind, the cliquey kind. They were. It was a genius idea that just...fell into place. All I had to do was pretend to be the vicar of this church, a new type of vicar, very hands-on, so relaxed, so welcoming. The church was where I'd been squatting for a while anyway, as I had the keys." He swept his hand around. "The keys to a kingdom. You worried me, you know, because you were the last to appear that day, but when you did, you had tears in those lovely big eyes of yours because you were so frightened. As I said, perfect. Fucking perfect."

A fly in a web, she was indeed that, and Ben the spider. If only the diocese had replied when she'd emailed them! Did the wheels of such an organisation grind so exceedingly slowly that a man like him could do what he'd done and get away with it? There was simply no one checking up on these properties, not until they had to? That was an act of faith in itself, that all would be well. Ben, of no fixed address, was homeless no more. Prayer upon prayer being answered.

Another question, one more, perhaps the most important of all.

"Are you going to hurt me?" she asked. "Like you hurt Sarah?"

"Fuck's sake! I understand, I do, that this is a lot to take on board. But how many times must I say it? I don't *want* to hurt you. Not unless…"

She braced herself further. "Unless I don't comply?" When there was silence, something in her exploded. "I've a husband and a baby, Ben! A husband and baby I love. I can't be your…your what? Your willing disciple. Your acolyte!"

"My partner! My equal!" he screamed right back at her. "And don't be a hypocrite too. Your husband and baby mean nothing to you. You've made it very fucking plain."

She cursed the sob that escaped her. "Not true, Ben. It's not true." But all too well she understood how he'd got that impression.

She would not comply, entertain his lunacy further. He hadn't said he *would* hurt her, even if she rebelled against him. Maybe he truly did revere her, this man who was as lost as she was. *That's* what had attracted him to her, and she to him, not the darkness. She would not – could not – accept that. Enough now. She wanted all darkness dispensed with, to climb out of the abyss once and for all.

Briefly she closed her eyes, fighting back the terror of her situation. There was no one to help her, to hear her screams if she retaliated, maybe not even God, but she was still going to do it. End his madness and hers. One way or another. Whatever dark path she'd found herself on, she hadn't wandered as far down it as he had, and never would she. Strangely, in this, her darkest hour, the world was no longer a bleak place but the most wonderful it had ever been. The *real* world, not the one Ben had created and was trying to draw her into. *Breathtakingly* beautiful. Bright. As was her love for Paul, Jamie, and Jed. The family she'd always wanted. That's what was perfect. Where she truly belonged. She'd lived a blessed life. *All* her life. And now here she was, not herself cursed but face-to-face with someone who was. A young man. A fit man. Could she really outrun him?

Her eyes fixed on the wound he'd sustained.

He was wounded, but, as yet, she wasn't.

Ben caught her glance, reached down and lifted his shirt.

"Really such a worrywart," he said, his mouth curving with delight.

As he lifted his shirt higher, she said nothing. There was blood there, yes, but from scratches rather than the disabling wound she'd hoped to see.

"See?" he said. "It really is…nothing."

"You did it yourself?" It was the last question she'd ever ask of him.

Ben laughed some more, such a ghoulish sound in the otherwise stultifying silence, almost comedic if she had a mind to laugh along with him. "It's there for authenticity, that's all. A bit of a ploy, yeah? I didn't want you panicking about this setup, not straightaway. I wanted you to feel sorry for me, give me the chance I needed, you know, to make you understand. It worked, didn't it? To an extent. You'd have turned on your heel sooner if not."

He was right, she would have. He'd reeled her in, bit by bit.

Madness for ever allowing it.

Ben sprang, literally *sprang* at her, as agile as a panther, perhaps seeing something in her eyes when the gloom prevented her from seeing anything in his – an intent, a complete *lack* of understanding, and, other than fear, contempt.

If she'd run before, it was only ever *to* him. Now she had to turn swiftly and – with the memory of her family foremost in her mind – run in the right direction this time.

Chapter Twenty-Five

For one terrible moment, Ava thought the door would resist her, that the key he'd used to lock it would comply with Ben, not her, and refuse to budge. Whatever diabolical plans he had, she'd be entirely at his mercy in a church due for deconsecration, in which the darkness had replaced divine light.

The key turned easily enough, though, and trying not to think further, to give her mind any opportunity to create any more scenarios, she hurled herself through the doorway, into the main body of the church. Not a large church nor a cathedral, she reminded herself, and therefore not a huge distance to the oak doors. She'd reach them quickly if she didn't falter, just kept on running, head down, staring at the floor, only that.

There's freedom out there, Ava. An escape from all this. Finally.

So, so dark! No ounce of moonlight filtering in. If it tried in a place like this, it would be devoured. A Satanist. That's what Ben fancied himself as. Again, something laughable if it wasn't so terrifying, if she wasn't caught up in the midst of his delusions, regarded as something of a key player. *A madman. Just that.* Not someone who, because of his beliefs, could suddenly wield some magical power. Satan was a tall tale, maybe even as much as God was, tools used down the ages to maintain control. She didn't believe in either, *still* didn't.

Despite the sound of her own heavy breathing and the pounding of her feet against stone, she heard it: a creak and a scrape. In front of her. *Definitely* in front.

Ben was behind her, though.

Wasn't he?

Despite her mind urging her not to slow, to keep up the pace, her feet would not obey. She'd reached the centre of the church, had run forwards from the vestry, then turned right into the middle aisle, rows and rows of empty pews either side of her.

If she slowed further, Ben would be upon her, would bring her crashing to the ground. Unless…he'd run further than she had, to the far aisle, faster, harder, even more determined, for he had everything to lose, whereas she had everything to gain, and now he was doubling back, taking her for a fool again.

She stopped. There was *no one* behind her. Ben had done exactly what she'd thought. If she kept going, she'd run smack bang into his arms.

Furiously, her mind calculated. What to do next? How to avoid him? If she ended up in his embrace, no way he'd let her go, not again. He'd clamp his mouth to hers, and that leviathan tongue would indeed choke the life from her.

No other option but to backtrack. There must be another exit! A back door of some description. And maybe, just maybe, by some miracle she could prise it open. Not a believer, but she prayed for the existence of something benevolent, some divine intervention, happy in this instance to be proved wrong, *begging* for that.

She tried to quiet her breath, to develop preternatural hearing instead, listening out for him creeping around here, a shadow man chasing a woman who was also a shadow of herself. Soulmates indeed.

The altar now in front of her, there seemed to be no cross suspended above it, upside down or otherwise. But – as her eyes adjusted – she spied something else. Items on the altar? *His* items, Ben's. What kind, though?

If he was behind her again, he was continuing to creep rather than lunge, the game far from over. The altar… Despite herself, she was curious to see what was on it. What was *beyond* it too, the door she hoped for. No way she'd go towards the vestry, a room he'd keep her hostage in. She must pass the altar, and so her curiosity would be satisfied – Ben, for now, keeping his distance, perhaps also wanting her to see what was there so she could understand further the extent of his devotion.

Several wide steps led to the altar. The first she almost tripped over, her hands flailing as she struggled for balance. More tentatively, she negotiated the second, third, fourth, and fifth until there it was, much closer now, the altar – the vicar's special domain. Moira's, not Ben's, never *rightfully* Ben's. A place to break bread and drink wine – the flesh and blood of Christ. A ceremony. A ritual. For over two thousand years. Now out of favour. Cancelled. Other options coming to the forefront, those no longer deemed frightening or obscene but cool, trendy, *effective*.

There was a Bible on the altar. A travesty, a mockery. Like the notebook, if she opened it, she knew what she'd see, scrawls in there that were anything but biblical, preaching hate not love. Another item: a cross. Placed so that if you stood behind the altar, it would, of course, be inverted. And Ben *had* stood there, when he'd had no right to. Calling on his God, summoning Him.

Other things too. Knives, several of them, varying in length and sharpness, and a bowl, round, ordinary, meant for what? Blood? A *filthy* bowl, she realised. Because of the darkness, it was hard to determine the substance that coated it, but there could be blood in it already. Sarah's or the blood he'd drawn from himself? Provided as an offering or a promise? *I'll do your will if you do mine.* Blood that wasn't enough; an entity such as Satan would need an endless flow.

Not just horror and fear, but rage also stirred. When she'd asked Ben if he'd hurt her if she didn't comply, he hadn't answered. Naïve to think he wouldn't, though. If she didn't join him, she'd be his next victim, and he'd do the job properly this time, no hospital bed for her in which to recover. And then after her, who else? He wouldn't stay here; he'd already said that. He'd move elsewhere, seize other opportunities, and he'd kill and kill and kill, having developed a taste for it. *Honour* killings, in their own way. As fantastical as it all sounded, even now in the circumstances she'd found herself in, Ava didn't doubt that, at least. If only Sarah had gone straight to the police with her suspicions, raised the alarm that way. But there was proof of nothing, and belief in your own convictions wasn't always easy. You could read about monsters in the papers, in news articles, and then make the mistake of thinking you were safe, that they'd never enter your world, find a way…

A noise from behind her, another scrape quickly hushed.

Rather than continue running, she wanted to turn and scream defiance at him: *I'm not scared of you, Ben, you freak! I trusted you. I thought I loved you. That you understood me. Because, yes, we were alike, but not in the way you meant. I don't want the darkness as my ally. I hate it! There's something wrong with me, I agree, I accept that now. I'm ill just like you're ill. We both need help. Or perhaps you're beyond help. I'm not, though. I can't be. Shit! How could I be this stupid?*

Tears gushed from her eyes and nose, but she didn't bother to lift a hand and wipe at them. Instead, she drew closer to the altar and grabbed a knife, the biggest one, the handle as cold as she was, as Ben, as this church had become. The fact he'd left them there, out in the open, where she could find them, was he that arrogant? Did he think she wouldn't have the courage to use them, frightened little mouse that she was? That if he flew at her, she'd drop the knife in fright rather than brandish it?

Just let him fucking try!

Footsteps behind her again. He was coming for her. No more delay. He'd *herded* her this way. She had to get beyond the altar, find a door, at least try.

Veering to the right, she maintained the distance between them, making headway. She had to escape, not die this way, someone ordinary in such an *extra*ordinary manner.

Making good headway, and then...she was flying like she had out in the street, something in her way, an obstruction of some sort, no way to keep upright, nothing to break the fall either, the hard stone floor rising up fast to meet her. She landed heavily, awkwardly, and felt rather than heard something snap, although what bone it was, she had yet to determine. There was no immediate burst of agony as she'd expected, but the knife had also flown right out of her hand. Scrabbling for it, the agony came at last. She'd broken her wrist, the very hand holding the weapon.

He was on her. Ben had closed the gap, lunged again, and now his body covered hers completely. The weight of him expelled any air she had left in her lungs, his breath hot against her cheek, *searing* it. He was snarling and hissing, something feral indeed. Making sounds beyond human, the very beast he wanted to be.

"Bitch," he said, "you stupid, stupid bitch! We could have had it all, you and me, if only you'd listened. *Really* listened. There's darkness in you, Ava, so much darkness! We're alike. We are!" A crack in his voice as he continued. "Now look what I have to do. What you're *making* me do. All because you won't fucking listen!"

Despite the pain in her wrist, she placed both hands out in front of her and tried to crawl from beneath him. Impossible. His hands covered hers and grabbed her wrists, the pain from the broken one so great she wondered if she'd faint.

She screamed instead, and it was bloodcurdling.

Mercifully, both her hands were released, but there was another explosion of pain as he grabbed hold of her hair and yanked her head back further than it should ever go, Ava fearful she'd hear another snap – her neck. She sobbed rather than screamed this time, a sound just as wretched. So easily he'd overpowered her. Without the knife, she was no match for him.

Spittle sprayed her cheek as he hissed at her again. "You listen, now, okay? Fucking make sure you do. If you scream again, if you try to escape, this will all be so much harder for you, so much more painful. Keep quiet and listen, just listen, and maybe, just maybe, we can salvage something from this mess you've made. My way is the *only* way. Perhaps there's still time for you to accept that. These are different times we live in, Ava, *exciting* times. Why fight it?"

The pressure was relieved as he lifted himself off her, but then she was turned, flipped over like she was nothing more than a rag doll, and thumped down on the stone floor as hard as she'd fallen against it, more pain in the back of her head, white-hot, adding to the injuries she'd already suffered. How was she ever going to survive this? She couldn't. Maybe that was all she had to accept.

As she stared into his face, into blackened orbs for eyes, she knew he'd do it: kill her. He'd drag her to the altar, hoist her onto it, cut her open, and watch her blood pour into that already filthy bowl. Her blood would mingle with his; she'd be his first successful kill. A sacrifice. No longer disappointing him, on the contrary, she'd give him the greatest thrill.

The altar would be cleaned afterwards, scrubbed spotless, all items removed, any duplicate keys disposed of. Ben would move on. And her body? That would be dumped somewhere too, in a canal or in some field, buried deep. Never to be found.

Oh, Paul! No matter how their relationship had deteriorated, she still meant something to him. To disappear like that would cause such agony. He'd blame himself, remembering how their last exchange was full of anger and accusation. That night in the hotel, their chance to talk, interrupted. Of course Ben was the man in the garden, spying on them, but had he done so by day as well? And if so, he'd known she and Paul were going away somewhere, had seen them leave, their excitement as they'd waved goodbye to Carol and Jamie, Carol telling them to have a good time, to 'make the most of it', that she'd see them the next day. Didn't take much for him to put two and two together, to be more visible as a spy – to Carol, at least, who would then phone her daughter in panic. There was such blinding pain in Ava's wrist and her head, but her vision had never been clearer.

As she'd predicted, Ben's hands reached down to curl around her torso so he could lift her and drag her. She had one broken hand, but one good one.

One last chance.

She twisted her body, balled her good hand into a fist, and swung it right into the side of Ben's face. Maybe it would have no impact, but she wouldn't succumb without at least trying – for Paul's sake, for Jamie's, Jed's, and for her own sake too because she wanted a second chance to make everything all right, not hurt those she loved further, only him, only Ben.

Somehow, someway, the blow connected as harshly as her knee had in the vestry. Another roar left his mouth as he let her go and lifted his hands to his head instead. Again summoning every ounce of strength, she wriggled away from him, putting as much distance between them as possible. Everything hurt, *everything*, but adrenalin was king, enabling her to move and keep moving.

There were more knives on the altar, closer than the one that had flown from her hand. Smaller knives, but still lethal. She had to grab another, do what Ben thought she couldn't, and what *she* thought she couldn't – until now. Paul would not be tortured by guilt for the rest of his life, Jamie would not grow up without the woman that gave birth to him, and Jed would not return to cages to be constantly overlooked. Her family would be together again, Ava the glue that bound them all.

With the altar before her, she reached out blindly and searched, found another knife. She only wished she had two working hands so she could drive it deep when the chance came, a *thirst* for vengeance developing. And for justice too.

On her heel, she swung around, began stabbing at nothing but thin air. And then, finally, connected with something more solid as Ben rushed at her, the darkness having concealed her actions, conspiring with her at last, not him, *loving* this new intent within her, encouraging it. But who knew flesh could be as hard as granite? Ava continued stabbing, though, drawing on the rage inside her, the wild energy it provided, screaming like a banshee. Ben was screaming too, a cacophony of sound, the swell of a hymn, the Satanic kind, the kind he loved.

"Praise be," she screamed, still stabbing, "praise be to my God, Ben, not yours! Whatever you intended for me, you haven't won. I have."

Ben slumped. He was clutching at himself again and groaning.

"Ava," he said. "Ava, what have you done?"

It was over. The only sacrifice today would be his. Although he was alive still, albeit breathing raggedly, he couldn't follow her, not anymore. She could run down that aisle again, head towards the oak doors, pull them open and escape. Once on the streets, she'd bang on someone's door, anyone's, hurriedly explain she needed the police, and they'd call them. Hand this whole sorry matter over.

There was no time to waste.

Exhilarated and horrified in equal measures, she turned. Life would be hers when she'd thought only death awaited. A life she'd make the most of.

No longer such a fool or a victim, she'd triumphed instead.

"Ava!"

Still Ben was calling for her, but she ignored him, darted forwards, then stopped.

The sight that met her eyes was a mistake. It had to be. An illusion. Her mind playing tricks on her again in such gloom. Not allowing her to see clearly at all.

Far from empty, the church was full. Every *pew* was full. The congregation having gathered, the spectators, enjoying the show. And every one of them a shadow.

Ben must have seen it too, the fruits of his labour.

"It's not over, Ava." She was sure she heard him say that. "It can never be over."

Chapter Twenty-Six

The knife fell from Ava's hand, made a clattering sound as it hit the floor. Frozen in place again, all she could do was blink, desperately hoping that each time she refocused, the shadows would be gone, that they wouldn't continue to sit there, so many of them. Ben had smashed her head against the stone floor, so it *could* be illusion. But a shared illusion? Because Ben could apparently see them every bit as much as she could and, despite his wounds, had straightened, sighing with wonder.

Whether they were illusion or real, they were sitting silently for now, heads covered with hoods like monks of old, bowed as if they were indeed in the act of worship. To which God? As cold as she felt, as tired and as scared, she couldn't keep standing there. She needed help, a doctor, and so did Ben. She'd stabbed him several times. How deeply, she didn't know, but she'd pushed the knife in as hard as she could, had had to in self-defence. He'd intended killing her, his wayward disciple, and so there'd been no choice. But she wasn't a natural-born killer even if he was, the rage that had provoked her already on the wane, allowing for more horror.

More fear.

If she could escape this wretched place and, as hurt as she was, as drained, find help, get the police *and* an ambulance, he could survive the attack.

If not...

She'd be a killer — someone who'd taken the life of another. A darkness in her soul, indeed, that would never depart, not once that line was crossed.

And so, Ben was right: if he died, this would never be over. In many ways, it would be the beginning.

That thought gave her the impetus she needed. She'd get help. He could not be allowed to die, because if he did, his would be the triumph. She began to move back to Ben. With her good hand she reached out and shook him gently, as he was murmuring now, his eyes half-closed, in raptures, as if he'd seen angels not devils.

"Ben. Ben! Stay awake, stay with me. Try, okay? Stay conscious. *Alive.* I'll find us help, I promise. We'll be okay." She looked down at the knit jumper he wore, a little too tight, actually, as if it were a hand-me-down, secondhand, and a cry left her as she saw how saturated with blood it was. It *covered* the jumper and was clearly still oozing, dripping onto the stone floor beside him, creating tarry black pools. Her handiwork this time. She who'd never hurt anyone or anything before, who trapped spiders in glasses rather than crushed them underfoot, and delivered sugar water to struggling bumble bees in summer.

She grabbed his jumper tighter. "Ben, is there another way out? At the back of the church? If you know, tell me. We haven't got much time."

No use. He *was* talking, but it was nonsense, a jumble of words, *beautiful, so beautiful* amongst them. *True. Knew it was. Saviour.*

Should she try to move him? Force him to come with

her? He wouldn't, she knew. More time wasted. A young man, that's all he was. Could he change? Just like she wanted, be given a second chance? A third, a fourth, and a fifth, what did it matter? "It's okay, it's all right, Ben. *I'll* find the door."

No way she'd go out the front, run between those pews. The shadows would rise and encircle her. They'd do so before she even got halfway, and then what? They'd suck the life from her? Leave her nothing but a husk? It was the stuff of fantasy, of horror novels and films, not real life. And yet right now it seemed like the only truth.

It was so dark towards the back of the church, the chancel, a place reserved only for the holy, those carrying out the work of Christ, his soldiers. Now *she* was the saviour, not Christ, and she wouldn't fail Ben; she'd fulfil yet another promise.

Place one foot in front of the other, that's all she had to do. Take a step and then another, and another. All the way through the darkness, another shield wall.

She kept speaking as she moved, not sure who she was trying to comfort, herself or Ben. "It's all right," she continued to say, "everything's all right," wondering also if she should grab another knife and take it with her, just in case…? *In case of what?* Ben was the only physical danger. What good would a knife be against something nonphysical, ghosts or shadows or whatever they were? Besides, she was done with knives, with this entire situation.

She'd have to negotiate such darkness; she'd already resigned herself to that. But a darkness that *writhed*, just as the shadows once had?

She was a little beyond the altar when she saw it,

movement in what lay before her, something that swayed, first one way and then the other. Sometimes the movements were smooth, free-flowing, at other times they were jagged, as though causing great pain. There was something in there trying to break free, something far bigger than shadows, far worse. Something that would never take human form. That *despised* such a notion. It was being given birth to – the swaying, the writhing were all some kind of pushing. A *spawning*. An energy able to enter the souls of humanity and wreak havoc.

Despite this terrible realisation, Ava was enraptured. She simply could not tear her gaze away. Was it real? All she was seeing and thinking? Any plans for escape futile because she was already at the bottom of the abyss, she and Ben both.

A shriek. A roar. Dual sounds that sliced the air. Not her own scream, for that was stuck in her throat, but the sounds of birth, nearing completion. Whatever it was, it'd be here soon, not a mewling, weak thing but all-powerful from the off, turning around, viper quick, devouring its host and, after that, everything in its wake.

Ava was moving, backwards, not forwards. How, she didn't know; she couldn't feel her legs. She'd take her chances with the congregation after all – the offshoots of this thing, its servants – run down that aisle, the path of the hopeful, the lovers, the sinners, and those in need. *Never* had she been so in need. *God, listen to me now, please. Help me.*

Another step and another, her eyes closing, *feeling* her way. *Keep going*, she commanded herself, *and have faith. God will help. He will.*

She'd escape, she'd still try. But if not, she'd refuse to

look on the face of what was emerging from the chrysalis. For if she did, she'd forget love and light entirely.

It was a plan. The only one she had. Being carried out until she backed up against something solid. Not the altar – Ben. The stink of him unmistakable.

Yelping, she swung around to face him, fearful he'd also picked up a knife, that while something was given birth to, something must die. Her.

He seemed to have no knife, though. If he did, he wasn't thrusting it forwards. Wasn't even looking at her or registering she was there. His eyes, no longer half-closed, were focused, laser sharp, on what was happening in front of him.

His mouth was also moving, words that once again she had to work hard to catch.

"...listened...here...true God."

Ava wished she could close her ears *and* eyes. This was *worse* than madness.

And she was growing more tired still, a part of her wanting to give up, be torn apart or swallowed whole, because afterwards, surely there'd be nothing?

Even more strange, she didn't retreat from Ben or try to bypass, taking advantage of the fact it wasn't her he was interested in during this moment. Instead, she laid her head against his chest. He didn't react, bring his arms up to hold her tight, *crush* her. He simply continued to stand there, muttering, as she was muttering too.

"Oh, Ben, Ben," she whispered. "What's happening here? What have you done?"

* * *

The roar that had shaken the very foundations of the church, shaken Ava to the core also, ceased. So abruptly and so completely, she wondered if she'd been mistaken, if it had never occurred, only in imagination. Wondered too, as she'd done before, if this was simply a nightmare. Another possibility: Ben had crashed her head into the cold stone floor harder than she'd previously thought, and she was unconscious, her mind running wilder than it ever had. Or she was dead. And hell truly existed.

Silence reigned. Ben caught up in wonder still, Ava in confusion. And then she felt Ben's body jerk as he took a sharp intake of breath, followed by a ragged exhale.

So it was here, then. It had been born, the thing Ben helped sire.

How proud he must be of himself. *Insanely* proud.

Instead of leaving him, taking her chances, running out of there, she'd gone to him and made contact. Now, finally, his hands came up to hold her too, but not in the way she expected. Ben gripped her by the shoulders, shook her, spittle once more spraying from his mouth and covering her face as he frantically spoke.

"Oh no. Oh no, no, no. Ava…it…it's not what I thought it was. What was promised. It's wrong. Shit! All wrong. Oh God, oh no, it's coming closer!"

He was speaking to her, addressing her, and yet his eyes remained fixed on what was behind her, nothing evil in them, not anymore – no cunning, no sign of triumph, just the very thing he'd see in her own eyes: utter horror.

As he continued to shake her, his fingers digging into flesh, bruising it through the clothing, Ava's teeth felt like they were rattling in her head, and she frowned, her confusion only growing. This was what he'd wanted. He'd played with the darkness, coaxed it forwards, guided it. Now he'd changed his mind? What was behind her, exactly? How strong curiosity could be! It was so tempting to turn and look, but she'd made a pact with herself that she wouldn't. If she held fast to one thing tonight, it must be that.

She had no idea how close the entity was to them, only that it *would* come closer.

With her good hand, she pushed at Ben, surprised when he immediately dropped his hands and collapsed against her, muttering still, murmuring and crying.

"I didn't realise...truly, truly, I didn't know. I thought...I thought it'd be...different. Better. It isn't what I want. *That* isn't. Help me, Ava. Sorry. Sorry. Help me."

Was he duping her again? He'd dragged her into this unearthly situation, gone to such great lengths to groom her, someone as vulnerable as he'd hoped she'd be, and now here he was, begging for the help he so clearly needed. Because he was vulnerable too? Damaged.

He was also a burden. If she were to help him escape alongside her, she'd have to practically carry him – impossible, even if she had all her bones intact.

More temptation. This situation was entirely of his making, not hers. If she had to leave him behind and run, what of it? Better that one of them survive than neither. And as things stood, she had the greater chance.

Temptation could be so overwhelming! Born not entirely from selfishness, for it would mean Jamie still had a mother. But what of Ben? Homeless Ben. Troubled Ben. Misguided, even though those like Moira had done their best by him, her protégé, gone the extra mile, never letting go of the hope that something they did, somewhere along the line, might have the impact they desired. What had Ben himself said, about motherhood being the greatest job of all? His words returned crystal clear: *Too many are left to run feral, and, well...problems occur because of it. Far-reaching problems.* And what had she said, when she and Paul had first mentioned rescuing a dog, Paul worried about the nature of it, the unknown: *If you hit something enough, could you blame them when they eventually hit back?*

She didn't know his history, only snatches of it, yet for every Ben, there were a thousand others, *millions*. Roll up! Roll up! Take your place.

The place of the damned.

Even so, it was just so easy to add herself to the list of those who'd abandoned him. Ben, who was whimpering, clutching at her, and begging.

Along with every other emotion that tonight had wrenched from her, there was still rage and flashes of hatred too, contempt for the way he was acting now, this man who was more confused than she was. The hatred was almost as black a thing as that which was behind her. A part of it, perhaps, that she was absorbing.

"Don't leave me. Don't leave me."

Ben was second-guessing what she intended, must feel how her whole body had stiffened as she braced herself, ready to tear away.

"Oh, Ben. Why didn't you realise what you were doing? How dangerous it was. Is it because you never believed in it either? Not really, not deep down. And now here we are, you and I. Trapped. Ben, all evil ever wants to do is to chew you up and spit you out. It is not your friend. *I* was. And look what you've done to me."

She *was* moving forward, dragging him with her as best

as she could, the weight of him like lead, weighing her down as much as the darkness did. No choice but to head towards the congregation, all sitting so still, worshipping what was at her back, which kept gathering strength and further sensibility, a force beyond reckoning.

Five steps led down from the altar, Ava and Ben tackling each one. Just as she'd stumbled going up, she stumbled going down, almost fell and sent her and Ben crashing to the floor. Only desperation kept them upright. Still, she had no idea how much distance was between them and what had newly hatched, something ancient, older than time itself, even. It could be feet away, inches, or had already attached suckers, amused at the hope they harboured.

How far the shadows in front were, she could gauge perfectly well. She and Ben were amid them, continuing to stagger forwards as they remained so, so still. Inanimate? Incapable of movement? Nothing of substance to them after all? As weightless as a cloud? Such a possibility fuelled the hope she clung to. Even Ben had stopped whimpering as much, had raised his head and was looking around as wondrously as before, but this time perhaps because he too felt escape within reach.

"Just keep moving, Ben." Although a whisper, her voice echoed, hurling itself back at her over and over. *Just keep moving. Just keep moving.*

Ben gave a grunt and nodded. "Ava—"

"Save your strength. You're going to need it."

He wouldn't be told. "Sorry. Am sorry. For Lou. Sarah. All of it. Lost. So lost."

An apology seemed so pitiful in the face of what was happening. Or was it the very opposite, a bravery to admit a mistake of such colossal proportions?

Why were they being allowed to escape? That was the question that truly occupied her mind. Could it be that evil had only so much power? That if you kicked back against it, were *repentant*, it couldn't touch you after all?

They were halfway down the aisle. Ava could almost taste freedom. The air outside would be so fresh compared to this, able to cleanse them both inside and out, a baptism of sorts, heralding a new phase. What Ben's new life would be like, she had no idea. A spell in an institution, most likely, a prison or a psychiatric unit. Harsh, but he'd get the help he needed in there. And her life? It would be *wonderful*.

Not far. It really wasn't. The oak doors were so close, and still the shadows remained static. There were no creaks, no scrapes or shuffles, no noises at all. How *expectant* the silence was, although she tried not to notice.

They were past the pews, and a sob escaped her, filled with relief. She could admit now she'd *never* thought they'd be allowed to pass. Perhaps it was true: evil couldn't touch you if you didn't give it permission. An insight. A *glorious* insight. Another revelation that heartened her.

Neither of them were victims in this. And after it all, if darkness tried to cling to her, she'd expel it, get all the help she needed in order to achieve that.

"Are we there? Are we safe?"

"Almost, Ben," Ava replied. "Almost. That's it, you're doing great, keep going. I can see the doors. Freedom. It's within reach."

Perhaps the cruellest thing about evil is the hope it gives you. Such…*false* hope. A precious gift which is then snatched away, leaving you emptier than before, not just incapable of summoning further hope but trust.

Of course they wouldn't be allowed to leave. Ben, the father of something unholy, and she, its intended stepmother, could not simply abandon what they'd helped to create. And she *had* helped it, even though she hated to think it, no matter how unwittingly. She'd played right into Ben's hands. Yet more irony: had been hell-bent on doing so.

Hell was coming for them. Rushing down the aisle with sickening speed.

The congregation, no longer static, rose and turned to face the aisle, threw themselves at the entity as it passed, adding to the sheer might of it.

"Don't!" Ava said, grabbing at Ben, even with the hand with the broken wrist, doing everything she could to stop him from looking. "You mustn't. Not anymore."

The scream that left his mouth could shatter those arched windows; certainly, it made them rattle in their frames.

"Ben, we have to reach the doors!"

A lost lamb who'd seen the error of his ways, but too late.

He remained where he was, his head turned and body now twisting too, staring, staring, staring, his mouth wide open still, although rendered silent.

For now, he was lost to her. And she'd be lost too if she didn't act quickly.

With no choice but to leave him, Ava headed to the doors. If she got them open, she could then try to double back, grab him again, yank him out of there, over the threshold, pray this thing couldn't follow them outside, that somehow it too was trapped.

She reached the doors, did as she'd planned and pulled and pulled and pulled. They were stuck. Both of them. How? They'd opened readily enough before.

"For fuck's sake, open!" She'd been the last one through these doors. They weren't locked. Unless...Ben *hadn't* retreated when he'd opened them for her, just stepped to the side, then stepped back and locked them. *Entombed* them.

Any prospect of freedom vanished.

Behind her, Ben was forming words again. "Sorry. Sorry. Sorry." Not apologising to her this time, but to it. As if it wasn't a futile thing to do, as if it would honestly lend an ear and listen. "Don't hurt me. Please don't hurt me."

As he screamed, his *final* scream, Ava stopped pulling at the doors and leant her head against them as she had with Ben.

The sound broke her heart to hear it. Shutting her eyes, she held in her mind a vision of him – not what he'd become but what he could have been, his potential. A handsome man with an air about him, charisma. A man who could have cared for others because he could see what so many were blind to, and who would indeed reach out but only with good intention. All of that possibility was in Ben, in anyone, and it remained there despite what life threw at them, whatever path they chose, whoever's example they followed, a kernel that remained in the depths, something glittering, *boldly* untarnished. *That* was what she'd responded to, that something precious in him. She had to believe it was so. He was a shadow of a man, and she a shadow of a woman, true – like calls to like – but as long as that ounce of goodness remained, so would hope. She'd had a good life, ordinary, normal. In his life there'd likely been trauma, neglect, and abuse. And yet they'd met, she and him, and there *had* been a bond between them. If they ever met again in another lifetime, she hoped she'd recognise him. If she did, she'd give him all the love he needed, this man who was really only a tortured child.

Ben was gone. The life sucked out of him. The darkness hungry still.

Coming for her.

The doors wouldn't open. There was no point in trying anymore. Visions of Ben gave way to visions of Paul and Jamie, and she wished them well too. Only the best.

And then turned.

Chapter Twenty-Seven

A low sound, a rasp. She was right in thinking this thing she'd soon face was primeval. It might suck the life from her too, as it had done with Ben, but one thing it would never have was her understanding. From whatever source it had sprung, it was alien to her and would remain so. If she had to spend an eternity battling against understanding something such as this, so be it. It'd be an eternity well spent.

Slowly she turned, oh so slowly. It had dragged the moments out when following them, teasing them, so she'd return the favour. So much churned within her. Fear, fury, acceptance, despair, loathing, but above all, loss. Just as well there was no escape, because if there were, there'd be no recovery. The icy cold that had lodged deep within her this night, the darkness that had found a way in through the cracks, would continue to increase. No way to forget such extremes, to be normal again.

Simply put, it was possible to know too much, stuff you weren't evolved enough to deal with. Be careful what you wished for, for it might come true. Ben was testament to that. And herself. Soon, in another half turn, she would see more than her mind could ever cope with. Then it would all be over. This hell, at least.

One more bright thought before darkness reigned so

completely. Of Paul on their wedding day, the way he'd
looked at her when they'd exchanged vows, the pride in his
eyes, the words he'd whispered later when all guests had
gone and they were alone: 'This is forever, you and me.
We've found each other.' Forever didn't last as long as you
thought it might, though. In the blink of an eye, it was
gone. But they'd had Jamie; he'd go on after she was gone,
and Paul too, as would Jamie's children, and so on, and so
on, a kind of forever, anyway. She pictured her baby with a
sweet smile on his face. Funny how the tears didn't matter
anymore, those he'd cried that had wrung tears from her
also. She'd only take smiles with her, the love that had
bloomed, hesitantly at first but was now fully there in her
heart, overflowing. Finally, she thought of Jed. Darling
Jed. The dog that had saved her in so many ways and saved
Jamie too. She remembered his velvety brown eyes, his soft
black fur, *his warmth*, the way he'd chase his tail when
excited. And he was *always* excited, greeting each day with
unbridled enthusiasm. Remembered too his kindness with
Murphy, how he'd met aggression not with equal
aggression but love. Such a lesson in it that everyone
should take on board, the *power* of love. For love was all
that mattered. In the end, the only thing you could take
with you.

She'd experienced love, and this thing she would soon
gaze upon hadn't. It was incapable. Fuelled solely by hate,
so hate was all it could return. No point in doing what Jed
did with Murphy, trying to show it what else existed. Some
things were beyond redemption.

Fully turned now, and despite promises to herself, she
would open her eyes. Not because it demanded that of her,
although certainly it waited to see if it would be so, but to

remind herself in the split seconds that remained that she was forged from something different, and in that knowledge there'd be solace at last. She pitied those who found Ben the next day, the state he'd be in, but on her face, there'd be a smile.

She was arctic cold, and yet her heart continued beating, deliciously defiant.

Not as quick to destroy her as it had Ben, it perhaps found her defiance delicious too. Was intrigued by it. Keen to see how far she'd take it. Whether she'd really be brave enough to stare into its face, something *beyond* imagining, and smile.

Useless. A failure. Unnatural. She'd felt all of those things. An outcast who would never belong. But the fact she didn't belong to this buoyed her. Remaining on the edges wasn't always so bad. That she was ready to face it, feel sorry for it, *laugh* at it, spawned something else that night: pride. She was *not* a weak woman. She was strong. Stronger than Ben. As ancient as this thing was, as enduring and as relentless, she was still something better.

Envy overcame it.

There was no intrigue anymore, no enjoyment of the game, only fury.

Like a Gorgon, as venomous, one look and she'd be dead. And if it were true, if she was made of better stuff, it could never devour her.

She fixed her smile in place, would hold fast to it no matter what. One day, this building would not just be deconsecrated but wholly destroyed, every brick smashed to pieces. Let the land lie fallow, though, at least for a short while. Time in which to heal.

Do it, Ava. You can *do it.*

Breathing in, not expecting to breathe out, she obeyed her own instruction, her eyelids slowly lifting. In that same instance, that very same second, there came a thud behind her, a roar, but this one infinitely more powerful than all the others she'd heard that night – a sound that forced her to shut her eyes tight again and bring her hands up to cover her face, her legs finally giving way beneath her.

She thought she knew what to expect, but not this. Whatever was happening now, she couldn't part her hands to look, because every time she tried, she was blinded, not by darkness this time but the brightest of lights. A light that *filled* the space before her, behind her, and all around. *Engulfed* her. A light as dangerous as its counterpart? Like fire, able to burn her?

There was no more pain. At least not yet. And there was the *warmth* of fire, banishing the icy cold that had sunk through Paul's jacket. *Glorious* warmth. The kind that didn't sap your energy but enlivened you. A warmth that gave you such hope, that reminded you that however bad it got in winter, with rain pelting, storms raging, and grey clouds hanging so low, it would always give way. It had to. Because that was the way of it. The cycle.

Here, in this church, there was no supreme reign, not yet. And she'd never got the chance to gaze upon the true face of darkness, which she was grateful for, for – despite what she'd told herself – she could not have borne it, kept smiling, not unless it was a rictus grin, a slash that had been torn from ear to ear. Hideous.

Another scream resounded, worse than Ben's, infinitely more pitiful, Ava scrabbling to the side, as far away from it as she could get, leaning against the wall there, her chest pounding, her head throbbing, and her wrist too. The

271

thud she'd heard must have been the oak doors opening at last, someone blasting them apart. That ensuing roar – so unlike the roar of the other – was one of ecstasy.

If only she could see what was happening, if only she wasn't beginning to doubt again. Was any of this real? Was she mad? Delusional? Imagining all this?

She had to shield her eyes as she opened them. So much light, but darkness remained at the outer edges. A battle. That's what she was witnessing. One that had taken place time and time again and would continue. In this realm and others.

The darkness did its utmost to regain ground, the shadows in the pews – the congregation, as she'd dubbed them, an army of minions sent before their host, far more than she'd seen before, a legion indeed – rushing full pelt, all those who'd sold their souls, believed the lies. Lies that were, she had to admit, seductive.

Poor Ben. He was in the midst of it all. If only he'd found his way through the darkness to the light. She could only pray it would reach him now, the realisation that it wasn't just the devil that listened. If ever she'd wanted proof, this was it.

Another roar, several of them, and from both sides. So loud, how was it that the neighbourhood hadn't come running? The people that lived nearby, were they really oblivious to all that was happening around them? Was everyone in every town, city, or country as unaware? Just because you didn't believe, didn't mean it didn't exist. But, yes, it was easy to turn a blind eye.

Sometimes.

She'd go blind if she continued to stare; her retinas would burn.

Please let the light win. Don't let the darkness return.

But even as she thought it, she knew: the darkness would stay there on the periphery. Would be inside her too, and not just her but in everyone. Humans were in themselves battlefields. Like mould, would the darkness grow again if she survived? Continue to find ways to torture her, *insidious* ways? It was possible to know too much; she'd already concluded that. *This* was too much. The dark *and* the light.

The darkness was gaining ground. The outcome not assured. Not yet. Such a vast place before her, as cavernous as before, no boundaries. A pit of chaos. More roars, screams, and desolate cries. She'd seen enough, heard enough. Her body crumpled, and she fell to the ground, curling her legs beneath her, foetus-like, wishing she'd never been born. And that Ben hadn't either.

She was crying, rocking her body, had reverted to the infant she was in all this. As helpless as Jamie. Her beloved Jamie.

Who would win, if not the battle, this war? *Why* did it have to happen? So much war. In the news, on the streets, in people's hearts. The eternal push and pull.

Her tears had dried. But she was still rocking, still praying. *Please. Please. Please.* What she meant, she no longer knew, only that all horror, all wonder, had left her. She was tired. Only that.

A touch, a sensation of something. A *nudge*? Her eyes jammed shut still, she had no idea what it was. Couldn't even begin to comprehend. Another nudge. Against her cheek this time. Something…cold? But hadn't the cold been banished? The light she'd seen was so strong! But not strong enough?

Ava refused to open her eyes, carried on praying; there was comfort in that one word – *please* – the repetition. Perhaps the only comfort she'd ever know. A one-word prayer she'd murmur all her life if she survived, and always with such desperation.

This madness had started before Ben.

Before she'd even set foot on church grounds.

In a living room, in front of a wood burner, that's when all this had begun, life perfect, *too* perfect. Not just Jamie growing but fear too. *Nothing* should be so perfect.

Another nudge. Still cold. And something else too. Wet. *Wet?*

Her eyes snapped open to the last thing she'd expected to see, the most glorious sight of all, the oddest and most welcome.

A dog. A black Labrador. A *glowing* black Labrador.

Exactly like hers.

Jed.

Something perfect after all.

Chapter Twenty-Eight

Ava struggled to sit up, forgetting about her wrist and pushing down on it, almost whiting out with the ensuing pain. Straightaway Jed issued a series of nudges and a few good licks. *Be careful!* If he could talk, that's what he'd say, eyes brimming with so much love, so much concern, they prompted more tears from her. A torrent.

Once she was fully upright, the dog jumped up, placed both paws on her shoulders and hugged her every bit as hard as she hugged him, his name – *Jed! Jed! Jed!* – the new mantra on her lips. Aside from the tip of his cold wet nose, he was so warm! Pulsating with life, with everything that was good and true. As warm as the light that had been there earlier, *gorgeously* warm. A pertinent reminder.

It felt like an age before Ava could let him go, and still she feared doing so, but Jed was pulling away now, urging her. *We have to go.*

Funny how she felt like she could read his mind, but then she'd always been able to do that to an extent. Now, though, the messages he conveyed were crystal clear.

"Okay, Jed. Fine. I don't know how you got out, how you knew I was here, but I'm glad to see you, so, so glad. And you're right. We need to get away. Get help."

There was no police station close by. She had to reach home, if her legs would carry her, to use the landline there.

Knocking at a stranger's door was also an option, although if they pressed her for an explanation…

Ava took a step forward. Her legs carried her well enough. Before she left, she had to take one last look, make sure the darkness really had been swallowed and not her, that this was really over – at least for now. Ben. She had to see him too.

Only a church met her gaze. Just a gloomy, dusty old church. Empty. *Cleansed.* She was certain of it. She had no sense of being watched by shadows residing in dark corners; those that *were* there were harmless. You couldn't banish the darkness, live in a world made entirely of light, not in the world she was a part of, but, unlike Ben, you didn't have to breathe life into it either and, unlike her, make more of it than you should. There was only one place you could keep the light burning constantly, in your soul. But not without effort. Always it took effort.

Her eyes shifted from the far corners of the church to the aisle, to where Ben lay. For the merest second, she hoped she *had* imagined him, that he wasn't real. The aisle would be empty, then. Ben, however, was all too real, lying there staring.

Despite Jed barking at her, pleading with her – *We have to go!* – Ava rushed forwards, needing to see Ben up close one last time. Yet again craving that.

"Ben," she whispered as she knelt beside him, then with more reverence, "Ben."

He didn't deserve such reverence! If she hadn't complied with his wishes, he would most certainly have killed her, then offered her as some kind of sacrifice. And there was Sarah; he'd tried to kill her and badly injured Lou. But whatever he was capable of, he wasn't any more. He was stone-cold dead. His eyes wide open and...*horrified.* In those last moments she'd spent with him, he had indeed changed. And it was change for the better.

Jed was still barking, her supposedly ordinary dog, but she'd seen it, how he'd glowed. Somehow, he'd got inside this church and brought the light with him. She would wonder more deeply about this later, all of it, but for now, there was only one thing on her mind. She reached out and gently stroked Ben's cheek. She'd thought he had a kind face, and she *still* thought it. Despite what he'd done and what he'd seen. Time to close his eyes against it all.

Jed was beside her, nudging. Of course she'd obey him, her good dog, leave this place to rot.

She rose and followed him back up the aisle, towards the oak doors, didn't look back, not again. In the porch, she pulled the doors shut. In there, she'd seen the darkness push back. And it *would* do so again. On fresh battleground next time.

Such quiet streets. As empty as they'd been when she'd journeyed to the church. An otherworldly silence. Lights from inside houses had indicated life before, but now all were switched off. Only the pallid glow of the streetlamps remained, a gentle breeze blowing, the clouds still low, forming something of a swirling mist. No matter, she could see her way through it well enough. And, of course, there was no one following them. They were alone. Quite alone. Despite a niggling doubt. Her imagination still active, going into overdrive. She pictured Ben again. He had risen, with not one shred of humanity left, a vessel purely for hatred.

He'd risen and was following her, as he'd followed her before.

And behind him, an army of devils.

* * *

They'd done it! Reached home. A place that mere hours ago – *minutes*, even – she'd thought she might never see again.

Ava half expected the front door to be wide open, but it remained shut. She withdrew the key from her pocket, her fingers clumsy, even dropping it at one point before finally ramming it into the lock and scraping the barrel round.

Jed waited for her to enter, and then once he was safely inside too, she slammed it shut, leaning against it, breathing hard.

The Kent family home was as empty as the church.

Ava felt like she'd cried a river that night, but more tears came. If only Paul were here, rushing forwards and holding her in his arms! She also wanted to press Jamie's sweet cheek against her own, feel the softness of it. That would come, though. It would happen. That's why she'd fought so hard.

That Jed had come to the church wasn't a mystery. They'd gone there several times recently; he knew the way, could easily have picked up her scent as she'd rushed there tonight. But how had he got out of the house in the first place? The front door had been locked, so Jed couldn't have got out that way.

She pushed herself away from the door and staggered through to the living room. Jed had been in the garden just before she'd left, as the texts from Ben had come hurtling through. Preoccupied, had she closed the doors fully behind her or accidentally left them ajar? She who was so worried about safety.

The patio doors *were* ajar, just a fraction. Enough for Jed to have squeezed himself through? Clearly. It was another mystery solved. Jed had acted the contortionist, entered the garden, jumped over the wall – a low wall, *too* low – and wrapped round before heading to the church. But then to have forced open the heavy oak doors there, that had been stuck, *definitely* stuck, locked even, and brought so much light in?

She looked at him. He was looking back at her, wagging his tail.

Dog was *god* spelt backwards. Perhaps for a reason.

So much fog in her brain, and the injuries she'd sustained screamed at her.

"Jed," she said. "I need to sleep."

Although Jed whined, gave a single bark, she retraced her footsteps, going via the kitchen in search of the cordless phone – which was neither there nor in the living room – to the foot of the staircase, then hauling herself upwards.

The landline phone was never on its cradle; it was always left somewhere random. Not downstairs, so it had to be in one of the bedrooms. But the thought of speaking to someone… She wasn't sure she could do it, string the right words together.

If only she could sleep. Just for a short while. She'd feel more together then, more able to explain events. *At least some of them. Not all. No way.*

She didn't go to her own bedroom but Jamie's, just to make sure… He wasn't there, was he? Sleeping soundly. She couldn't just…magic him up?

The cot was empty. Sheets pulled back when Paul had

taken him from it only this morning, the sleepsuit he'd worn hanging over the rail. No hope of all this being a dream. Every last bit was real. Paul had taken Jamie and left. But he was coming back. He'd said so. Or was she wrong? That was just what she'd *hoped* he'd said? Would her husband ever want her again once he knew what she'd gone through? She knew too much. Her mind wouldn't settle, no matter how much she might want it to. Would he sense that well enough?

A scream erupted, no way to stall it. Hands flew upwards too, one clutching at her head, the other held uselessly against her chest. What she'd experienced! The congregation. A darkness that just kept on reproducing. The horror in Ben's eyes when he'd realised some gods must never be worshipped. It was all in her head, trying to sap the wonder of what else she'd seen, the light that had triumphed, her dog, Jed, coming to rescue her, bringing her home. *Being* home.

The darkness turned it all into such bitter triumph.

You know too much. And so you can never sleep again. Because that's when the darkness will strike back. Always, it'll strike back. It will try. Never let go.

As Ben had said, this wasn't over.

She, Ava Kent, once normal, had strayed too far. The damage done. How could she pick up the phone to the police, to Paul, to anyone, and explain any of it? No sane person would believe her.

Panic flared.

What to do? Where to go? Should she stay here or, as injured as she was, run again? Find some other place to hunker down, far from her family.

Stay away from me, Paul. Don't try to find me.

If she did pick up the phone, that's what she'd say. *Demand* it.

I'm taking the dog, and I'm going. You cannot follow me.

She thought she'd been saved, but what if she was more lost than ever?

Of course Paul would try to find her; he'd corner her, throw question after question at her, chip, chip, chipping away until she exploded, revealed everything. Oh, she could imagine it now, the way he'd look at her when it all came tumbling out. All love diminished. The only thing left: contempt.

How had it come to this? That mystery couldn't be solved or unpicked even if she spent a lifetime trying, descending further into madness.

She was home. Jed had brought her back. And she was grateful to him for doing that. But she wouldn't stay. That was the only decision that made sense. She'd flee and do so alone, not take him with her either, make sure she locked him in good and proper this time. He was pure. She was not. They no longer suited each other.

Another decision: she wouldn't run to an alternative place, somewhere she could lie low. She'd go to the beach, to the sea, face a roaring white ocean that had undiscovered depths too. There, she would fill her pockets with stones, then walk into the sea. *Please, please, please*, back on her lips, a request only for oblivion. Then when it finally came: *thank you.*

Paul would be wifeless, Jamie motherless. The very thing she'd feared. But she loved them, with all her heart and soul she loved them, and so the kindest thing, the most *selfless* thing she could do was to let them go.

A calm settled over her that she welcomed.

One last look around Jamie's room was all she'd permit herself. A glance back at the cot with its wooden bars and white and blue bedding, at the mobile that hung over it, cars, trains and planes swaying gently, that he'd stare at whilst lying in his bed with such wonder in his eyes. What a wonderful thing innocence was! A gift everyone was blessed with when they entered the world but very few retained. The walls of his room were brightly painted, two yellow and two green. She remembered how, when decorating whilst pregnant, she'd wanted his life to *burst* with colour. Not for him, soft or neutral shades. Let him see what the world was capable of, what it could produce. The good stuff. Only that.

Time to leave it all behind, for her innocence was wholly destroyed.

A final touch of the blue blanket on Jamie's bed, made of the softest lamb's wool. He'd rub the edge against his cheek when drifting off to sleep, his eyelids gently closing. A comfort blanket. Able to soothe him when she couldn't.

Enough. She must leave. No need to phone the police, to explain anything to anyone. Ben's body would be found soon enough. Maybe hers too.

Sorry, she mouthed as she stepped forward, still calm, because what she longed for – oblivion – would be hers soon enough. "Jed, move out of the way."

He was in front of her in the doorway. The light from the hallway lent him that glow again, the one she'd witnessed in the church. A trick. Likely then as it was now. The product of a fevered mind. He was *just* a dog.

One that didn't obey her command, that continued to stand there.

A few more steps and she was directly in front of him,

and still he wouldn't move. He was looking up at her, her gentle dog, but he was powerful. It was like she was seeing it for the first time, the sheer bulk of him, how solid he was – a creature of huge proportions that not only stood in the doorway but filled it entirely.

Delusion. Illusion. All of it.

"Move, Jed! You have to. And this time, stay here. You don't come looking for me either. Jed! Come on. I know you understand me. Move!"

He wasn't going to. If she wanted to get past him, she'd have to *shove* past. So be it. God, she'd miss him! He was the one there whenever she needed someone, not Ben, and not even Paul. Who saw what she'd become, the transformation, and still held no judgement in his eyes, just love and adoration.

Perhaps she *could* stay, pretend like nothing had happened.

But it did. You'd never *be able to pretend otherwise.*

"Jed, move," she repeated. "You're not going to stop me."

Her glowing dog.

Ready to do as she'd planned and shove past him, she drew closer. Once she was out of the house and back in that cold, silent night, away from everything that belonged to her and to which she also belonged, this would all be so much easier.

The cold, silent night would *make* it easier.

"Jed? What the—?"

No way to push past him. Not when he'd reared up, standing on two legs not to give her his usual Jed-hug, but to hurl himself at her.

Ava had only seconds to register what he was doing, to

wonder at it, *split seconds*, before she was falling backwards like she had in the church, hard, her head catching at something – the edge of Jamie's chest of drawers?

What she *did* have time to register was a similar bolt of searing pain as she hit it, damage already done being compounded. There was also a flash of light that once again blinded, but in it she could see – she *swore* she could see – her dog's face. Not just a dog, but something else entirely.

Magnificent.

And then the darkness came for her.

Soft darkness.

Chapter Twenty-Nine

Hazy. Impossible to think straight. There was darkness, and there was light. But not…intense darkness. Or intense light. Not a constant struggle between the two. *Glaring* light, for certain, courtesy of several fluorescent lights recessed in the ceiling above her. Ava attempted to lift a hand to shield her eyes but couldn't. Something was attached to her arm, preventing her. She frowned. Struggled harder. Panicked.

Only when a hand touched her in such a gentle manner and a voice spoke, just as gently, did she calm.

"It's okay, Ava, it's all right. You're safe now. You're in the hospital."

Hospital? That couldn't be right. She'd been at home. Intending to go somewhere. To do something. But what? Everything was just so hazy!

Her vision blurred too as she tried to focus. "Paul? Is it you?"

"Of course it's me, sweetheart. I'm here. I'm just…I'm sorry I ever left, that's all. It was wrong of me, so wrong. All of this…it's my fault."

Paul was there beside her, which was even more confusing. Hadn't she thought she'd never see him again? Another surge of panic.

"Jamie! Where's he?'

A slight squeeze of her hand. "He's fine! He's with Carol. Ava, we're *both* fine. And thank God you are as well." There was a slight pause before he asked the question she was already busy asking herself. "What happened?"

Something *had* happened, something big – huge, in fact, overwhelming. But what? She tried to sharpen her mind, peer through fog's curtain to find an answer to his question, for the dozens she had too. She simply couldn't remember. Not yet.

"How did I get here? In the hospital?"

"You were attacked. There was someone in the area targeting women. There's another in the hospital too. They think she's a victim of the same person who attacked you. Her name's Sarah Savery."

"Sarah Savery?" Ava quizzed. The name seemed familiar.

"Ava, do you remember that night we went to a hotel and your mum phoned, certain someone was in the garden, spying, and was going to break in? It could have been him, that same person spying again." Such anguish in his voice when he added, "The bastard must have known you were alone at the house. We played right into his hands. I really am so, so sorry, Ava. I don't know how I'm going to ever make this right, but I'll try. I promise you. I'll spend a lifetime trying."

"The patio doors…" Ava whispered. "I got distracted. I don't think I locked them."

"Distracted? By what? Can you remember?"

She tried, she really did, but had to admit defeat. "No. So…I was attacked at home?"

Paul nodded. "That's where I found you. I came home early," which, again, he thanked God about, although there was a hint of sheepishness too as he elaborated. "Jamie wouldn't settle. Nothing I could do was making any difference, or Mum either. 'He needs his mum,' she kept saying. And she was right. It was like…in a blinding flash, I knew it. It wasn't just Jamie that needed you, we both did. We're a family, and whatever difficulties we face, we do it together. Oh, Ava," he continued, sighing. "I know you've been having a hard time lately, and…and…I suppose I didn't want to admit how hard. I know what I'm guilty of. I'm completely aware how I've tried to ignore stuff, wanting it all to be perfect when the world isn't like that, *parenthood* isn't. So, yeah, anyway, I came home early and found you upstairs in Jamie's bedroom." His voice cracked. "I couldn't believe it. Was beside myself. But, Ava, the good news is the attacker's been found, or so the police believe. And he's dead."

"Who was it?" Ava asked, unsure if she really wanted to know. All that Paul was saying, what he was trying to explain, it just added to the fog, not cleared it.

"A vagrant. A drifter. Ben Miller was his name. You…well, you know him."

"Ben Miller? Do I?" Like Sarah Savery, his name sounded familiar, his first name, at least. Did she know a Ben? Had she *ever* known a Ben? *Think, Ava. Think!*

"He was pretending to be a vicar at a local church, St Luke's. Not that anyone ever saw him in vicars' clothing, it turned out, but I suppose things are different now, aren't they? The clergy is often more casual. He also ran that music class you'd started going to with Jamie. Peculiar, isn't it? Why he went to those kinds of lengths."

Ben…music class… Again, familiarity but no clarity. An echo of a memory, a whisper, something ghostly, flickering, and then it was gone.

"How does anyone pretend to be a vicar?" she asked.

Paul shrugged. "I don't know the ins and outs of the case, just that the police have stopped searching for who did this to you and Sarah. They believe they have their man. Maybe…God, it doesn't bear thinking about, but maybe he was trying to get to the kids, not sure why, but…as I've said, I can't think about it, Ava, go there. It's too dark. Those aren't the kind of thoughts I want knocking around in my head. Thing is, if he was spying on you like before, he knew there was no Jamie in the house and no husband. So, in that sense, it *was* you he came for. He attacked you, knocked you senseless. Your wrist is broken too." He shrugged again, tried to smile but failed. "A fact you're probably very much aware of. He wasn't at the house when I arrived home. If he was, if I'd caught him… I'm not sure what scared him off. Maybe he thought he'd succeeded where he'd failed with Sarah, that he'd killed you. Jesus, Ava, *I* thought you were dead. You were lying so still, barely had a pulse. I don't know what went on in his twisted mind, but he scuttled back to the church, where he'd apparently been living in a room there, the vestry. The church had been closed down, you see, the land deconsecrated, then sold to developers, most likely, but that's where the police found him as dead as they come. He'd been stabbed, over and over, not by you, Ava, oh no, no, no. The police don't think that, not for a minute. There were knives at the church, a selection, the only fingerprints on them his own."

"You mean…he stabbed himself?"

"Seems like it. Suicide, and good riddance to him. He was very disturbed. There were…shit, Ava, there was evidence he was into some kind of devil worshipping. He'd turned it into a shrine for Satan, not God. The police won't reveal exact details about all that, but it's enough to say the guy was as deluded as they come. Completely warped."

A devil worshipper? Was Paul serious? Wouldn't she have known if the guy who ran the music class she'd attended had been into all things Satanic? Wouldn't she or someone else there have sensed something wrong about him?

She swallowed hard. "Paul...will the police want evidence from me?"

Rather than answer her straightaway, he leaned into Ava and held her. She breathed him in, his clean soap-and-water smell, cherished the warmth of him.

"Paul?" she prompted after a few moments. "Will they?"

"The thing is, Ava, as well as your wrist, you received blows to the head, back and front. The doctors said you might not remember everything straightaway, that it could take time." A slight pause before he continued. "They said...you might *never* remember certain things. Obviously, we're going to have to wait and see, but if you're struggling right now, that could be the reason. Ava...do you remember Ben at all? I think you must have known something was off about him, because you emailed the diocese and asked about him. The police found correspondence on your computer."

"Did I?" Again, all news to her.

"Yeah, and they replied, although a good few days later, and said they didn't know who you were talking about and had alerted the police, but...it was too late by then. If they'd acted sooner, things might have turned out differently. But, no, they took their own sweet time, just like all these institutions do. They get too big, too busy for their own good." From being righteously angry, he looked more hangdog, *hurt*. "You were texting someone, Ava. Recently, I mean, just before the attack. You were texting someone *a lot*. I mean…could it have been Ben? Was it because you didn't trust him?" His cheeks suffused with colour. "Or because you did? I mean, who doesn't believe a vicar? Society's trained to believe them. I'm only bringing this up because, before I left, we talked about whoever it was you were texting, and you were cagey about it, wouldn't answer. I wonder now if it was him."

"Surely there's an easy way to answer that. Check my phone."

Paul shook his head. "We can't. There's no sign of it."

She frowned. "What? It's gone?"

"Uh-huh. Look, shit, forget about whoever you were texting, my stupid jealousy—"

"Your jealousy? What do you mean? You think I wasn't investigating Ben but that we were having an affair?"

"No! Of course not. I know you wouldn't do something like that, betray me, and I'd never betray you either, okay? Like I said, let's focus on the good stuff, not the bad. Whatever he intended to do to you, he failed. You're here, you're alive, and we have another chance to be a family. We're blessed, you, me, and Jamie." His voice cracked. "No way I'll lose sight of that again."

He was right; they were. Whatever had happened – no matter how terrible, how out of the ordinary – was over. Their lives started from this point onwards, and she felt good about that, great, in fact. Couldn't wait to see Jamie, hold him in her arms, and breathe in his sweet smell too.

She *loved* being a mother. She knew that for certain. And a wife. A normal life that was actually pretty spectacular. As well as amnesia, Paul told her the doctors thought she might suffer from PTSD – post-traumatic stress disorder – but it was strange, because she doubted it somehow. As she looked into Paul's eyes, so full of love and concern, she knew she'd be all right, that *they* would be, and maybe, just maybe, if it blotted out all the bad things, the amnesia was a blessing too.

"I'll look after us," he murmured as he held her again. "We'll be all right."

"I know," Ava replied. "You, me, Jamie, *and* Jed."

Paul pulled away, looked at her. "Jed?"

She almost laughed. "Yes, of course Jed! Our dog. I remember you've never been as fond of him as me, but that might change. He's such a good dog, the best. I don't even know how Ben got into our home, not with Jed as a guard dog. Oh shit, Paul…" Another surge of dread. "Did…the attacker hurt him too?"

"Hurt Jed?"

"Yes!"

"No. No, he didn't."

"Oh, thank God he's okay as well. Then how did—"

Paul had taken her by the shoulders now and was looking into her eyes.

"Jed wasn't hurt because we don't have a Jed. Ava, we've *never* had a dog."

* * *

It was a bright day in May, and the air was warm. The dark, cold days were gone; there was to be some respite, and, yes, the cold would return, the darkness would, but Ava had lost her fear of the latter, if she'd had any fear at all. That was the thing, amnesia *had* affected her. There were certain things about the past she couldn't recall, but what remained stuck in her head was a notion she'd been afraid of the dark somehow, of shadows. And yet, when she struggled to find out why, there seemed to be no good reason. Certainly, it wasn't an affliction from childhood. In her parents' home at night, with all the lights off, she'd slept soundly enough; Carol had confirmed that. She simply *wasn't* afraid of the dark. It was a misleading notion.

But her memories of Jed…they were still so real. She and Paul had adopted him, from the building she was standing in front of now on this fine spring day, their local animal rescue centre. Whilst she'd been pregnant, six months or so, she and Paul had walked in there with the intention of owning a dog someday, and there he'd been, Jed, making such a fuss, barking, but it had caught her attention, was *designed* to, she was sure of it, and it had worked. She'd turned to him, and her heart had soared. A black Labrador. With eyes the deepest shade of brown. As she'd headed over to him, he'd stopped barking, began to wag his tail hard instead from side to side, hopping from foot to foot in excitement. She'd knelt down, stared into his eyes through the bars of the pen that contained him, touched his wet nose, and the bond was there.

Instantly.

Iris, an assistant at the centre, had told her he was new in, that they didn't have much information on him; he was a stray who'd just…appeared. Iris had christened him Jed because she'd thought the name suited him, simple as that.

Paul hadn't been keen; Ava could remember that clearly too. He'd had in mind a much smaller dog that wouldn't need so much exercise. She'd stood her ground, though, even when Paul had stormed off in a temper about it, persuaded Iris it'd be okay, that she could talk him round. And she had. They'd gone back a few days later, signed all the paperwork, and he was theirs.

Jed had come home with them and was a part of their family, an *integral* part. He'd saved her when she was giving birth to Jamie, had somehow alerted a midwife, of all people, who'd rushed into the house to see what was going on and saved not just Ava but Jamie too. How he'd escaped the house, she didn't know, but it wasn't the only time he'd saved them. Jamie had stopped breathing in the middle of the night, she remembered that, had been alerted to it because she'd heard barking, Jed below them in the living room, going frantic. And yet Paul's version of events that night was entirely different: Ava alone had sensed something wasn't right. Jamie snuffled in his sleep, and it was that lack of snuffling that had pulled her from her own shallow sleep.

Such a muddled mix of memories. So frustrating.

She was indeed suffering from amnesia, especially when it came to more recent memories of the past few months, but what she was also doing, apparently, was inventing *false* memories. The doctor had told her this, and Paul *kept* telling her.

"There was a Labrador at the rescue centre. You're absolutely right about that, a yappy thing, and you *were* taken with it. But no way would the centre let us have him, a dog with an unknown history, just when we were about to have a baby. We *had* to leave him there, Ava. It wasn't because I'd stormed off. We simply had no choice in the matter. Had to shelve any plans for adopting a dog until well in the future."

It wasn't true; it couldn't be. But Paul wouldn't lie to her.

The most recent time they'd talked about it, they'd been downstairs on the sofa, Jamie slumbering peacefully in bed, such a good boy, always a delight to look after, just so easy, and she and Paul had gone over everything for the umpteenth time, Paul as patient as ever, trying hard to disguise his own frustration.

"So the midwife just…blew in through a door that was wide open suddenly, a midwife who was also, incredibly, called Jamie. It had nothing to do with Jed?"

"You know it didn't. You've emailed her several times about it already."

"But I remember asking if it was Jed's barking that had alerted her, not just a wide-open door, and she nodded. Now she denies it. I remember talking with you about it too, afterwards, mentioning Jed and what he did."

"*False* memories, Ava! And, by the way, don't email Jamie about it again, okay? She'll think…"

"Think what? That I'm mad if I do?"

"Well…"

"And then the night the intruder, that may or may not have been Ben, tried to get in when we were away and Mum was here babysitting, I heard the racket Jed was making down the phone, barking and barking. It was deafening."

"Ava, if a dog was here barking, no way an intruder would hang around."

Even though that made sense, she still protested. "Here's

294

the thing, Paul, how can I be conjuring all this simply from desire? I wanted a dog, *really* wanted one. I wanted *him*, Jed, from the rescue centre, and so many scenarios exist in my head in which he was there. Walks that we'd take, the times we'd sit together on the sofa when you were at work, before Jamie was even born, the pair of us snuggled beneath a blanket. I can *feel* his fur beneath my hand. I used to love just staring into his eyes, those deep brown eyes. He was my saviour, he really was. And then…then I remember a glowing dog. Not here. Somewhere else. I keep thinking it was at the church, that I'd gone there. It's like the last memory I have. Funnily enough, I don't remember the music class that much, although I know I went a handful of times or whatever. But my last memory is that I was at the church, where Ben was later found, and Jed was there too, doing something, something *hugely* important, saving me again, and, Paul, I'm telling you, he glowed so bright!" The smile she gave Paul was decidedly watery. "My beautiful dog. My angel."

As Paul held her, another thought occurred.

"Paul, we need to go to the rescue—"

He cut her off at the pass. "Why? What do you think it will achieve? I've checked with Iris about Jed. Yes, he was there the day we went in, and, yes, you were smitten with him. And, okay, all right, I did get the knock about it, went outside for a breather. But we couldn't have him, even if I'd agreed, because you were *pregnant*, Ava, soon to have Jamie. And Jed was an unknown. We know all this. No reputable shelter would let us have him with a baby on the way. He's not there anymore. He escaped whilst out on a routine walk, slipped his collar and bolted. No one's seen him since. That's something else you know as well."

It was true, she did, although one thing she hadn't checked.

"When did he bolt? Did Iris say?"

"Oh God, let me think. It was a couple of days after we'd gone to see him, like the Monday or something."

"The day of collection," Ava murmured. "We'd gone to see him on the Friday, and I'd arranged with Iris to pick him up on the Monday, asked her to give me the weekend so I could make you see he was right for us. That's how I remember it."

Even Paul looked confused when she'd said this, as if succumbing to her version of events. But no, he couldn't be. It was as he'd said: she was creating false memories, jumbling everything up, reality and desire, making a mess of it. It made you question, though – Paul too, it seemed – just what reality was, if it even existed.

And now here she was, for the first time since the attack, out for a walk on her own and heading to the rescue centre. She didn't know why, exactly. If she went in there asking the same questions Paul had, Iris might look askance at her. Like Jamie the midwife, if Ava continued to badger her about it, she'd think she was mad. She wasn't, just recovering from something terrible, trying to make sense of it. Considering what had happened, the gravitas, she couldn't believe she was as sane!

If a dog called Jed wasn't in there, then there was no point in going in, none whatsoever. Really, all she wanted to do was see if standing there outside it prompted a memory that went *against* those in her head. Of her and Paul – and Jamie in her tummy – walking away from the shelter empty-handed, no dog on a lead bouncing excitedly in front of them. The experiment failed. The false memory remained, made her smile, even. The happiness the dog had felt, that she had too, knowing they'd found each other, that they were *right* for each other. For a moment in time. If only she had her phone, one that had mysteriously disappeared and hadn't surfaced since, she could have checked it, sifted through photographs, because one thing was for sure: if she'd had a dog, she'd have taken as many pictures of him as she had of Jamie. Paul had already shown her the photos on his phone. None of Jed. Zero.

Ava heaved a sigh as she checked her watch. It was almost two o'clock. Jamie would wake round about now; she had to go home, be with him and her mother too, who was looking after him. The three of them were planning to spend the afternoon together, just a quiet one in the house, but she was looking forward to the simplicity of it, just watching TV, chatting, letting Jamie roll about on his playmat, days away from crawling. Carol spent a lot of time at the house now whilst Ava was recovering, then Paul would return from work and take over. She was rarely on her own, both of them guarding her every bit as much as a fictional Jed had. But she was getting better every day, and she looked forward to some alone time with Jamie and all the things they would do together: swimming and heading to the park for playtime on the swing. At the weekend, Paul would join them for bigger trips to the seaside or into the country. He used to work a lot at the weekends, but things were different now; he wasn't going to. They'd forge memories instead, ones she'd never forget. No point in hanging on to delusion, although, she had to admit, it was a *pleasurable* delusion.

As she turned from the rescue centre and walked away, Ava continued to muse. She'd miss their house when they left it. But they *would* leave it soon. Already, it was up for sale. Paul's idea, not hers. He said the house 'stored trauma', but, in truth, it was more traumatic for him than her, how he'd returned home to find her in the state she was in. She felt no trauma simply because she couldn't remember, amnesia definitely akin to blissful ignorance. The estate agent had assured them it would sell quickly, describing it as 'an ideal family home'. No way he'd say that if she'd died there! She wouldn't object to any of Paul's wishes, but…when they left, would memories, false or otherwise, of Jed fade too? She felt him most upstairs, where she'd lain injured. She imagined him standing over her, keeping guard still, wagging his tail, barking, *magnificent*. Her beloved dog, who was just so loyal.

So deep in thought, she didn't register straightaway that someone was calling her name.

"Ava? Ava, is that you? It's Sarah."

Ava's entire body jolted as she looked up.

Immediately, Sarah apologised. "I'm so sorry. Did I startle you? I honestly didn't mean to. Do you remember me? From the music class. You're out for a walk on your own too? Managed to get some 'me' time. Look, I heard…you know…you'd been attacked too by that bastard Ben Miller, that *imposter* masquerading as a vicar, of all things. I'm so glad to see you're okay!"

When Ava didn't respond, only stared, Sarah continued. "But, look…I know what you're going through. The terror that remains. It just…it doesn't go away, does it? That fear that he'll come back, even though he can't because he's dead and buried. Crazy. All of it. So hard to make sense of, although I knew something was wrong with him. When I confronted him that day, you were there, remember? You'd stayed behind with him for some reason. I was so worried for you because…like I said, I knew there was something off about him the minute I laid eyes on him. He denied having anything to do with Lou and Jenna's mother, and with the latter it was true – they found the kid that mugged her, did you know that? Sixteen, that's all he was! There's no hope for some, is there? I still think Miller was responsible for Lou, although, admittedly, Lou isn't as sure. She questioned what his motive would be. It wasn't like she'd accused him of anything or—" only briefly did she hesitate "—got closer to him than she should have."

Ava frowned. Was that a dig at her? Had she got close to him? Was that why she'd stayed behind with him that day when Sarah had come in and allegedly confronted him? That was one of the memories lost.

"Look," Sarah continued, "I know we didn't get off to a good start, you and I"—again, this was news to Ava, yet she continued to listen—"but…we could try again. Meet up and go for coffee." Sarah chanced a laugh. "Especially now we've got more in common than just having babies the same age! Maybe we could meet up with Lou and Jenna too. They're reeling from all this as well." She laughed a second time. "God, I don't know, we could form some sort of survivors' club or something. A bit more interesting than a music class, at least!" She grew serious again. "I really would like to get to know you, Ava. I think we could…help each other."

Sarah continued to talk, to babble, actually, full of nervous energy, but it wasn't her Ava was looking at anymore. It was the dog by her side. A black Labrador.

She reached out, desperate to touch him.

"Oh!" Sarah exclaimed. "Look at that. He's happy to see

you."

As Sarah relaxed the lead, he bounded towards Ava, licked her hand profusely. He then looked *beyond* her, small barks and yelps escaping him as his tail wagged and wagged. Yelps of confusion?

"See," Sarah said, "he's a good boy, really, so loving. What all that was about in the café, I'll never know."

Ava's head shot up, the memory of that meeting suddenly becoming clear. "He saw something in me," she said, frowning, "something...he didn't like. It frightened him. And then...then...my dog, Jed, diffused the situation, calmed it right down, got your dog – it's Murphy, isn't it? That's his name? Yes, yes, I remember! Jed got Murphy to calm down by...licking him, nudging him, the way he always used to nudge me when I was down or anxious. You remember, don't you? What Jed did?"

Sarah, with her bright blue eyes and blond hair curling past her shoulders, just looked at her the way Paul had, the way her own mother had: *mystified.*

"You didn't have a dog with you," she replied, slowly, carefully, as if explaining to a young child. "I was there with Leo and Murphy, and you were there with Jamie...*just* Jamie."

Another confirmation Ava was wrong, and her lip started to tremble because of it, but then...Murphy was trying to circle her and sniffing the air.

"Murphy," Ava said, leaning down towards him, "Murphy, come here, boy."

Murphy stopped what he was doing, leant his head to the side, then jumped up at her – exactly the way Jed used to – so that they were at eye level. In the background, she heard Sarah protest, telling him to get down, to do so at once. But that's where she remained, in the background. Murphy was who Ava focused on.

Entirely him.

His sleek black head and his deep brown eyes.

Jed was here, wasn't he? I didn't invent him?

Murphy inclined his head again, as though she'd spoken aloud.

As though he understood.

A bark. Just the one. A lick of Ava's face. A nod, even.

The dog in front of her was nodding.

Yes. He was here. I remember him too.

Love the story of Jed and want to meet him again?
You can find him within the pages of all nine books
of the Psychic Surveys series, where he first makes an
appearance in Book One: _The Haunting of Highdown
Hall._ Everyone needs a Jed, right? Especially when
they _really_ need him.

Happy reading!

A note from the author

As much as I love writing, building a relationship with readers is even more exciting! I occasionally send newsletters with details on new releases, special offers and other bits of news relating to the Psychic Surveys series as well as all my other books. If you'd like to subscribe, sign up here!

www.shanistruthers.com

Printed in Great Britain
by Amazon